The Menehune Murders

**Other Penny Spring and Sir Toby Glendower Mysteries
by Margot Arnold**

MARGOT ARNOLD

The Menehune Murders

A Penny Spring and Sir Toby Glendower Mystery

A Foul Play Press Book

The Countryman Press, Inc.
Woodstock, Vermont

First Edition
Copyright ©1989 by Margot Arnold

Library of Congress Cataloging-in-Publication Data
Arnold, Margot.
The menehune murders.
"A Foul Play Press book."
I. Title.
PS3551.R536M4   1989   813'.54   89-15803
ISBN 0-88150-149-2

A Foul Play Press Book
The Countryman Press, Inc.
Woodstock, Vermont
05091

Printed in the United States of America

To Lani Gail Nickerson,
Who loves the Islands

The Menehune Murders

WHO'S WHO

GLENDOWER, TOBIAS MERLIN, archaeologist, F.B.A., F.S.A., K.B.E.; b. Swansea, Wales, Dec. 27, 1926; s. Thomas Owen and Myfanwy (Williams) G.; ed. Winchester Coll.; Magdalen Coll., Oxford, B.A., M.A., Ph.D.; fellow Magdalen Coll., 1949-; prof. Near Eastern and European Prehistoric Archaeology Oxford U., 1964-; created Knight, 1977. Participated in more than 30 major archaeological expeditions. Author publications, including: What Not to Do in Archaeology, 1960; What to Do in Archaeology, 1970; also numerous excavation and field reports. Clubs: Old Wykehamists, Athenaeum, Wine-tasters, University.

SPRING, PENELOPE ATHENE, anthropologist; b. Cambridge, Mass., May 16, 1928; d. Marcus and Muriel (Snow) Thayer; B.A., M.A., Radcliffe Coll.; Ph.D., Columbia U.; m. Arthur Upton Spring, June 24, 1953 (dec.); 1 son, Alexander Marcus. Lectr. anthropology Oxford U., 1958-68; Mathieson Reader in anthropology Oxford U., 1969-; fellow St. Anne's Coll., Oxford, 1969-. Field work in the Marquesas, East and South Africa, Uzbekistan, India, and among the Pueblo, Apache, Crow and Fox Indians. Author: Sex in the South Pacific, 1957; The Position of Women in Pastoral Societies, 1962; And Must They Die? —A Study of the American Indian, 1965; Caste and Change, 1968; Moslem Women, 1970; Crafts and Culture, 1972; The American Indian in the Twentieth Century, 1974; Hunter vs. Farmer, 1976.

Chapter 1

On high, all was serene: the Hawaiian sky of early morning a pale, untroubled azure, across which a helicopter skidded like a water beetle across the face of a limpid pond, and a lazy trade wind stroked the trees with warm fingers as they moved sensuously under its tender touch. Only below was an element of discord, an intrusion into this harmony of blue sky, green foliage and red earth, as a small, virulently-yellow car drew up with a savage shudder on the black tarmac strip of road that signalled man's intrusion into idyllic nature. The car disgorged its two very disparate occupants, one tall and lanky, the other short and dumpy, who stood looking around them with the nervous uncertainty of sightseers in an unfamiliar locale determined to get their money's worth.

"It says 'No trespassing' on that sign. Are you sure this is the place?" the tall man queried, his voice a deep, irritated rumble. He pointed to a discreet sign bearing the familiar trademark of Del Monte Pineapple Company.

"Yes, this is it," his small companion said firmly, her voice a little shrill with nervous tension. "We've passed the Del Monte experimental station and the Dole fruit

1

stand, and over there I can see some tin roofs: those'll be housing for the pineapple workers in harvest time. But I don't see why we have to stop out here, there's supposed to be a service road running almost up to the Birth Rocks and it would save us quite a walk." She, in turn, pointed to a large grove of trees in the distance beyond a vast field of spiky pineapple plants. "The Birth Rocks are in that clump of trees."

"I'm not going to risk breaking an axle of a rental car on some damned dirt road or of getting stuck in this be-nighted place. It's costing an arm and a leg as it is to rent it, without paying out a fortune in damages," her escort grumbled. This was merely an indication of his deep disapproval of the whole undertaking, for Sir Tobias Glen-dower had never had to give two thoughts about money in his entire life, and was notorious for his absent-minded generosity.

"Well, have it your way," his small companion muttered crossly. "We'd better get going, or we'll be late." She launched herself onto one of the corridors of red, crumbly earth that ran like rivers of blood between the sentinel-straight rows of dull green pineapple plants.

Sir Tobias hung back. "What about this 'No trespassing' sign?" he growled.

"Oh, it's all right so long as you don't pick the pine-apples," she called back over her shoulder. "Do come on, Toby!"

With an exasperated sigh, he set off on another red slash, parallel to hers, his long legs rapidly bringing him abreast of her. "I really don't know how you get yourself into these things, Penny," he grumbled. "I fully expected this to be a relaxing and enjoyable holiday, and now this! Dragged from bed at the crack of dawn to this God-for-saken spot to arbitrate what must be the most addlepated dispute the academic world has seen to date."

"*You* didn't have to come at all," Penny Spring retaliated grimly. "And, as I said last night, once this meeting is over, I'll be as free as a bird."

Sir Tobias, that archaeologist extraordinary, drew himself up to his full height and snorted. "And let you go alone with two apparent maniacs who came to blows at their last meeting? Out of the question! They might do you some harm, or worse, they might, after it's all over, insist that their respective version of how things went was the correct one, and without a witness you'd be back to square one. Anyway, before we get there you'd better fill me in on all this Menehune nonsense, and what this fight is all about."

"I told you last night on the way to the hotel from the airport!" she exclaimed.

"I was half dead with jet lag, so none of it made any sense," he said loftily.

"You mean you were too pickled on all that free booze to take anything in. Traveling first-class indeed!" she snorted. "Oh, well, here goes! What do you know about the Menehunes to start with? That may save some time."

"The 'little people' of Polynesian legend, akin to the leprechauns of Ireland, and the stories about them are found throughout all the Polynesian islands including Hawaii," her companion came back glibly. "Probably folk memory of aboriginal types found on some of the islands by the Polynesians during their great trek eastwards, and who quickly succumbed to or were absorbed by the larger stock, but who have now been incorporated into Polynesian legend as 'luck-bringers' capable of remarkable feats of work, rather like Santa's elves," he concluded with a hint of sarcasm.

"Yes, well that's about the size of it," Penny Spring muttered. "However, in Hawaii it's a little more complicated than that. Although no *physical* signs of them have

3

ever been found, in the first census taken after the Europeans came here some 'Menehunes' were actually listed as such. This, apparently, is what started Giles Shaw off."

"Oh, yes. You'd better fill me in on him too." Toby paused in his stride, got out a very battered-looking briar pipe and lit it up with slow deliberation. "Something to do with a friend of yours?"

Penny was glad to catch her breath, for he had been setting a brisk pace. "Yes, Emily Vernon was my best friend at Radcliffe—studying anthropology, like me. She met and married Giles Shaw, a wild Irishman if ever there was one, when she and I were out in Tahiti doing some field work. He was more into archaeology back then, but they set up as an anthropological team, and spent most of their time here in the Polynesian area."

She paused and gave a wry grimace. "He was always a real handful, but she loved him to distraction, so all went well enough until she died suddenly a couple of years ago. Since then he seems to have gone to pot. Dived into a bottle, and his work got more and more erratic and out in left field. All this present business started when he wrote an article for some crackpot psychic magazine about the Menehunes, claiming they were still 'at work' in Hawaii. Most of his colleagues did the sensible thing and ignored it, but this man, Helmut Freyer, who also works at the University of Hawaii like Giles, jumped in with both feet and wrote a scathing criticism. This just egged Giles on. He wrote a whole book making even more extravagant claims, and the yellow press got hold of it, with choice headlines like 'Noted anthropologist claims Menehunes still exist in Hawaii' et cetera. Helmut Freyer got even more hysterical at this point, and some of the rags, scenting blood, published interviews with him that were intemperate to say the least. Since then it's just gone from bad to worse, and has culminated in this latest claim of

Giles' that he has *found* some Menehunes on the big island and will produce them. By this time, the University of Hawaii had become alarmed by all the unfortunate publicity, and they did try to cool the feud, with no success. So they called me in."

Toby started off again with loping strides. "That's the bit I don't see," he grumbled. "Why you of all people? If both of them are faculty members of the university, why couldn't they just squelch them?"

"Giles just isn't very squelchable. He's not a full-time faculty member like Freyer. He has plenty of money— Emily's money, I might add—and just teaches when and what pleases him. They have only managed to get this far because he did one of his rapid mind-changes and decided to sue for peace. He *asked* them to call me—as an old friend." Her attractively ugly little face softened. "He always was a great charmer, so I really don't mind. They both wanted secrecy: hence this meeting at a remote spot like the Royal Birth Rocks—another bit of Giles' whimsy, I suspect."

"And this Freyer fellow—what about him? German, is he?"

"Despite the name, no. From Michigan originally, I believe. But a bit on the heavy Germanic pedantic side. I've met him at a few conferences, and he does take himself very seriously. Just the type that Giles would love to bait, and also one to hold a long-term grudge. I was surprised that he seemed every bit as keen on this peace conference as Giles."

"Hmmpf," Toby grunted. By this time they were almost up to the grove of tall trees, among which were scattered some curiously-shaped, reddish-black volcanic rocks. They looked about them, but apart from a few startled birds that flew up on their approach, there was no movement in the grove, nor any sign of life.

5

Penny sank with a relieved sigh into one of the saddle-shaped rocks. "Remarkably comfortable!" she exclaimed. "No wonder the royal Hawaiian women came out here to have their babies! Much more comfortable than squatting on a stool in a hut." She patted the adjacent rock. "Why don't you try one while we wait?"

Toby glowered gloomily. "I don't think I have the right anatomy. Where is everyone?"

Penny looked at her watch. "Well, we're only about ten minutes after the appointed hour, and Giles never was one for promptness." This did nothing to mollify him.

"I suppose whilst I'm here I may as well look around and take a few photos." He produced a complicated-looking mini-camera from one sagging pocket of his linen jacket and strode off.

Penny leaned back with a relieved sigh and closed her eyes, savoring the warmth and the quiet. She hoped fervently that the meeting would go off with the minimum of fuss and fury, and that she could get back to the original plan of a Hawaiian vacation and of smoothing down her eminent companion's ruffled feathers. It had been nothing short of providential when Benedict Lefau, who credited Toby with his present happily married state, had offered him the chance to "break in" the new Lefau yacht now bobbing at anchor in the Honolulu marina, prior to his own descent on the islands to establish yet another branch of the ever-growing Lefau commercial empire. Penny herself had welcomed the chance to touch base with many old colleagues and to tidy up odds and ends of fieldwork in the islands, but had known that without this alluring bait to dangle before her eccentric companion she could never have tempted Toby so far away from home: and now this mess! She sighed faintly, and hoped that Giles Shaw would be on his best behavior—but where were the combatants?

Bushes rustling caused her to open her eyes in hope, but it was only Toby returning. She was about to close them again when a certain tenseness about his lanky frame caught her attention, and she looked up enquiringly as he towered over her.

"What does this Shaw fellow look like?" he asked, a shade too casually.

"Big, shambly, and with flaming red hair. Why? Do you see him coming?" she said quickly.

"No. Er, would this Freyer fellow be about five ten, stocky, with black hair and a rather large nose?"

"Why, yes!" she scrambled to her feet. "Good. At least one of them is here. Maybe I should have a word with him before Giles shows, to see how the land lies."

"I'm afraid not." Toby's round blue eyes behind his equally round glasses were stricken. "Helmut Freyer won't be talking with anyone anymore. He is lying on the ground behind some rocks over there, and he is *very* dead."

"Oh, my God!" she choked out, as they looked at each other in consternation for an agonizing pause. "How?" she managed to force out through stiffened lips.

"Well, it's hard to say, but it's a rum-looking setup. You'd better come and see." Toby turned abruptly and loped back through the bushes, Penny hard on his heels. Behind a jumbled mass of volcanic rocks, he stepped aside and Penny found herself looking at all that remained of Helmut Freyer. He was stretched out on the ground, his arms neatly at his sides, face up, eyes closed, and but for a grimace that twisted the flaccid mouth looked as if he was quietly napping. "He's still warm," Toby said gruffly. "Can't have been dead more than half an hour."

"A heart attack?" she hazarded.

Toby shook his head. "I'm afraid not. Look to the right of his right leg. There, where his trousers have ridden up a bit and you can see a patch of bare skin above his socks."

She looked and gasped in disbelief. "That's absurd!" On the bare shin was a purplish patch and a small scratch from which ran a trickle of blood, that pointed like an arrow to something that glittered dully in the sunlight: it was a tiny, finely-flaked spearpoint of obsidian attached to a small shaft of polished wood.

"Is that what I think it is?" Toby asked mildly.

Penny peered closer, "If you mean is it a so-called 'Menehune point,' why yes! But nothing like that could cause anyone's *death*."

"It could if it were poison-tipped," he said quietly. "The Hawaiians did use poisons sometimes for hunting, didn't they?"

"Well, yes, but . . . it's still absurd. To think Helmut Freyer would have held still while someone stuck a poisoned fake Menehune spear into his leg—without any sign of outcry or disturbance!"

"I think I can explain that," Toby said grimly. "I felt around at the back of his head. There's quite a bump on it. This is a setup all right, but I think whoever did this knocked Freyer out first and then scratched him with the spear as he lay on the ground; the trickle of blood tells us that. The idea being, presumably, to give the impression that this Menehune hater was slain by one of the 'little people': a very whimsical touch, perhaps by a man much given to whimsy?" He stared hard at his shattered partner.

"You think *Giles* . . . ?" She shook her head. "I can't believe it. Giles isn't a violent man, at least, not in that way."

"Then where is he?" Toby rumbled. "It's way beyond the meeting time and there's not been a sign of him. But that's beside the point now. We've got to get the police. I don't know what the drill here is, but there must be a police post in that village we drove through or a phone at least." He fished in another sagging pocket and produced the car keys. "You hightail it back there and get help, and I'll stay here to guard the body."

She hesitated, then shook her head again. "No, you go and I'll stay. For one thing you'll make it a lot faster, and for another, when you produce your credentials, you're likely to get much quicker action. You know how most policemen seem to hate me on sight. I've no idea how something like this is handled, but I think since we're outside the city that this sort of thing falls into the domain of Hawaii Five-O."

"I can't leave you here alone with a potential madman roaming around," he protested.

She was adamant. "I don't believe your theory for one little minute, and Giles would never hurt me, I know that. So, get going—you're wasting time."

"Well, alright," he grumbled, "But if he does show up and acts strangely, bean him with a rock and run for the road." He wheeled about and loped away.

Penny propped herself up against a rock and lit up a cigarette with a shaking hand. She looked pityingly down at the still figure and tried to remember if he was a family man. She had never liked Freyer, whom she had classified as a pompous pedant, but whatever he had been he certainly had not deserved to end up like this. A snatch of conversation with him from some long-ago conference floated into her mind. "I'm a widower, but my daughter lives at home and helps me with my work." So there was a family: she felt even more miserable.

A sudden thought struck her: how had Freyer got here? There had to be a car around somewhere, and maybe that would tell her something. Rather than stand around doing nothing, she hastily stamped out her cigarette and made for where the service road ought to be and, sure enough, just beyond the small wooden barrier marking its end stood a jaunty-looking silver Porsche. She tried the doors, but they were firmly locked, then peered inside, but could make out nothing untoward in the black leather interior. The keys had to be in the dead man's pockets. She grimaced. "Well, in for a penny, in for a pound," she murmured. "I'll have a quick look-see, and then tell the police what I've done."

She began to make her way back toward the body, following a slightly different route, and on rounding another group of rocks recoiled with a yelp of fright. There on the ground lay what looked like a gigantic dark green chrysalis with a red head, that transformed itself into an oversized sleeping bag out of which stuck a thatch of flaming red hair. As she approached it cautiously, her foot hit something that clinked and rolled away: it was an empty cognac bottle. "Giles?" she quavered. "Giles, is that you?"

A ripple stirred the sleeping bag, followed by a faint groan. Alarmed, she knelt down and shook the form within the bag. "Giles, are you alright?"

There was a louder groan and a major upheaval in the bag as the head reared up blindly and the eyes opened: they were bright blue and extremely bloodshot. As they dimly focussed on her, a broad grin split the red-stubbled face, revealing strong, nicotine-stained teeth. "Why, Penny, me old darling, what a wonderful sight to greet me tired eyes! Top o' the morning, to you." A huge meaty hand appeared and fumbled with the zipper on the bag and the hulking torso struggled its way out.

Penny got up, backed off a little and looked down at the heaving body. "Giles, what are you doing here like this?" she said weakly.

"Why, it's a meeting we have to have, isn't it? And I didn't want to be late for it now!" He ran a hand through his wild mop of hair. "They took me license away, y'see, so I got a friend to drop me off last night, with me bag and a drop of comfort for the cold, so I'd be right on the spot." Having finally disentangled himself from the bag, he stumbled to his feet and winced with the pain of his hangover. He gave her a bear hug and planted a very scratchy kiss on her forehead. "It's just grand to see ye again. Just like the old times. We'll put this Freyer feller in his place, the two of us. A real old Mary-Anne he is, but you'll straighten him out, I know."

Penny disengaged herself and looked up into his guileless eyes. "Look, Giles, I'm afraid something has happened; something very bad, and we haven't much time: so just listen. Freyer's dead: murdered—over there by the Birth Rocks. My friend has gone for the police, and should be back at any minute. You've got to be honest with me, and I'll help you all I can. Did you do it?"

He looked blankly at her. "Me? Why I niver laid a finger on him!" His next words were drowned out by the roar of a helicopter that suddenly appeared above the grove, stirring the trees to frenzy. It proceeded to settle down in a clearing next to the grove like an ungainly dragonfly. Penny saw with a sinking heart that Toby had been his usual efficient self, and that time for Giles had already run out.

Chapter 2

For Giles Shaw it was certainly not his lucky day. Toby's remarkable speed in getting results had been due to the unlikely presence—and on quite a different pursuit—of a state police helicopter in the neighboring village. The state police came, looked and listened, then summoned Hawaii Five-O, who promptly arrested Giles Shaw "on suspicion of murder, pending further investigation." To them it seemed an open-and-shut case: there had been no robbing of the body, and the man on the spot had overwhelming motive, means, and opportunity.

It did nothing to lift Penny's already low spirits that the testimony she and Toby had, perforce, to give only helped to seal Giles' fate. They had neither heard nor seen any other living human being in the vicinity of the murder, and when, on Penny's anguished urging, the police had made a halfhearted search for signs of another car, the only tracks they had found in the soft red earth had been those of the Porsche. Unless Freyer had brought his murderer with him, and then that murderer had managed to vanish into thin air within the space of a few minutes, there was no possibility of a third party. In vain did Penny expatiate on Giles' unconscious and soggy state when she had found him, and on the fact that he would never have committed the murder in such a way as to point directly back to himself. In the face of all the other evidence, the police brushed these objections aside, with but thinly-veiled contempt for her evident partiality.

Giles Shaw did little to help himself. He was so dazed by his hangover and the sheer speed of events that he stood blankly uncomprehending and silent throughout the investigation. Only when they had cuffed him and were leading him away to the police car did he finally rouse himself. He twisted around in the hands of his captors, a desperate gleam in his clouded eyes. "Penny," he shouted. "For the love of God, help me!"

She was so upset she could not get a word out, and could only nod violently as he was dragged away. When peace had settled back on the grove, she looked up at Toby, who was regarding her with gloomy concern. "I believe him," she managed to get out. "But what on earth can I do for him?"

"Well, if you'd take my advice—which you probably won't—you'll get him the best lawyer in the islands and leave it at that," he said. "We came here for much-needed rest and recreation, and I, for one, am going to do just that. It's absolutely no use fretting. There's nothing else you can do for him."

They set off back toward the rental car in silence. When they reached it, she said, "Maybe the autopsy will show something. It may even be suicide. Giles swore to me that he never laid a finger on Freyer."

"And may, for your sake, have been speaking the literal truth," Toby said, coiling himself into the driver's seat and starting the engine. "If you bean a man with a rock and then scratch his leg with a poisoned spear, you *wouldn't* lay a finger on him, you know." And with this gloomy thought to chew on, they drove back to Honolulu.

Toby was so obviously elated and happy at the prospect of fitting out and trying out the new yacht—for which Benedict Lefau had given him a free rein to do as he wished—that Penny did not have the heart to ask for his further help. Accordingly, she dropped him off at a ship chandler adjacent to the marina, into which he dove with all the excitement of a small boy in a toy shop, before driving back to their hotel, the Hawaiian Prince; one of the smaller, less pretentious hotels, but chosen by her because of its proximity to the marina. Once there, she busied herself for a while in finding out the most prestigious lawyer available and retaining him on Giles' behalf. That done, she found herself pacing around and around her room in an agony of frustrated energy. What should she do?

"This is no good whatsoever," she chided herself fiercely. "Gather your wits, sit down, and think straight!" She made herself a pot of coffee in the small kitchenette, took it out onto the lanai, and sat sipping the black brew, as she gazed unseeingly out over Pearl Harbor and sorted out her priorities.

The more she thought about the whole Menehune controversy, the less sense it made. Giles had obviously not given a damn about his reputation since Emily's death, and if the university had bounced him out on his ear, would not have given a damn either, since he was well fortified with money. So why, on the eve of a peace conference that *he* had instituted himself, should he have killed Freyer? It made no sense at all.

And Freyer's actions were just as odd. Knowing that he had Giles backed into a corner as far as the academic world was concerned, why should he not have continued on for the "kill"? And yet, apparently, he had been as anxious for this meeting as Giles had been. So, item one, find out when and why he had undergone this sudden change of mood and mind.

If Giles were innocent, then somebody else had to be guilty, so, item two, find out if Freyer had any other enemies, academic or otherwise, who would have had cause to kill him. How to go about it? On item one she would obviously have to find out a lot more about the whole Menehune controversy: at the moment all she knew was the main sequence of events that had culminated in a punch-up between Giles and Freyer in the lobby of one of the ritzier Honolulu hotels. For this she decided to approach an old friend in the Bishop Museum, who was also a part-time faculty member of the university, but who was less likely to be as discreet about the affair as the full-time faculty. Item two was likely to be a lot more sensitive, and the only thought that came to her on that was to approach Freyer's daughter to offer sympathy and support, in the hope of drawing her out on her father's activities. She grimaced with distaste at the thought of this, but could see no other alternative.

The coffeepot drained, she leapt into action. She called for an appointment with Chris Bullard at the museum, left a note for Toby at the reception desk as to her whereabouts, in the unlikely event he should wonder or worry about her, got out the car and zoomed across town to the museum.

The Bishop Museum lay drowsing in the midday sun, and its familiar ambience, that drew her back into a Polynesian world with which she was more familiar than the modern bustle of the islands, soothed and comforted her. Chris Bullard was run to earth in the bowels of the museum, and emerged from his office blinking like a bear newly-roused from hibernation. He was a tall, stooping, greyish man, whose all-absorbing passion was for the more obscure dialects of the Polynesian area, and who rarely

15

talked about anything else. He was, however, a good listener.

On this occasion, he was a rapt one, giving little exclamations of horror, disbelief, and concern at all the right places as Penny rapidly told her story. "I thought I knew enough to play the role of peacemaker," she explained, "but now, if I'm going to be of help to Giles, I've got to know *everything* about the row. What I need from you Chris, is a detailed account, and particularly about when and why their attitudes changed."

He let out his breath in a gusty sigh. "Quite a tall order, but I'll try. Let me see now. Well, things at the start were just standard academic bickering. Giles evidently enjoyed needling Freyer, whom he never did have much time for. After the publication of the book with his extravagant claims about the 'modern' presence of Menehunes in the islands, Freyer got a lot more vocal and a lot nastier. But it was only when Giles specified that he *knew* of Menehunes on the big island of Hawaii, and hinted at leading an expedition of journalists and TV people to a certain locality there, that Freyer really blew his stack. He called Giles a raving maniac, as well as other less complimentary names, and said that such an expedition would bring nothing but ridicule to the islands and should be officially banned. Everyone thought this was a bit extreme, since there are plenty of other half-baked searches going on around the world—for Bigfoot, Noah's Ark, 'Nessie,' etcetera—and these do no harm. They give the participants a lot of pleasure and are—and this is the bottom line, I think—extremely *good* for the local economies."

"So it was after that when Freyer started to back down?" Penny enquired.

Chris Bullard shook his head. "No, Giles was the first to change his mind. You know how volatile he is. Anyway, he gave an interview on a local TV station and said he'd decided that he had no right to intrude on the privacy of his little friends, and that he would produce 'visual' proof that would justify his claims, but would not let the rest of the world in on their habitat. Strangely enough though, it was *after* that that he and Freyer had the punch-up. No one knows what passed between them at that meeting, but it was after that that Freyer went to the university authorities, all sweetness and light, and said that he thought the dispute had gone too far and that if a third party of some stature could be brought in, he would be prepared to make a joint statement with Giles to settle the matter."

"I see," Penny said thoughtfully. "And how long ago was this?"

"About a month ago—maybe a little less."

"Did Giles ever specify the area of Hawaii the expedition would go to?"

"Only in a very general way." Chris uncoiled himself and ambled over to a huge map of the islands on the office wall, and vaguely sketched in an area towards the eastern part of the big island. "Just in this area between Mauna Kea to the north and the eastern shore. It's largely undeveloped terrain in which looking for Menehunes would be slightly worse than looking for the proverbial needle in a haystack, and which would make a lot of sense if Giles was just having us all on."

Penny frowned, because it still seemed to make no sense to her. "Did you think Giles was at all serious about this whole thing?"

Chris shrugged. "I did point out to him that the word 'menehune' was often used just to designate a plebeian or even just an artisan in many other parts of Polynesia, and that might be a simple explanation for the presence of the menehunes in the first Hawaiian census. He just laughed and said he knew all that."

"So what did you think?"

"I thought he had something else in mind. Giles is pretty devious, you know, and I had the feeling that the menehunes were just a smokescreen for what he was really after."

"Any idea what that may have been?"

Bullard shrugged. "No. Behind that facade of the professional Irish clown that Giles cultivates so assiduously lurks a very keen mind, as well as some very strongly-held beliefs. He's rabid on some issues, in fact, I think he'd like to see every *haole* and oriental cleared out of the islands and the whole kit and caboodle handed back to the original inhabitants—himself excepted, of course. He's been keeping some pretty strange company since Emily died, including some of the more extreme and less savory Polynesian nationalists. I know he has joined some of their more violent protests about developers . The very mention of land being taken over for construction of any kind is enough to start him foaming at the mouth."

Penny worried away at this thought in silence, while Chris Bullard threw wistful glances at the page of manuscript he was working on. Finally, she sighed and said, "Well, I still don't make too much sense out of it, but I've taken up too much of your time, Chris, so I'll go and chew this over and leave you in peace. May I call you again if I think of anything else?"

He got up with alacrity and evident relief. "Of course, Penny—anytime, anytime at all."

As she emerged into the bright sunlight, her prompt stomach growled at her with the warning that it was way past her usual lunch hour. To comfort herself she went to a nearby restaurant, ordered a large and expensive lunch, and ate every scrap of it absentmindedly as she mulled over what she had learned from Chris Bullard. If only she had had more time to talk with Giles! There were a thousand questions seething in her mind that only he could answer, but not, she realized, under the sharp ears and eyes of the police. Perhaps his lawyer had managed to arrange bail, and then she could get to him for that all-important talk.

Feeling decidedly over-full, she staggered to the nearest phone, and after being passed from secretary to secretary, as befitted the action in the august firm of Rogers, Yokamura and Feldstein, was told that Mr. Rogers was unavailable. His personal secretary, however, did unbend sufficiently to inform her that bail in the Shaw/Freyer case had been set at $60,000, which the client had refused, electing to stay in jail. This again puzzled her, for Giles was not one, she would have thought, to take incarceration lightly, and the money, however much of Emily's fortune he had managed to get through, should have presented no problem. For some reason it suited Giles to stay put—why? she puzzled.

Baffled on her first project, she turned to her second. Hunting up Freyer's number in the book, she made her second call, but after several tries could only get a busy signal. From this she concluded that Freyer's daughter, understandably in the circumstances, had probably taken the phone off the hook. Nothing daunted, she noted down the Freyer address, which lay in a residential section not far from the university, and set off on her second hunt.

The Freyer house turned out to be one of a multitude of identical modest one-story houses in a new development, its only distinction from its neighbors lying in the immaculate neatness of its front yard, where not a blade of the short-mown grass was out of place and not a weed visible in the flowerbeds, where the plants and shrubs were stiffly arranged with a military precision. In the carport beside the house stood a venerable Ford station wagon, whose faded paint also shone with cleanliness and careful waxing. She was a little surprised to find the street completely deserted, for she had half-expected a small crowd of reporters and the inevitable TV van laying siege to the Freyer household, but on Lalani Avenue nothing stirred. She drove slowly down the whole length of it, nerving herself to the unpleasant task ahead, then turned around and parked on the opposite side of the street across from the house.

Only Giles' desperate face as he was led away drove her up the swept cement path to the front door, to pound on the sparkling brass knocker, which, she noted with grim amusement, was of a grinning Menehune. But in spite of all her pounding, the door remained firmly shut, although she could have sworn there had been movement of some kind inside the house, movement she sensed rather than heard. Her stubborn streak aroused, she made her way around through the carport and pounded on the side door that led off of it: still no result. She toured around the back of the house, where the minute back yard was every bit as neat as the front, and came out on the other side with a sinking feeling of anticlimax.

Getting back into the car, she decided to wait and see if her quarry would either emerge or return, and lit up a cigarette. Looking up and down the quiet street, an anomaly suddenly struck her: this was a relatively humble neighborhood but, granting the high price of Hawaiian real estate and the none too generous salary of an associate professor, quite in keeping with Freyer's means. The few cars outside of the neighboring houses were all of an age and price range with the Freyer station wagon, but the Porsche Freyer had driven to his rendezvous with death would stick out in such a setting as this like a sore thumb: it was brand-new and expensive. Maybe it was not his car at all. She frowned. Perhaps she was clutching at straws, but this was something else to be checked into.

A tall, skinny Polynesian emerged from the carport of a house several houses down from the Freyers', and after a swift glance toward her slid into a very battered and dusty convertible and roared away from the curb. Excited by her new idea, she was just about to follow his example when another car roared suddenly down the quiet street, drew up with a scream of brakes before the Freyer house, decanted a tall, young fair-haired man, who raced up the path and proceeded to pound energetically on the Menehune knocker. Penny took her hand off the key and sat back to watch. Who was he?—boyfriend, plainclothes cop, other? With no more success than she had had, he repeated her actions by going around to the carport side and emerged on the other side in due course looking baffled. He stopped, took a notebook out of his pocket, looked around eagerly and started to scribble in it: so that was it—the press had undoubtedly arrived. She felt it was time to go. But before she could get the key in the ignition, he had spotted her, and racing across the road stuck his head in the open window on the passenger side, the notebook still in his hand and pencil poised. "Excuse me, madam, Brad Field of the *Hawaiian Gazette*. Have you heard about the Freyer murder?"

"Yes," she said reluctantly.

"Any idea where Miss Freyer might be?"

"None."

"Then may I have *your* reaction as a neighbor to the news?"

"I'm not a neighbor," Penny said shortly, starting the engine.

His vivid blue eyes narrowed. "Hey, wait a minute! Don't I know you from somewhere?"

"I doubt it," Penny said firmly. "Now, you must excuse me," and put the car in drive. He hastily withdrew his head as it began to move, but she could see him in her mirror gazing fixedly after her as she drove away.

She drove aimlessly for a while, trying to figure out how to find out about the Porsche, but came to the conclusion that that information could also only come from the elusive Miss Freyer, so rather grumpily decided to take a leaf out of Toby's detecting technique of consulting source material, bought herself a paperback of Giles' book on the Menehunes, which she found had been put out by one of the smaller Hawaiian presses, and, driving back to the hotel, settled down on the lanai to read it.

She was still at it several hours later, when Toby returned, his face bright with sunburn and enthusiasm. "How about dinner?" he boomed. "Been hard at it all day, and I'm starved!"

Never one to refuse a meal, she was soon seated across from him at a seafood restaurant overlooking the marina, but when the enticing seafood platter she had ordered was put before her, she found herself pecking at it with none of her usual zest as her excited companion raved on about flying jibs and spinnakers and the wonderful array of gadgets he had found for the new yacht. It finally penetrated to Toby's mind that she was not giving him her full attention nor was she interested in eating. At this last and most unusual phenomenon, his spate dried up and he looked at her with lively concern. "You look really down in the mouth. What's up? More nails in Giles' coffin come to light?"

"No, not really. I just did not accomplish much today." She briefly related the events of the day, ending up with her concern about the Porsche.

Toby did not appear impressed. "It's something to check on, yes, but there could be a lot of natural explanations. Maybe he'd been saving for it for years—after all, it's not too unusual for a man to crave a 'dream car.' Or maybe a rich relation died and left him a legacy and he sunk it into something he'd always wanted." Seeing the gleam in her eye and the grim set of her mouth, he went on. "You know I do appreciate the fact you want to do everything you can for an old friend, but have you thought about the other side of it? If Giles *isn't* the man, then we are faced with an impossible murder. One done by an invisible person who appeared out of nowhere and disappeared the same way. Much as, for your sake, I'd like to believe otherwise, I swear that no other person could have got in and out of that grove while we were there without us seeing or being aware of him."

"There *has* to be another explanation," Penny said stubbornly. "And I'm going on until I find it." She pushed away her half-eaten dinner and got up, hoisting her capacious tote bag over her shoulder.

"Where are you off to now?" he demanded.

"Going back to dig out the Freyer girl. There's a lot of questions to be asked."

"Do you want company?" he said reluctantly.

"No. You'd better do something about that sunburn or you'll be peeling like crazy by tomorrow, and then you'd best sleep off your jetlag. I'll be all right." She left him glooming into his Mai-tai.

Back on Lalani Avenue, she was relieved to see, as she parked across the road, that the Freyer house was ablaze with light. She marched resolutely up to the front door and pounded on it. After a short pause a young voice quavered on the other side "Who's there?"

"Miss Freyer? My name is Penelope Spring, Dr. Spring. You may have heard about my part in the sad events of this morning. I came to extend my condolences and to offer to help in any way I can. May I come in?"

There was something between a gasp and a sob from the other side of the door, and then it was opened a cautious crack and Penny's eyes widened in surprise. A tall, slim, pretty girl was looking at her out of large dark, red-rimmed eyes: eyes that were stricken with fear. But she was clad incongruously in a wraparound work apron, her hair hidden beneath a bandanna to protect it from dust, and in her free hand she was clutching a pile of untidy files. Seeing the shock in Penny's face, her pale face flushed and she hurriedly tore off the bandanna, letting loose a flood of ash blond hair that cascaded down to her shoulders. "I was just doing some tidying up," she faltered. "Er, you'd better come in, Dr. Spring. Yes, of course I've heard of you. I'm Griselda Freyer." She fell back from the door and Penny went into a small square hall. Griselda Freyer shut and locked the door before mutely indicating an open archway leading into the brightly-lit living room. Penny walked in and stopped dead in her tracks. The room was furnished with cheap rattan furniture that nonetheless looked bright and attractive because it was so impeccable and well-cared for. The one very discordant note was two large empty book cases that stood on either side of the fireplace, and from which every single book had been tumbled into untidy heaps on the polished parquet floor. She looked in amazed enquiry at the girl, who stared back with fear-filled eyes. "I found them like this when I got home this evening," Griselda forced out through ashen lips. "But that's not the worst of it." She led Penny toward another door at the far end of the living room and threw it open to reveal a small, book-lined study. This looked as if a cyclone had hit it; books and papers were scattered everywhere and every drawer in the large desk and the filing cabinet gaped wide.

Coming out of her own shocked stupor, Penny put a comforting arm around the trembling girl. "How did they get in? Do you know what was taken?"

"They forced the study window. I've wired it shut again, but . . ." the blond head rolled helplessly. "So far as I can make out nothing is missing, nothing. . . ." The voice rose to a hysterical pitch.

"You've called the police, of course," Penny said, a wild gleam of hope expanding in her own heart, for this vandalism could be none of Giles' doing.

The girl drew away from her, her eyes dilated. "No," she whispered. "I haven't. I daren't. Oh, you don't understand, but I'm just terrified!" and she burst into helpless, hysterical tears.

Chapter 3

Penny ended up staying the night. She had led the sobbing girl back to the living room, deposited her on the brightly-cushioned couch, and then had foraged around in the cupboards until she found some brandy. Getting a stiff shot of this into Griselda, she again left her to have her cry while she went into the kitchen and made a pot of strong tea for them both. By the time she returned with the tray Griselda's sobs had died down to a quiet crying, and as Penny settled down in a chair opposite to her, she mopped at her eyes, sat up straighter, accepted a cup of tea, and declared, "I'm not behaving at all well. I'm sorry, Dr. Spring."

"You've had a series of great shocks today, my dear," Penny said gently, "so you're having a perfectly normal reaction. But I think it's very important we have a long talk. If you like I can call the police, tell them what's happened and to put a guard on the house, and you can come back to my hotel for the night—there's an extra bed in my room. Or, I can keep you company here tonight. I don't think you should stay alone until we have got to the bottom of this."

"Oh, *would* you stay?" Griselda said pleadingly. "I can't face any more policemen tonight, I just can't!"

Penny felt that the girl had already probably messed up any evidence the police might have found useful, so there would be little point in summoning them before morning anyway. "Alright," she said soothingly. "We can wait until tomorrow. Now, perhaps I'd better explain something. I expect you know I was supposed to arbitrate the dispute between your father and Dr. Shaw? My colleague, Toby Glendower, and I found your father's body this morning, and then *I* found Dr. Shaw, and the condition he was in when I found him makes me certain that the police have made a great mistake and that Dr. Shaw did *not* kill your father."

Griselda's beautiful brown eyes were puzzled. "But if it wasn't Dr. Shaw, then who?" she asked.

"Well, that's what I intend to find out," Penny said firmly. "And I hope you can help me. What has happened here today clearly indicates that there is someone else involved. Giles Shaw is in prison so he couldn't have done this. Suppose you tell me the events of today just as they happened to you, unless you're too tired?"

"Oh, I couldn't sleep a wink. I'm far too keyed up. We can talk all night if you like," Griselda said earnestly.

Penny, who was beginning to feel more than a little weary herself after her long day, greeted this with resignation, and to bolster her own waning energies poured a large slug of brandy into her tea. "Fine," she said. "Go ahead then."

Griselda put down her cup and let out a quivering sigh. "Usually on Tuesday mornings I do some secretarial work for Professor Ebert at the university, but this morning, because of the meeting, my father asked me to stay here and finish up some notes he'd been working on, and he was supposed to come back here and take me with him to the university later on. When he didn't show up I didn't worry, because I thought the meeting was just going on longer than he had anticipated. Then the next thing I knew Professor Ebert came here, along with the police and . . ." her voice quavered and broke for a second, ". . . they told me what had happened. I had to go down and identify my father, and they questioned me, and then Professor Ebert insisted I go home with him, because he wanted to spare me from 'the hyenas of the media' as he terms them, he was certain would be laying siege to this house. He and Mrs. Ebert were very kind, and I stayed with them all day. But they are both rather frail and elderly, and I didn't want to impose on them, and besides, the police had asked for some of my father's papers here, so when it got dark I suggested they bring me home. Professor Ebert drove up and down the street a couple of times to make sure there were no reporters lurking around, and then dropped me off. And I came in and found . . ." she made a helpless gesture with one slim hand, ". . . this. I was so upset that all I could think of was clearing up all the mess."

Penny looked at her curiously, for to her it did not seem a normal reaction at all, but she said, "So you've no idea when this could have happened?"

Griselda shook her head. "None at all."

"You didn't go to your neighbors and ask for help or if they'd seen anyone?"

Griselda flushed faintly. "We don't know our neighbors," she stammered and looked down. "We were always so busy at the university, you see."

A sudden thought struck Penny. "Do you have a Polynesian family living three houses down?" she asked.

Griselda looked positively shocked. "Oh, no, this is an all-white neighborhood."

Penny felt a small surge of excitement. "Then I think I might be able to pinpoint the time for the police. I was here looking for you earlier today—about two o'clock this afternoon. I thought at the time there was someone in the house and that you probably just didn't feel like answering the door, but shortly after that I saw a young Polynesian come out from the carport of a house further down and drive off like a bat out of hell. It *may* just be a coincidence, but it's something the police should check on. Perhaps I disturbed the intruder and he took off without finding what he was looking for. Have you any idea what that might have been?" She gazed directly at Griselda.

The girl looked completely baffled. "None. There is nothing of value here—except to us."

"Other than Dr. Shaw, was your father on bad terms with anyone else? Anyone who bore him a grudge?"

Griselda bristled. "My father was a man of peace. He wasn't very sociable, but no, he was not on bad terms with anyone."

Either the girl didn't know or wouldn't say. Penny decided that now was not the time to press this particular issue: she changed tactics. "Did your father's work habits or patterns change at all over the past few months? Anything, anything at all out of the ordinary might help."

"No, nothing," Griselda began, then hesitated. "Well, yes, there was one thing that puzzled me rather. My father has been seeing a lot of a Hawaiian called Hapili recently."

It was Penny's turn to be puzzled. "Your father was an anthropologist, why should seeing a native Polynesian be strange?"

"Well, you know my father was a social anthropologist and his main field was the integration of native peoples into urban societies, and the impact Western culture had on theirs?"

"Yes. So?"

"Well, Hapili was a *kahuna*," Griselda said wonderingly. "A *kahuna ana ana*."

"A *black* magician! A killing priest! Why, I didn't know any such still existed in Hawaii." Penny was thunderstruck.

The girl glanced at her quickly, her tense face closing up. "It probably isn't important," she muttered.

It opened up a whole new vista to Penny, but again she decided this was not the moment to pursue it. "And what is going to happen about your father's lovely new car?" she challenged.

Griselda looked amazed at this non sequitur. "Er, the police have it in their garage, and are bringing it back here tomorrow. I suppose I'll have to sell it, although we've only had it a month, but I don't know how to drive a stick shift car."

"Maybe the finance company can help you with that," Penny said craftily.

"Oh, my father would *never* have anything to do with one of those!" Griselda was horrified. "Why, we never even had a credit card of any kind. He did not believe in them."

"You mean he paid *cash* for such an expensive item?"

Griselda gazed at her in bewilderment. "I suppose so. He always did for anything we bought. I'm afraid I don't know much about it. My father always handled the finances. I just kept house and helped out at the university." She was beginning to wilt, the eyelids drooping over her pansy-brown eyes. A few minutes more, Penny decided, and she would be ready for sleep. "I think we've both just about had it, so enough of this catechism," she said. "Just tell me all about yourself—nothing to do with all this, but I'm just incurably nosy about people."

Somewhat to her surprise, the girl appeared to unfold

like a flower as if no one had ever asked her about herself before. She greeted the change of subject with a naive eagerness, her energy reviving in the process. But as she talked on about her childhood in Michigan, her mother's early death, and her life since she came to the islands, Penny felt an upsurge of compassion for the lonely girl. Reading between the lines of Griselda's murmured narrative, a none-too-pleasant picture of Helmut Freyer was emerging. He had been a heavily Germanic and demanding father, using the girl, even though she had somehow contrived along the way to get a Master's degree in sociology, as a combination household drudge and general dogsbody at the university for his own work. He was an extremely parsimonious man, who doled out the money for the household with a very sparing hand, and the only money the girl had ever had as her own was the small sums she earned by doing secretarial work for the other professors at the university. His tight-fistedness had excluded socializing, so in this crowded, colorful and busy island they had led a curiously isolated existence with no real friends, no close contacts.

Griselda had been well-named, Penny reflected grimly, for she closely resembled the Patient Griselda of Germanic folklore who also had had a lot to bear. The spate of confidences faltered and died as the girl's head drooped and she slipped down on the couch and curled up like a child into sleep.

Penny stood up, acutely aware of her own weariness, then staggered off and gathered a couple of blankets from the girl's bedroom, covered the sleeping Griselda carefully with one of them, and settled down on the smaller couch, thankful for once for her small size. Before she drifted off, the anomaly of the Porsche still nagged at her. It could be as Toby had surmised, a single wild indulgence of a man who had been frugal for a lifetime, but somehow she could not see a man as penny-pinching as Freyer evidently had been ever doing such a thing. It was a lead, a definite lead. So thinking, she too slept.

By the morning, her energies restored, she went into high gear. The Honolulu police were summoned, the situation explained, and leaving Griselda in their—she hoped—capable hands, she bustled off, promising to return later for the apprehensive girl. She drove like an arrow toward the headquarters of Hawaii Five-O, intent on laying all this new extenuating evidence at the feet of Chief Inspector Lyons, who had been placed in charge of the case. With any luck, she hoped that Giles would be let out before the end of the day and she could, at last, have that heart-to-heart talk.

As she walked into the venerable building that housed this super unit of law enforcement, she felt completely at home, for she had been an avid fan of the TV series when it had been shown in England. When the familiar dark mahogany door of the chief-inspector's office opened, she half-expected the dark-suited figure of Jack Lord to appear, and it was a definite anticlimax when a small man with mouse-colored hair akin to her own, and with a mild, nondescript face came out and said, "Dr. Spring? I'm Inspector Lyons. What can I do for you?"

"A lot, I hope. I have new evidence in the Freyer case—something that will exonerate Giles Shaw," she announced. He looked mildly surprised and none too impressed, but ushered her wordlessly in and seated her before his large mahogany desk. He fixed her with shrewd grey eyes that belied the mildness of the rest of his face. "And what is the nature of this evidence?"

Rapidly she told him. He heard her out in silence, making little doodles on the yellow pad in front of him as she gabbled on. When she got to the part about the Polynesian, she was a little disconcerted to see an amused smirk play around his firm thin lips, but she struggled valiantly on.

When her story was done, he carefully put down his pen and said with quiet irony, "Am I to take it then that you and your distinguished colleague are acting as amateur detectives in this case?"

Penny bristled. "Amateurs we may well be, but we have a hundred percent success rate in the investigations we have been involved with. A lot better average than your own department has, I might point out. And no, Sir Tobias is not involved in this, but *I* am. Very much so. Giles Shaw is not your murderer, and surely this evidence proves it. He cannot have been involved in this break-in."

Inspector Lyons sighed faintly. "Dr. Spring, I applaud your zeal in coming to the defense of your friend, but I'm afraid this new development proves nothing of the kind, and I would strongly urge you to go on about your holiday and leave this business in our hands. We *do* know what we are doing, whatever you may think." He had been leafing through a folder on his desk and took out a photograph which he handed to her. "Is that the man you saw yesterday?"

A huge face that seemed carved out of lava and bore a startling likeness to the statue of King Kamehamea glared out at her. "No," she snapped. "Not a bit like the man I saw. And I don't understand what you're getting at."

"No matter," he murmured, patting the photo back into the folder. "Kaowa would have plenty of stooges to do the job for him. And what I am getting at, Dr. Spring, is that Giles Shaw has a lot of friends besides yourself, and friends, I might add, who are not as law-abiding as you are." He tapped the folder with a stubby finger. "This Kaowa is one of them: an ardent Polynesian nationalist who claims descent from the old royal line and who is not above putting salt on the tail of *haole* officialdom. I wondered why Giles Shaw was so unwilling to meet his bail: I imagine he was anticipating Kaowa would take some action like this to throw dust in our eyes."

"Oh," Penny said blankly, her own reservations about Giles returning in full flood. "But surely you will look into this, won't you?"

"Naturally. You have raised some interesting questions, especially about the Porsche. But all of them will be dealt with, by *us*." His voice had become like steel.

She was on the defensive, but far from defeated. "Have you the results of the autopsy yet? I'd like to see them."

For the first time he seemed disconcerted. "Yes, the report is in, and a copy will be sent to Mr. Rogers, the defense lawyer. You can get the details from him."

"Mr. Rogers is an extremely difficult man to reach," she retaliated. "So, if it doesn't strain your resources *too* much, I'd like to have a copy myself. Was it poison?"

"Oh, definitely." Now he was downright uneasy. "An unusual one. Luckily we have very sophisticated equipment in our crime lab, otherwise we might have missed it."

"Then I'd very much like to see it," she repeated.

He hesitated, evidently torn between official caution and the desire to get rid of her. "Oh, very well," he switched on his intercom and gave some terse orders. "You can pick it up at the desk on your way out," he said.

Dismissed, she got up. "Thank you, Inspector Lyons, for all your help," she said as sweetly as she could manage, and hurried out to get the report. Its medical jargon meant little to her, but she tucked it safely away, hoping Toby would be able to make some sense out of it. She drove back to Lalani Avenue to find the police gone and Griselda again resolutely tidying up. "Do you want me to come with you to the university and help you look through your father's things there?" she asked.

"Oh, yes. That would be nice." Griselda hastily put away her cleaning materials, patted her shining fair hair into some kind of order, and followed her out, after carefully locking up. "The police said they are going to keep an eye on the place in case the intruder returns," she informed Penny as they drove the short distance to the university. "But they don't seem to think the break-in is very important."

Penny sniffed at this. "A lot they know. Will you be all right if I leave you after this for a while? I really ought to get back to my hotel and let Toby Glendower know what I've been doing."

"Oh, yes. The Eberts have invited me over again, and I think I'll stay with them tonight. I'll finish up the work for him I was supposed to do yesterday first, while I'm here." They parked in an almost deserted parking lot, for it was vacation time at the university, and Griselda led her small companion through a maze of sterile-looking corridors devoid of life. Finally she stopped before one of the closed doors and produced a bunch of keys. "My father didn't keep much here," she explained as she fiddled with the lock. "He preferred to work at home, because it was so much quieter." She flung open the door and stopped dead, as they took in another scene of devastation—books and papers were strewn everywhere. A neat hole cut out by the latch of one of the windows, still standing ajar, announced the point of entry. Griselda gave a little moan of despair. "Oh, *no!*"

"Damn! This time don't touch a thing," Penny ordered, and made for the phone, being careful to wrap a handkerchief around it before she called. The same police were summoned, the same squad arrived, looking considerably disgruntled, and the same routine begun. "This will take hours," Penny informed the shocked Griselda. "So I think I'll be off and touch base with you later. Maybe this time you will find something missing, and that will give us a lead."

Driving back to the hotel, she thought with satisfaction that this latest episode might make the smug Inspector Lyons sit up and take notice, though she realized it was but a continuation of the same theme. The intruder had been after *something* of vital importance among Freyer's papers: the problem was, what? Until she knew that she was no further ahead.

She was a little startled on entering the hotel to find her partner-in-crime pacing moodily up and down the small lobby. On spotting her, he came over and hissed, "Where the hell have you been? I've been worried to death."

"Good heavens! I thought you'd be out on the boat," she hissed back. "You ought to know by now that I can look after myself!"

"Ha! With your track record of getting into trouble, *that's* a laugh," he snorted. "Why didn't you leave me a message?"

"Well, things have been going at a rather fast clip. Come on up to my room and I'll explain." As they rode up in the elevator, she fished out the autopsy report and handed it to him. "Here, you read this, while I talk—I couldn't make head nor tail of it."

They had settled down and she had launched into her recital and was really warming to her subject when she realized she had completely lost her companion's attention. He was glaring fixedly at the report, a look of utter disbelief on his round face. "What is it?" she demanded.

He came to with a start. "Wait!" he commanded, and disappearing out of the door, returned shortly with a large, battered-looking book, which he started to leaf through, muttering to himself. "Has Giles Shaw been in Africa recently? Kenya to be precise," he demanded at length.

"Africa? So far as I know he has never set foot on the continent. Why Kenya?"

"Well, this certainly does put a different complexion on things," he muttered maddeningly.

"*What* does?" She was squeaking with impatience.

He closed the book, keeping his thumb stuck in it to mark his place, and frowned at her. "The report says that Helmut Freyer died from massive cardiac failure."

"But Inspector Lyons said he was poisoned," she spluttered.

"So he was. Analysis of a sticky substance found on the obsidian spearhead revealed *ouibain*," Toby said slowly. He opened the book and quoted. "*Ouibain* is only obtained in Kenya. It is especially prepared by the Giriama tribe from branches of the Murija tree, which are sliced up and boiled with reptile intestines to make a sticky poison used in hunting. Its effect is immediate heart stoppage." They stared at each other for a long pregnant moment. "And that means," Toby went on, "if you are correct and Shaw has had no connection with Africa, we must look elsewhere."

"Does that mean you're in with me?" she said.

Toby made a helpless gesture. "What choice do I have now? You're certainly not going to leave it alone, so the holiday is shot down in flames anyway." He got up and started to pace. "We have an obviously premeditated murder. What is worse, an *impossible* murder; the report puts the time of death within twenty minutes of our own arrival on the scene." He stopped dead and smote his forehead. "My God, what a fool I am! We *saw* the murderer."

Penny looked at him stupefied "We did?" she said weakly.

"Of course! I'd been thinking in terms of someone on the *ground*. The police looked for car tracks on the *ground*. Do you remember now?"

"Ah!" she said, light dawning. "The helicopter: the helicopter we saw overhead as we were getting out of the car."

"Exactly!" Toby beamed at her like a proud parent. "Which probably had set down in the nearest open space to the grove, namely the same place the police helicopter set down, thereby obliterating any traces of the other."

"Oh, great!" she returned. "So now we know the murderer can fly a helicopter. I wonder how many helicopter pilots there are in the islands; it must almost be as common as driving a car these days."

"No. Think about it. We know more than that." Toby resumed his excited pacing. "In fact, we can start building our picture of the murderer. How long did it take us to dismiss the 'Menehune' setup as a phony?"

"About thirty seconds," Penny said reflectively. "I see what you mean. In other words, not an anthropologist or archaeologist. Just someone who had latched on to the Menehune nonsense and decided to use it."

"Not only that, but someone who knew so *little* that he used a poison native only to Africa. There must be scores of native Hawaiian poisons he could have used, but didn't. So he's either very careless or very stupid."

"An off-islander?" she queried. Toby nodded.

"So we're looking for a helicopter pilot who knows nothing about anthropology, has recently been in Africa, isn't too swift, and probably doesn't belong out here at all. That still must encompass one hell of a lot of people," she said gloomily. "And what possible *motive* could anyone like that have had to polish off Freyer, whose whole expertise and life has been centered here, or to frame Giles, for that matter?"

"We can't know everything at once; it's early days yet," Toby reproved. "Maybe if the Freyer girl finds out what is missing, it will show us the way. I think the best way for us to proceed is . . ." He was interrupted by a fusillade of knocks on the door. They looked at each other in surprise, and Penny got up and opened it.

One of the largest men she had ever seen loomed on the threshold. He topped Toby's six feet by a good nine inches, and his massive frame completely filled the doorway; his bronzed monolithic face glowered down at her, as she instinctively fell back and he advanced menacingly into the room.

"I am Kaowa," he announced in a deep bass rumble. "Benjamin Kaowa. And I must speak with you." His deep maroon eyes under craggy brows encompassed them both as they stood paralyzed, then his face split suddenly into an engaging, white-toothed grin. "I understand from the police that you are trying to help Giles Shaw, and I've come to offer you my services."

Chapter 4

"For heaven's sake, Toby!—the man is a known thug, how *could* you have hired him? He can't be trusted and what's more, when Inspector Lyons hears of this, he'll hit the roof and we won't get another scrap of information out of him," Penny fumed. Kaowa had just taken his massive departure, having helped Toby demolish a whole bottle of dark rum during which process the two so very disparate men had become bosom buddies under her horrified eyes. The door had scarcely closed upon him when she sailed into battle.

Toby, his round cherubic face flushed from the rum, his equally round eyes shining like blue marbles behind his round glasses, looked stubborn and unrepentant. "I need someone to help me with the crackdown cruise, and Kaowa knows boats and the island—not to mention all that's going on in the local native scene. He'll be very useful. For instance, he many be able to track down this Hapili character quicker than the police can."

"You didn't tell Kaowa about him, did you?" she squeaked in dismay. Their drinking session had gone on so long that she had been in and out, finding out about

Porsche dealers in Oahu: there were so many of them that she was already discouraged. And she had missed a lot of the conversation.

Toby was all offended dignity. "Of course not!" he snapped. "Not before I had talked over our plan of action with you, but so far as I can see we don't have one. How would *you* go about finding Hapili?"

"Well, I was hoping Inspector Lyons—or even Giles, come to that—might give us a line on him," she said.

He snorted. "I gathered that you had had your usual negative effect on the police, and that Lyons had more or less told you to butt out. I can't see him being of much help."

"He gave me the autopsy report, didn't he?" she cried. "And if I trade him off our information about the helicopter he might cooperate."

"We were the only ones who saw it, and there is no other proof it was ever there, remember? He'll probably think we made it up as an afterthought to get Giles Shaw off the hook," Toby pointed out grimly. "No, if I were you, I'd keep that dark until we can get a better idea of what this is all about."

Penny decided to change her line of attack. "Toby, you're very good at research and digging things out, but when it comes to knowing about people and how they act you're often a babe-in-arms. As an anthropologist, people are *my* bag, and I know one heck of a lot about Polynesians. Kaowa is an *alii*, an aristocrat, who claims to be of the blood royal of Hawaii. He thinks himself above the law. He's one of those people who'd like to put the clock back and clear out every non-Polynesian from the islands: in other words, a fanatic. And one who would gladly twist the tail of the authorities and double-cross any *haole* just for the heck of it."

Toby looked out from the lanai with profound distaste

towards the towering skyscrapers of Honolulu, the crowded harbor, the beaches thronged with a seething mass of holiday-makers. "And I can thoroughly sympathize with him," he said somberly.

"This is no time to indulge in your Celtic weakness for lost causes," she snapped. "We're here to help Giles."

"And Kaowa is Giles' *friend*," Toby retaliated. "If of nothing else I am certain of that. And he is not a wild-eyed fanatic, he's a realist who is trying to halt this terrifying process that is turning Hawaii into wall-to-wall hotels and retirement homes for the rich. You should have stayed around and listened to him. . . ."

They were interrupted by a series of brisk raps on the door, and Penny, unable to think of a retort, hurried to open it. Brad Field stood on the threshold, a bright smile on his young face, a notebook and folder clasped in his left hand. "Ah, Dr. Spring, I *knew* I recognized you when I saw you out at the Freyer house! Brad Field of the *Gazette* again." With an agile side step, he was past her into the room and making for Toby, hand outstretched. "And you must be Sir Tobias Glendower, her celebrated partner-in-crime. How do you do, sir? Brad Field of the *Hawaiian Gazette*. I was hoping you would grant me an exclusive on your involvement in the Menehune case."

Toby had recoiled against the railing of the lanai and was looking desperately around for a means of escape. His hatred of publicity of any sort amounted almost to a phobia, and in the face of the brash eagerness of the reporter he was reduced to a series of panic-stricken, incoherent gobbles. Brad Field had whipped open the folder, which was full of press clippings, and brandished it under his nose. "As soon as I remembered who Dr. Spring was, I did some digging in our files, and just want to check over the facts with you to get them straight for my article. Now this will be your seventh murder investigation, I believe?

There were the two in America—in New Orleans and
Cape Cod; the affair in Brittany, the one in Scotland, and
the two in the Middle East, Turkey and Israel—weren't
you buried alive in that one, sir? How does this case
compare with the others? And what progress have you
made?"

Toby let out a faint tormented groan, and Penny, feeling
he had suffered enough, said with some asperity, "Mr.
Field, we are simply here on vacation and are not about
to give any interviews on anything to you or anyone else.
But I would like to know how you tracked us here." She
almost added "so fast," but thought better of it.

Brad grinned at her. "Piece of cake! I noticed you were
driving a rental car out at the Freyer place, so, once I
remembered who you were, you were a cinch to find."

Impressed by this detective flair and vividly conscious
of the long list of Porsche dealers now nestling in her
purse, Penny favored him with a long reflective look. "I
see," she murmured as an idea burgeoned and blossomed.
"Very impressive. And while an interview is out of the
question, since, I repeat, we are merely here on vacation,
perhaps I do have something for you, something you might
want to follow up."

Brad Field brightened, his notebook at the ready.
"Great! Go ahead." Toby seized his chance to escape, and
with a few long strides was past them and heading for the
door. A series of deep, incoherent rumbles issued from
him, the only coherent sound coming as he reached the
escape portal, ". . . at the yacht," he growled, and was
gone.

"What yacht is that?" Brad said instantly.

Penny saw no harm in building up their image as innocent vacationers. "The one on which we'll be spending
our vacation—as guests of Benedict Lefau. Sir Tobias, who
is an expert yachtsman, is getting it ready for his arrival."

The reporter's eyebrows shot up. "You mean the multi–millionaire Lefau?" he said in awe.

"His son", she said crisply. "Now, are you interested in what I have to say or not?"

He collected himself with an effort. "Er—of course! Please go on."

She chose her words carefully. "Well, you may have heard of the car found at the scene of the murder at the Birthing Rocks? It is a brand-new Porsche, recently acquired by the dead man. Since it is a luxury car and somewhat out of keeping with his previous lifestyle, it occurred to me that it might be worthwhile checking up on. When, where and how he bought it—you might like to check on that."

Brad Field was busily scribbling away. "We could do that easily enough. When can we start?"

She did not care for the "we" at all; the last thing she wanted was a reporter dogging her footsteps, but then had a further flash of inspiration. "Oh, it's of no concern to me," she said carelessly. "Though I'd be mildly interested to know what you find. I don't know anything about it, but you could ask Miss Freyer—she may know something."

"I haven't been able to get as much as a glimpse of her, let alone an interview," he confessed gloomily. "She's a regular Vanishing Lady."

Penny hastily weighed the pros-and-cons. In a sense it would be throwing Griselda to the wolves of the press, but Brad Field seemed a very mild wolf and she would have to talk to a reporter sooner or later. More importantly, it would divert him from her own trail. "If I could arrange a meeting with Griselda Freyer for you, would you guarantee to handle her with kid gloves? She has had a terrible shock, poor child. And also to show her any copy you propose to print?"

His face lit up. "Sure! On a stack of bibles, if you like. If you could only get me in, why, it would be an exclusive!"

"Then I'll see what I can do," Penny said. "If you'll excuse me now." She went into the small bedroom, firmly shutting the door behind her, and applied herself to the bedside phone. She ran Griselda to earth at the university on her second try, and put the proposition to her as artfully as she could.

Griselda was understandably dubious and reluctant, but Penny persisted. "He's an amiable and bright young man who might prove very useful, and it's possible if you win him over, he might keep the rest of the press off your back. Once wind of these break-ins gets around, they'll be after you for certain."

Whether it was Brad's youth or his potential as a watchdog that appealed, Griselda allowed herself to be persuaded. "I'll be going back to the house now," she volunteered. "We could meet there if you like."

"Excellent!" Penny exclaimed. "By the way, where is the Porsche now?"

"Sitting in the driveway—the police brought it back this morning."

"Good. And did you come up with anything on Hapili in your father's files?"

"Only a telephone number—no address. It was tucked into my father's Roladex at his university office."

Penny almost crowed with delight. "Do you have it there? If so, give it to me and I'll get right after it."

The girl gave her the number, then whispered, "Please, Dr. Spring, do be careful! I only saw Hapili twice, but he frightened me. That man was *evil*."

"Oh, not to worry, my dear, I'm an old hand at this," Penny assured her. "See you in about an hour then?" and rang off.

She applied to Directory Assistance and discovered the

Hapili number was for a bar phone in an extremely sleazy native section between Honolulu and Waikiki. Not quite what she had hoped for, but at least a start, she told herself optimistically, and returned to the living room to find Brad Field sitting out on the lanai and immersed in Giles Shaw's Menehune book.

"Any luck?" he enquired and then, holding up the book, "Do you believe in any of this stuff?"

"Not really," she said drily. "And yes, Miss Freyer will see you—right away, in fact—but again I warn you that if you upset her in any way, this will be *it.*"

He sprang up. "Right on! Let's go. I'll behave—honest!" And they were on their way.

The minute the door of the Freyer house opened on Griselda, clad in a simple, sleeveless pale blue linen dress that showed off her full-bosomed, slim-hipped figure to perfection, and with her lovely hair falling in a golden cloud onto her shoulders, Penny knew that some of her troubles were over, as the young man beside her positively gaped at the gorgeous vision before him and his ears went a bright pink. Griselda, well aware of his vivid blue eyes upon her, blushed faintly, as Penny briskly made the introductions, thereby completing Brad's devastation and reducing him to a state of unusual silence.

"And there's the Porsche," Penny informed him unnecessarily, and to pull himself together he paced around it, a look of wistful yearning on his young face. "Beautiful car," he muttered. "Just gorgeous," with a sidelong glance at Griselda. Then brightened back to his normal self. "Look, it's got the dealer's name right on it! What say we take a spin out to them, Miss Freyer, and find out more about the car?"

"I can't drive a shift car," Griselda confessed, and looked deliciously helpless.

His chest swelled. "I can—if you would allow me the

privilege. And we could talk on the way. Perhaps you would also allow me to buy you lunch at the beach? It's a beautiful day."

Griselda blushed even more rosily. "Well, yes, that would be very nice." He let out an ecstatic sigh, and Penny, well pleased with the turn of events, said hastily. "In that case I'll leave you to it. Maybe you can let me know later what you find out." And she hopped back into her own car. She left them gazing into each other's eyes and headed, smirking, for Waikiki.

A few qualms assailed her as she cruised slowly past the bar—a mere hole-in-the-wall establishment on a rubbish-strewn street with more derelicts and winos than any she had seen on the islands. She found a parking space on a street nearby that looked a little more respectable and locked the car carefully, thanking her stars that she spoke enough Hawaiian to get by. She had the sinking feeling that in this neighborhood English would not get her very far.

She scurried back to the bar, acutely aware that she was the only *haole* around and that the sidelong glances she was receiving from the passing throng were anything but friendly. She plunged into the dusky interior and halted just across the threshold, to adjust her eyes after the brilliant sunlight of the street. She was thankful to see that the bar was almost empty, with only two clients at the counter and another slumped over a table in the rear. With more confidence than she felt, she sailed up to the bar, over which a stony-faced Polynesian bartender in a tattered t-shirt presided. "I wonder if you could help me," she said somewhat breathlessly. "I'm looking for someone, a patron of yours. A *kahuna* named Hapili. He gave me your phone number and it's urgent that I find him."

Not a flicker of response came over the impassive face before her, so she tried it again in Hawaiian. This time there was a flash of surprise in his dull, dark eyes, and the two men at the bar stopped their own conversation and turned to stare at her. The barkeep leaned towards her. "You buying something?" he said in English. "This ain't no information booth."

Penny meekly ordered a light beer which she had no intention of drinking, and was aware of their eyes on her as she fumbled in her tote bag for money. "Now about Hapili," she said firmly. "Yours was the number he gave me and I need to see him. Where is he?"

"He ain't here." The barkeep's tone was mocking.

"Obviously. But can you tell me when he'll be in or, better still, his address." To sweeten the pot she added, "A friend owes him some money and asked me to look him up and give it to him."

The barkeep's meaty hand thrust itself under her nose. "You can give it to me. I'll see he gits it when he gits back."

She recoiled. "No, that won't do. I have to get his receipt and give him a personal message. Where has he gone?"

"Hapili don't never mess with no *haoles*," one of the men at the bar observed. "You're lying, lady. What you really at down here?" He and his companion had moved away from the bar and were now blocking her pathway to the door.

"You got money for him, you give it to me, if you know what's good for you," the bartender said with soft menace, and started to come out from behind the bar.

"I don't have *cash*," Penny said icily, edging away. "I have a check. My friend's instructions were to take Hapili to my bank after I had delivered the message. So I need him in person. Where is he?"

"Gone," the bartender said. "And since we give you this information, you pay for it, see! We'll take what you got in that bag, lady, and then you clear outta here damn quick."

She was now backed against the opposite wall and feeling more than a little desperate as they converged on her, when the light from the open door suddenly darkened and she looked up to see a huge and unmistakable figure blocking it. She did not know whether to be relieved or more frightened than she already was, until Kaowa rapped out an explosive string of Hawaiian and the men froze in their tracks and slowly turned toward him. He advanced menacingly into the room and the bartender quickly retreated behind the bar and the two men fell back before him, then turned and scuttled out into the daylight.

Kaowa towered over her. "Okay, Dr. Spring," he said soothingly. "It's okay now. What did you want here?"

She collected herself with an effort, still uncertain whether she had exchanged the frying pan for the fire. "I was trying to find the *kahuna* Hapili and was given this phone number for him. The man here knows about him but won't tell me."

"He will now," Kaowa said softly, and with a single stride was before the bar and a ham-like hand shot out and grasped the bartender's t-shirt, bringing him forward with a jerk so that they were eye-to-eye. "Tell me where Hapili is before I shake it out of you."

"He's gone—gone away," the man spluttered.

The fist twisted on the shirt and rested beneath the man's chin. "Where?" Kaowa hissed.

"The big island—Hawaii—yesterday," came the choked reply.

The grip tightened further. "Where on Hawaii?"

"I don't know, honest I don't!" The man's eyes rolled in panic. "He jes' came and went in one hell of a rush. Said to hold messages till he got in touch. And there ain't been any messages. That's the truth, I swear!"

49

"If it isn't, I'll be back. You can count on it," Kaowa menaced, and released him. He turned to Penny who had edged towards the door. "That seems to be all of it," he observed. "Now is there anything else you'd like to do in this neighborhood, or shall I see you back to your car?"

"No, I'm all finished here," she said absently, her mind busy with the puzzling flight of her quarry. "Thanks, Kaowa. Very kind of you. Most helpful."

His huge hand under her elbow urged her across the threshold. "Sir Toby know you were coming here?" he enquired, as they walked back towards the car.

"No." She didn't elaborate.

"I thought not." His tone was grim. "Well, let me tell you something. Don't you *ever* come to this part again without a Polynesian with you. You were just asking for trouble and you damn nearly got it."

"I know," she conceded, getting back into the car which she was relieved to see was still all in one piece. "But I had to find out about Hapili. Anyway, thanks again."

"Any time!" he grinned broadly. "And tell Sir Toby I'll be at the yacht first thing tomorrow."

She smiled and nodded, but the thought that was uppermost in her mind as she drove slowly away was that his fortuitous arrival had not been a coincidence: Kaowa must have been following her, and she had to find out why.

Chapter 5

Penny wrestled with her new set of problems all the way back to the hotel. It was too much of a coincidence that Hapili had disappeared so quickly and conveniently after the break-ins—he just had to be involved in some way, and yet, for the life of her, she couldn't see how he could be tied in with the murder itself. A *kahuna ana ana*, part of whose stock-in-trade was a knowledge of native poisons, would never have used such a ridiculous anomaly as an African poison, nor could she see him piloting a helicopter, although changes in the islands were happening so fast these days she supposed it was an outside possibility. Nor could he have been the young Polynesian she had seen in the vicinity of the Freyer house, for the training of a *kahuna ana ana* was a long and arduous one, and she pictured Hapili as at least middle-aged or, more probably, elderly. But where did Kaowa fit in? She heaved an exasperated sigh as she drove into the hotel's parking lot. One thing for sure was that Hapili was now beyond her reach and she would have to try another line.

There was no sign of Toby in the hotel so, still boiling with unanswerable questions, she sought the consolation of a late, large and solitary lunch, and then wandered sadly back to her suite feeling singularly at a loss. Should she have another go at Inspector Lyons about the break-ins? Should she try and see Giles, whose continued refusal to post bail both puzzled and infuriated her? For a man who was facing almost certain life imprisonment, he was doing nothing to help himself she reflected bitterly, and for a moment was tempted to throw up the whole affair and take her much-needed vacation. The shrill of the telephone put an end to her gloomy, negative thoughts, and she snatched it up. It was Griselda, a somewhat breathless Griselda, who said, "Brad asked me to call you to tell you that we found the dealer who sold the Porsche to my father and his records show it was entirely paid for by a cashier's check from the Bank of Honolulu." Penny's eyebrows shot up in amazement. "Brad's gone there now to see if he can find out anything else about it. But that's not all . . ." Griselda became even more breathless. "I think I've found something. You see, after Brad left I thought I'd give the Porsche a good cleaning inside—we got some sand in it when we went to the beach . . ." for a second the young voice glowed ". . . and . . . well, I found this metal cigar tube stuffed way down in the crack of the driver's seat. It looks as if there are some papers inside."

"What are they?" Penny said, thanking her stars for Griselda's compulsive neatness.

"Oh, I haven't looked!" Griselda sounded shocked. "I thought the police wouldn't like that—should I take it to Inspector Lyons?"

"No!" Penny exploded. "Not before we've seen what it is ourselves. I'll be right over."

"What about fingerprints and things?" Griselda fussed.

"Handle it with a handkerchief, but if it was still where your father had hidden it, chances are nobody touched it but him. If the murderer had found it, it wouldn't even have *been* there," Penny pointed out. "And don't tell a soul about this until we've examined it—not even Brad Field if he gets to you before I do."

She scurried back to the car and whizzed back to the Freyer place at breakneck speed, her hopes recharging as she drove. She found Griselda gazing anxiously at the aluminum cigar tube which sat on the coffee table as if it were an unexploded bomb. The girl's first words were, "My father didn't smoke, it can't be his. What about Dr. Shaw?"

To Penny's knowledge, Giles smoked everything in sight, but she thought in the circumstances that this particular cigar could not be foisted upon him. "Not likely," she said, and gingerly unscrewed the cap with a handkerchief. "Got any tweezers?" she demanded as the tube revealed its tightly-rolled contents, and when Griselda had produced a pair of eyebrow tweezers extracted two thin sheets of tracing paper.

With extreme care she unrolled and flattened them out, then stood gazing in growing puzzlement—they appeared to be map tracings, one much larger than the other. The smaller was little more than a rudimentary sketch map and she could make nothing of it, but the larger teased at her mind for, despite the awkward sketching, there were the unmistakable hatchments for a volcano in the middle and a portion of coastline above. Somewhere, recently, she had seen something like that. Her attractively ugly face contorted in thought, she looked at Griselda. "These mean anything to you?"

The puzzled girl shook her head. "Not really, but . . . well, there is another thing I had to tell you, and this might fit in with that. On going through my father's things at the office for the inspector, I found a map folder missing. I always numbered them sequentially and there was a gap in the numbers, you see."

"Do you have a card index of contents for them?" Penny asked eagerly.

Again Griselda shook her head. "There really weren't that many of them, so father said it wasn't necessary. I just put the numbers on to file them right."

Penny suppressed an exasperated sigh. "And what did Lyons say about it?"

"Nothing. He didn't seem to think it very important."

Penny was gazing at the larger map through slitted eyes. "Do you have a copy of Shaw's Menehune book?" she said suddenly.

"Why, yes." Griselda got up and extracted a hardback copy of the book from one of the living room bookcases that had been restored to its normal soldierly neatness. "Actually my father had two—the other he kept at the office."

Penny riffled quickly through it, noting with grim amusement that it had been heavily annotated by the dead man, whose scribbled marginal notes got steadily more scurrilous and apoplectic as the book progressed. Toward the end she found what she was seeking and let out a sigh of satisfaction. "I knew I'd seen it somewhere—look!" She plonked it down beside the larger map and pointed. "It's part of the big island. There's Moana Kea in the middle and what looks like a sketch of some of the Parker ranch around it. Now here's Giles' sketch map of where he thinks the Menehunes still hang out; part of it on those deep, tropical canyons on the north shore lying on the ranch, part of it beyond its boundaries. Now, there seems to be an extra bit shaded on your father's map. See, just to the northwest of Hilo? And that partly overlaps that area. Any idea what that might mean?"

"None at all," Griselda said with certainty.

"Well, it obviously was important to your father," Penny said, "or why would he have bothered to trace it from the original?" She turned her attention to the smaller map, but other than it showed a different bit of coastline she could not make anything of it—maybe Toby would do better, she comforted herself; research, after all, was his department.

She looked quizzically at Griselda. "Now I am going to ask a big question and then a big favor. Do you trust me?"

Surprise brought the easy color up in full flood on Griselda's soft cheeks. "Why, er, yes," she stuttered. "You've been very kind."

Penny waved this aside. "Kindness has nothing to do with it—do you *trust* me?"

The girl looked at her for a long moment. "Yes—I do," she said flatly.

"Good. Then listen, for I'm going to confide in you and then ask my favor," Penny said. "Sir Tobias and I do not think Giles Shaw is guilty and believe the case is far more complex than the police suppose, for the following reasons . . ." and rapidly sketched out the main points about the helicopter, the bizarre poison and the sheer unlikelihood of an expert like Giles having staged such a phony murder set-up, apart from the apparent weakness of his motive for the murder. "I'm certain this is the only thing keeping the police from hauling him before a grand jury and charging him with murder one. If it had been a simple bludgeon slaying, with Giles' record of violent behavior, they'd have charged him before now, despite the weakness of his motive, but this had to be a *premeditated* murder and it makes no sense in the circumstances. Your father had more of a motive for murdering Giles than vice versa, because it was *Giles* who sued for peace and that extraordinary meeting. . . ."

"So, what are the police doing about the helicopter?" Griselda broke in, bringing Penny's harangue to a screaming halt.

"Er—they don't know about it yet," she confessed. "Had we remembered it immediately it might have helped, but we only recalled it later and, as friends of Giles, the police would probably not believe us *unless* we have some other evidence to back it up. And in light of these," she waved her hand at the maps, "it looks as if it is something to do with the big island and the *kahuna* Hapili, who is now down there—though I haven't the faintest idea what or why. We need time and we need information—will you help us? Giles Shaw did not murder your father, of that I am sure, and I don't think you'd want to see an innocent man railroaded. We *will* find out who killed your father—that I promise you."

Griselda thought it over. "Yes," she said at length. "I will. What do you want of me?"

"Well, first I'd like you to say nothing of the maps to the police until Sir Tobias has studied and copied them. Second, I'd like you to tell me all of your father's movements around the islands since this Menehune affair began, particularly any visits to Hawaii itself."

Griselda got up. "That's easy enough," she murmured. "I keep a diary." And she drifted off into the recesses of the house to reappear shortly with a couple of vinyl-bound page-a-day diaries and a pad of notepaper which she handed to Penny. "You may want to take down these dates. And if it's any help, he went more to Hawaii in the past eighteen months than he did in all the years we have been on the islands."

She sat down and began to leaf through the diaries and to read aloud as Penny scribbled busily away. At length Griselda said, "That's it," and shut the book with an abrupt snap. Penny looked at the list, "Hmm, six trips to Hawaii in the last fifteen months, the first fifteen months ago. . . ."

"That was just after Shaw had printed his first article in the psychic magazine," Griselda put in.

"Then a break, and three fairly close together between nine and six months ago. Then two, again close together, the last being a month ago. And all, apparently, to Hilo," Penny murmured.

There was a pregnant silence, then Griselda said reluctantly, "No, I don't think so—the first four, yes, but I don't know about the fifth, and the sixth and last definitely wasn't. I think it was to North Kona."

Penny looked at her in surprise. "Why would he go there? That's right on the other side of the island, isn't it? Away from Giles' Menehune country?"

Griselda shrugged her shoulders helplessly. "I've no idea—maybe to look at the fish-ponds on that side? You know how they're always being ascribed to Menehune builders."

"Well, didn't he *say* anything?" Penny was slightly impatient.

Again the girl colored faintly. "No, he never talked to me abut the trips. I only know about North Kona because, when I was doing his laundry after his return from that last trip, I found a matchbook with the imprint of Kailua-Kona bar in his pants' pocket."

A matchbook in the pocket of a non-smoker—but matchbooks also had addresses and phone numbers on them, and this put Penny in mind of Hapili again. "You don't happen to have it still?" she said eagerly.

"No, I just threw it out," Griselda admitted. "And I don't remember the name."

Penny was already on to another idea. "Now when, in relation to all this, did your father start seeing the *kahuna?*"

Griselda thought hard. "It was just about four months

ago. I remember that my father was intrigued because Hapili had sought him out after one of his lectures at the university and had asked to meet him here." She shivered slightly. "He came over one evening—very late."

"And what did they talk about?"

"I've no idea. They went into my father's study and I went to bed."

Penny sighed and looked at her notes. "So he appears *after* the first four trips but before the fifth and sixth, when your father apparently did *not* go to Menehune country. So those trips may have had something to do with the *kahuna*." She was thinking aloud. "Can you describe Hapili for me?"

"Easily," Griselda's voice was muffled. "Very tall, very thin—almost emaciated. He seemed old—over fifty anyway." Penny winced slightly. "He was tattooed across his cheekbones—you don't see much of that anymore in the islands—and he had eyes like a snake's, small and glittery, and his hands were like a bird's claws, all scaly." Again the girl shivered. "After that first meeting here, my father had several other appointments with him, but not here. And I only saw Hapili once more; he came to my father's office at the university, when he wasn't there but I was. He seemed very anxious about something. My father was quite upset and angry that he had been there."

"And that was when?"

"Six weeks ago."

"So that was shortly before that last trip to North Kona," Penny said thoughtfully. "And just about the time your father agreed to the arbitration between him and Giles. I really think we may be getting somewhere. . . ."

She was interrupted by the telephone ringing in the study and Griselda sprang up and disappeared. When she came back, some ten minutes later, her color was high and she said breathlessly, "That was Brad. He's so clever! He has found out the origin of the cashier's check already."

Penny's eyebrows shot up; knowing the ways of banks, she gave the young reporter full marks both for his enterprise and speed. "And?" she demanded.

"It was issued against the Norpark Corporation's account." Griselda sounded puzzled. "I've never heard of it and neither has he, so he's off to find out about it and he'll be around here in about an hour. "Her face lit up. "We're going out to dinner."

"Good—then you'll want to get ready, so I'll take myself off." Penny was now itching to share what she had learned with Toby. "Maybe we can get together tomorrow and go on with this?"

The animation died and Griselda looked stricken. "Tomorrow is father's funeral," she muttered. "A service at the university chapel at eleven and the interment in Honolulu Memorial Park. We didn't belong to any church and father didn't like burial rites or wakes or anything like that, so it will be very simple. I don't know if you'd be interested in coming?" It was something between a question and a plea.

Cursing herself for her own brash obtuseness, Penny said hastily, "Of course I'll be there. I just had not realized it was scheduled for tomorrow."

"So much has happened today—and so fast," Griselda murmured dolefully, "I've been sort of swept away. Maybe I should not go out to dinner tonight. Maybe that's a bad idea."

"Nonsense!" Penny said briskly. "It's just what you need. You have to eat, don't you? Much better to do it with someone of your own age than sit moping around here. You certainly should go."

"You really think so?" The girl's face brightened again. "You don't think it would be improper?"

What a word to hear in this day and age! Penny thought, torn between sympathy and irritation with the over-sheltered girl. "Anything but," she assured. "The last thing your father would have wanted is for you to be alone and miserable at a time like this." She doubted that the selfish Freyer would have wanted any such thing, but was more interested in Griselda's future than the restrictions of her past.

"Well, in that case I had better get ready," Griselda said in alarm, looking at the clock above the small fire-place.

"And I'll be off," Penny said, rising. "But, again I warn you, don't tell any of this to Brad—not yet. After all, he's doing excellently on his own line, and we don't want him distracted by possible red herrings, do we? If he has got anything else on the Norkirk corporation, maybe you can let me know later?"

"All right," Griselda agreed, but she looked doubtful, and Penny had the sinking feeling that it would not be long before Brad had wheedled everything out of the vulnerable girl. To emphasize her point she went on, "You see, bright as he is, Brad is still a newsman with his job to think of, and at this early stage we don't want him printing anything that might be hurtful to your father's reputation and which may prove totally irrelevant. I hope you understand that."

The girl nodded like an obedient child. "Oh, I do, I do indeed," and with that Penny had to be satisfied. "I'll be at the chapel tomorrow," she said and took her leave.

Back at the hotel she found Toby settled on her lanai, with yet another bottle of dark rum in front of him, glowing with sunburn and looking very disgruntled. "Where have you been all day?" he grumbled. "I really don't see the point of us coming on holiday together if we never *are* together."

Penny started to bristle but thought better of it. "Like you, I've been busy," she retorted. "And at last I've got some real meat for us to sink our teeth into. So, pour me one of those, have one yourself, and shut up and listen. . . ."

Her recounting took them through the drinks, through dinner at a nearby seafood restaurant on the marina, and back again to the hotel. As they ambled through the lobby, still deep in conversation, the receptionist called out, "A message has been left for you, Dr. Spring," and handed Penny a folded note.

It was written in an energetic, spiky hand, and read "Selda wanted me to pass this on stat. The check came from the Norpark Corporation and the Norpark Corporation is headed up by a South African businessman, Piet Van Norkirk, currently resident in Hilo (Don't know where yet!). How are you getting on? B.F."

Penny offered it to her interested partner. "Bingo!" she said softly. "We've just been given two magic words—Hilo and Africa. I think things are beginning to gel."

Chapter 6

"Our next step seems to be obvious—a trip to Hawaii," Toby Glendower observed mildly. *"The Dancing Lady* is all set to go, so we could leave tomorrow morning with the tide. It would be a great shakedown cruise."

Penny was momentarily diverted from her many preoccupations. *"The Dancing Lady?* Is *that* what Benedict Lefau has called it? How extraordinary!"

"Her—all ships are feminine, usually with reason," Toby corrected. "And I don't see anything extraordinary about it—it's the name of their New Orleans estate."

"Exactly, and when you think of all the ghastly things that went on there you wouldn't think they'd want to be reminded of it!" she exclaimed.

Toby dismissed this with an airy wave of his hand. "All past and gone. If the Lefau family had ever allowed itself to be swamped by the past they would never have survived so well or so long as they have." He went on the attack. "Anyway it's a lot better than calling it something silly like after Benedict's wife, what's-her-name." Ever since Benedict Lefau and the former Mimi Gardiner had unanimously credited Toby with their fortuitous meeting and happier marriage, he had reacted in typical misogynistic fashion by deliberately blocking out the second Mrs. Lefau's name.

Penny grinned at him knowingly. "What a phony old curmudgeon you are! Can't bear to think you may have played Cupid successfully, can you?" While Toby gobbled in outrage, she went on, "But okay, if you're willing and able, Hawaii is a great idea, but not tomorrow—maybe the day after that."

"What's wrong with tomorrow?" he demanded. "All our leads are to the big island, as you've already pointed out, so why waste any more time here?"

"Because I promised Griselda I'd be at the funeral, and I want to have one last crack at Giles, *if* I can get in to see him. I just can't understand what he's up to," she retaliated.

"And I suppose I just sit here and twiddle my thumbs," he grumbled. "Some holiday this is, I must say!"

"There's a lot you *could* do if you wanted," she fired back. "Research on those two maps, for one thing—you could spend tomorrow at the Bishop Museum. I could set it up that you have free run of the place by just one call to Chris Bullard, a man after your own heart, by the way—doesn't know what age he's living in," she tempted.

Toby heaved a resigned sigh but did not look ill-pleased with the idea. "Oh, very well—go ahead and set it up then. But we'll leave the next morning—right?"

"Without fail," she agreed.

It did not come as any surprise to her that the funeral service for the unloved Helmut Freyer was sparsely attended. The dean of the university delivered the eulogy with the air of a man determined to do his duty and not go one step beyond it, and the rest of the mourners, she discovered, consisted almost entirely of other professors and their wives for whom Griselda had worked, including the elderly Eberts. She was relieved to see that Brad Field, clad unusually in a sober dark suit, was there hovering solicitously behind Griselda, also clad in a black suit, relieved by a soft white blouse, its color almost matched by her ashen cheeks.

After the short service, Brad successfully fended off several of his fellow journalists, who attempted to corral the tearful girl, and they discouraged easily enough, for, with Giles already arrested for the murder, it was no longer a hot news item, and they did not even bother to pursue the cortege to the cemetery. In his press release Inspector Lyons had carefully suppressed all references to the unusual poison used, and this Penny found both intriguing and hopeful. Maybe he wasn't as convinced about Giles' guilt as he pretended, she mused.

When the inspector himself turned up at the graveside, she managed to sidle up to him without being obvious about it, and when he recognized her and nodded she said quietly and, she hoped, with convincing sincerity, "Well, Sir Tobias and I are off on our interrupted trip to Hawaii tomorrow, Inspector." And when that had sunk in, went on. "But I was wondering if, before I left, you could possibly arrange for me to see Giles Shaw? I feel so badly just going off without so much as a goodbye."

He looked duly relieved. "Yes, I see no harm in that. I think it can be arranged. How about this afternoon—say four-thirty? Would that suit you?"

"Admirably," she murmured. "Most kind of you. Where is he?"

"Oh, still downtown—he has not yet been arraigned, you know." He seemed slightly uneasy.

"Any progress on the source of the *ouibain?*" Penny pressed her luck.

Lyons glanced sharply at her and his face closed up. "No, but we're working on it," he said shortly. "Now if you'll excuse me?" He went over and said a few words to Griselda, cast a sharp eye over the people at the graveside and walked back to his car.

Penny transferred her attention to Brad Field, who was gazing wistfully after the departing Griselda, who had been cajoled by the sympathetic Eberts into returning with them. "Any update for me on that note of yours?" she asked, and he came to with a start. "Some," he admitted. "I could bring over what I've got tomorrow, if you like. Now I've got to rush back to the office—a deadline to meet on a couple of things."

"Tomorrow I won't be here," she said sweetly. "Off on the shakedown cruise of the yacht with Sir Tobias."

He looked surprised and disconcerted. "Oh? Where are you going?"

"Oh, just around the islands."

"For how long?"

"For however long it takes—I've no idea." Which was true enough. "I'm depending on you to keep an eye on Miss Freyer while I'm gone," she added slyly. "I was very impressed by how you handled your fellow newsmen at the chapel, and she should be spared any further grief."

"You can bet on that," he said with a sudden, charming grin. "I know a good thing when I see it. So you're giving up on Giles Shaw?"

She ducked that one. "The police seem to have things well in hand," she murmured. "But I'm still very intrigued about what you found out about the Porsche. Curious, wasn't it?"

He eyed her keenly. "Very. Why should the Norpark Corporation hand out an expensive under-the-counter gift to a professor of anthropology? Not exactly their style."

"What is their style?" she prompted.

"Oh, like most conglomerates they are into a lot of things—mines, oil, plantations, land development . . ."

"In South Africa, I take it?"

"Van Norkirk started as a Johannesburg businessman, but he's spread a lot since then—West Africa, Zambia, Kenya, Madagascar, something in the Solomons, Tahiti, now here."

Penny almost purred with satisfaction. "Kenya?—my favorite African country! What's he got there, I wonder. Can't be easy for him to get a foothold there, where a South African is generally so persona non grata."

"Well he always had local partners as front men apparently," Brad said in an absent tone. "In Kenya he has a tea plantation in the highlands and some hotel development center on the coast—near Malindi, I believe."

She suppressed a crow of delight, for this last was close to Giriama country. "And now he's settled in Hilo, or is he just visiting?" she prodded.

"He's built himself a house and set up an office—so it looks as if he's here to stay. Word is that he's negotiating for a plantation in Molokai and a motel franchise on Maui."

Which, if he was planning a land grab on Hawaii itself, would make an excellent smokescreen, she reflected, as the shaded portion of Freyer's sketch-map began to make some sense to her. "None of which seems to have much connection with Freyer, does it?" she said aloud.

This time Brad's look was heavily suspicious. "No, but I'm still digging," he agreed. "Got any ideas?"

"None," she said hastily. "But I'm sure you'll find out, you've done so well thus far. Well, I must be off and start my packing. Gook luck! Maybe I'll see you when we get back."

"You can count on it," Brad said, and stood looking thoughtfully after her as she hurried back to the car.

She had some time to kill before her appointment to see Giles, so, after a short dither, she had lunch and betook herself once more to the Bishop Museum, where she learned that Toby was still closeted with Chris Bullard. She peeked in at them to see Toby was happily immersed, almost up to his ears in maps, on one side of the desk, and Chris, equally submerged, on the other, so tiptoed away to the library on a project of her own.

She unearthed one of her own early papers on "Totemism in the islands" and noted down a couple of names of her native informants, then applied herself to the current telephone directory for the big island. She noted down a North Hilo number and an address and closed the book with a little sigh of satisfaction. "Everything's going my way" she hummed to herself, as she once more trotted out into the sunlight. "Let's hope that the aged Mama Luali is all in one piece and still has all her marbles. Nothing like a local informant, I always say, and she always did have a great knack for gossip."

She was surprised and impressed when, at the appointed time, she was ushered into a small interrogation room at the downtown headquarters, and was shortly joined by the shambling figure of Giles, escorted by a policeman, who then went out, shutting the door behind him but with the back of his head visible through the meshed glass window as he stood guard. She had not expected this much privacy, then wondered uneasily if the room was bugged. She eyed Giles critically as he slumped into a chair across the table and grinned at her. His eyes were now clear and, apart from a slight trembling in his large hands, he showed no great signs of strain. "Well, me darlin', you're a sight for sore eyes. How's it going? Got any cigarettes?" he said all in the same breath, thereby increasing her irritation with him and confirming her in her decision that shock tactics were the only solution.

She fished in her tote bag and plonked down cigarettes and matches, which he immediately pounced on and lit up with lively satisfaction. "I've come to say goodbye," she said in a loud voice, for the benefit of any listeners. "I'm off tomorrow. There's no reason to stay, since you seem dead set on destroying yourself."

His eyes widened in shock. "But why? What have I done? I'm innocent, I tell you, innocent! I was depending on you. . . ."

"Like hell you were. I don't know what the devil you're playing at, Giles, and I'm not sure that I care. If you're so damned innocent, why are you still here? Why haven't you posted bail like any sensible man would have, so that you could help us? Or is it that you've gone through every cent of Emily's money already and are too proud to admit it?"

He winced at that, but his bearded chin jutted up and he glared back at her. "It's not a question of money—I've plenty of that. It's the principle of the thing. They've arrested an innocent man—wrongful arrest, that's what I'll have them for! Persecution, that's what it is. Just because I've stuck up for the natives and twisted the tail of the whole rotten money-grubbing establishment!"

"There's a lot more to it than that and you damn well know it," she hissed. "If you think by staying in here you've helped yourself, you're dead wrong. Those break-ins at Freyer's home and office the police think were done by some of your Polynesian pals as a smokescreen—I don't believe that, but so far I can't prove them wrong. And if they can tie you into the poison used—the *ouibain*—your goose will be cooked for sure, unless you tell me right here and now the *truth* about this whole mess."

"What the hell is *ouibain?*" Giles was genuinely astonished.

Penny told him in a few terse sentences and was further confounded when he threw back his great head and roared with laughter. "So *that's* why they've been keeping after me about Africa!" he spluttered. "What a lucky man I am then niver to have set foot in the place! Better look out, me darling, or they'll be after you next—you with your globe-trotting ways."

"Look, we don't have time for such foolishness." She dipped into her bag and slapped his Menehune book down on the table, its pages open to the map. "I want to know three things. One: was the whole thing more authority baiting or do you really believe any of this Menuhune nonsense? Two: what is the significance of this particular area . . ." she indicated the portion that had been shaded on Freyer's map. "And three: why were *you* so anxious all of a sudden to call off this ridiculous feud?"

His face changed and he shot her a shrewd warning glance and shook his head slightly. "What a clever lady you are, to be sure," he said softly, and the phony Irish accent he so cultivated had vanished. "But I cherish my little Menehunes—the luck-bringers, the protectors of the islands, and, God knows, they all need protecting. The Menehunes still serve their purpose and, hopefully, always will. As to that area—why, it's a lovely bit of coast that—unspoiled, undeveloped, and where the Menehunes find the shrimp that's left for them by fishermen . . ." for a flash the impishness was back and gone again, as he went on soberly. "One thing you can say for the Parker ranch—even though Richard Smart, the Parker heir, had to go in with that Texas conglomerate to keep it going—is that they've always cherished the land."

"The land I'm talking about is not Parker Ranch land," she pressed. "To whom does it belong? The Norpark Corporation?"

Again he looked warningly at her, cementing her impression that they had an unseen audience—or that, at least, he thought they had. "No, nor will ever be, please God!" he said softly. "I think my Menehunes have seen to that. And to answer your third question—well, I was sick of the whole business with Freyer. It had served its purpose. Everyone in the islands knows about the place now—nothing like having the public eye focussed you know."

But a prickle of unease ran through Penny as, for the first time, his bright blue eyes shifted away from her and she scented evasion. She glanced in despair at her watch, for the twenty minutes allotted to them were almost up. "Then tell me why you had your goon Kaowa following me," she hissed. "And what *he* has to do with the *kahuna ana ana* Hapili who was in cahoots with Freyer."

Giles leaned forward, his face earnest. "Benjamin Kaowa is nobody's goon, but he is my friend and a true patriot in every sense of the word. I haven't seen him since my arrest, but if he has been following you, you can be sure it's for your own protection. One thing I can say for certain—even if you don't trust me, you *can* trust him. I beg you, Penny, don't give up on me. I don't think you have, but trust Kaowa. He can help and will, if he's given a chance."

The guard outside the door had turned and was peering in, and the handle started to turn. "And what about Hapili?" she whispered urgently.

The old Giles reappeared. "Faith," he grinned, "how should I know? Probably Freyer was hiring him to do *me* in!" And Penny knew he was lying.

"Time is up," the guard said gruffly.

She rose reluctantly to her feet. "Giles, *please!* Quit this nonsense and post bail. We're off to the big island tomorrow. On the outside you could help us here."

Giles looked up at her and shook his head. "For the moment this suits me well enough. Nice cell to meself, three squares a day and me on the cold turkey 'cure' at the same time! Don't worry, me darling, all will be well in the end—you'll see!"

"You go first, lady," the guard said sternly, and furious with Giles, the system and herself, she stomped angrily out.

That evening, as she related the events of the day to Toby, who, among his many virtues, was an excellent listener, her own budding theory of the case strengthened and burgeoned. She bustled around the suite throwing her belongings somewhat haphazardly into her suitcases, as she warmed to her subject. "As I see it, Van Norkirk is emerging as our most likely target. As head of an island-based corporation, he *must* have a helicopter at his disposal; he has a *definite* connection with the right area of Kenya, and we know he was paying off Freyer, probably to divert Giles from the land-grab the corporation was contemplating—something I'm sure Giles is well aware of. If, as you say, Kaowa is indeed coming with us, we may be able to get more out of him on that. It's all starting to make a certain amount of sense—don't you agree?"

Toby had been listening in pop-eyed fashion, while puffing up a miniature volcanic cloud of blue smoke that now completely encircled his knoblike head. He took the pipe out of his mouth, carefully knocked it out on the ashtray and cleared his throat. "Yes, I think you do have *something*," he said carefully. "Except for one major point. Your theory is that Giles Shaw got wind of a land-grab in the offing and started this Menehune business to draw people's attention to this remote area, and that when Freyer joined battle with him, Van Norkirk subsequently hired *him* to ridicule and disgrace Shaw. Then, when Shaw was on the run and had given up on the expedition idea, he told Freyer to settle the whole business 'out of court', as it were. All that's fine, but my question is, then *why* should Van Norkirk murder Freyer, at such a time and place and in such an improbable way? It just stirred things up again, not quieted them down—and, worse, it brought *us* in!"

"To get rid of Giles by framing him and silence Freyer, who was in a position to blackmail him," Penny said promptly.

"Possibly," Toby murmured, "but I have the sinking feeling it's a lot more complicated than that. There's that second sketch map, you see . . ." His gaze became fixed and inward and his voice dropped to a soft rumble. "That last trip to Kona and the interesting question of Hapili . . . No, Van Norkirk may well be part of it, but I don't think he's the whole of it. There's something else here, another pattern emerging, but at this stage I can't for the life of me see what it is." He came to with a little start and shook his head at her. "No, we've still got a lot of work to do, a lot of answers to find—on the big island. The key to all this lies *there*."

Chapter 7

"Isn't she beautiful?" Toby's face was rapt with love, as he gazed up at the sleek lines of the gleaming white yacht with its twin towering masts. "Some interior modifications but she's built on the lines of Sir Francis Chichester's *Gypsy Moth 4*—you've heard of that, of course?"

Penny murmured dryly that she had, as he rhapsodized on, "Fifty-four footer, sixteen tons, ketch-rigged. Fast, sleek, easy to handle—everything one dreams about in a yacht. Ah, what it is to be rich!" There was a note of longing in his voice.

Penny looked at him in utter astonishment. "My dear Toby, you *are* rich, remember? If you *want* a boat like this why don't you buy one? Absolutely no reason, as far as I can see, that you shouldn't. I mean, apart from the inordinate amount of money you spend on your wine cellar and assorted booze, and the equally inordinate salary you pay your housekeeper, you don't even spend your *salary* let alone your income from your inherited estate." She eyed with marked disfavor his nautical attire, which consisted of a shabby pair of khaki trousers, an old and yellowing cricket shirt and rope-soled espadrilles. "You certainly don't waste any money on clothes, that's for sure. You could easily afford something like this if you wanted it!"

It was his turn to look at her in astonishment. "What a ridiculous idea! What on earth would I want a thing this size for? When would I ever get to use it? I mean, at the rate you drag me around the world whenever we have a free moment, which is rare anyway, I'd never set foot on it!"

She decided to be tactful and change the subject. "Well, it's very nice I agree but, not being a sailor, I'm more interested in the domestic arrangements. Where do I sleep?"

"You can have the main cabin, which has a bathroom of its own. There's another head by the aft cabin, which I'll take. Both of those are double-berthed, then there's another single berth in the bow."

"Is that where Kaowa is going to be?" she asked, looking up to where the huge figure was busy checking the rigging of the main mast.

Toby chuckled suddenly. "No, they don't build below decks for anyone Kaowa's size. I can *just* stand upright below, so he'd be bent like a pretzel if he had to spend any time there—as it is he has to go sideways down the hatches, otherwise he gets stuck. He'll sleep on deck and probably eat there too—said he'd prefer that. Doesn't like to be cooped up."

"Am I to be chief cook and bottlewasher?" she enquired.

Toby shrugged, "Just as you like. The galley is fully equipped, as you'll see. But we may as well keep it to a minimum, after all—after this first long leg down to Hawaii—we'll be port-hopping mostly and can eat ashore." This sounded fine to her. "With a good wind we should be in Kailua by early evening."

"Why Kailua? I thought we were making straight for Hilo!" she exclaimed.

"Oh, we'll get there eventually," Toby said, turning a bland face to her. "But I thought I'd like to check out the Kona coast first. Kamehameha country and all that. Besides, that's Kaowa's native heath—he has all sorts of relatives scattered around in the vicinity. I thought we may pick up a line on Hapili."

She eyed him suspiciously. "Are you up to something? On to something you haven't told me about?"

"If I were, I would have told you," he returned. "All I have at the moment is a lot of nebulous ideas."

"Such as?" she prompted, but he refused to be drawn and became the brisk skipper. "We'd best get on board and underway. Kaowa's taken your things to the main cabin. Why don't you get stowed away while we're getting out of the marina? It's so damned crowded with traffic that we'll need a clear deck for action."

Penny knew how to take a hint, and went below to explore. Her cabin she found to be almost luxurious, for it boasted a double bed instead of the two berths she had expected, and its adjoining bathroom had a shower as well as handbasin and toilet. She stowed her things away in the big drawers built in beneath the bed, as she listened to the deep rumble of the men's voices above and the thud of their feet on the deck as they raced up and down casting off the mooring lines and starting the auxiliary engine that would power them out of the strait confines of the marina's mooring-slips. She was mildly thankful when the yacht slowly glided into motion for, when moored, it had the tendency to roll from side to side with the monotonous regularity of a huge pendulum. She had already remarked on this, and Toby had brushed it aside with "It's because of the height of the masts—Benedict wants to try his hand at racing whilst he's here, and so she's rigged for that, rather than just plain sailing, so, while at the dock, she will roll. You won't even notice it when we're underway." She fervently hoped this would be so, since she was not at all sure how good a sailor she was: seasickness was not the best way to begin an investigation, she reflected.

Her unpacking done, she turned her attention to the main cabin and galley, and found to her delight that it did indeed have all the modern conveniences Toby had promised; a gas stove, with a tiny oven, a well-stocked refrigerator built under the stainless steel sink, and even a miniature washing machine. To her further delight she found that the fixed swivel chairs around the teak-topped table, and indeed the table itself, were gimballed, so that no matter at what angle the yacht was tilted they remained on an even plane. She hastily made herself a mug of instant coffee and sat down, as *The Dancing Lady,* freed from the restraints of the inner marina, started to live up to her name as she leaned into the wind and picked up speed.

The voices and the footsteps died away into a silence broken only by the soft shurring of the waves against the hull, and so, her coffee finished, she ventured up the companionway for a peek outside. Her eyes widened as she saw the cockpit was empty, with no one at the tiller: she hastily emerged all the way and looked frantically around. Toby was in the bow helping Kaowa run up another jib sail. "Shouldn't someone be holding that thing?" she yelled, pointing to the tiller. Toby laughed at her and shook his head. "Not to worry! We've set course and put the Hasler self-steering device on." He pointed to the rudder. "It's on that. Could you get us a couple of bottles of beer? This is thirsty work!" The warm wind snatched at his words, but she nodded and ducked back down to the galley.

Not fancying balancing herself and the beer along the pitching deck, she explored further through the bathroom and the single-berth cabin beyond it and popped up the forward hatch, like some genie from the abyss, almost at their feet. "You all right?" Toby enquired, as he collected the bottles. "Oh, fine, just fine," she gulped, and beat a hasty retreat.

Secure in her comfy chair at the table, she got out a note pad and settled down to work out her plan of campaign against Van Norkirk. Her first priority would be to see Mama Luali and find out how the local land lay. Then there was the question of the helicopter and whether Van Norkirk was a pilot. Also his movements at the time of the murder. . . . But how was she going to meet him? She scribbled busily on, and then found her eyelids drooping into drowsiness: the soft swishing of the waves against the hull, the warm silence, the gliding motion of the boat, all were lulling her into a semi-comatose state. She yawned and stretched luxuriously. "Maybe a little nap?" she murmured, and tottered off to her cabin. She stretched out on the downy bed and was almost instantly asleep.

When she awoke she was completely disoriented as to both time and place; when awareness of her surroundings returned she had no idea how long she had slept, and was amazed to see by her watch that her short nap had actually been for more than three hours. Staggering up, she dashed some cold water on her face to complete the awakening and tried to comb some order into her unruly, mouse-colored hair.

Still yawning, she made her way back up to the cockpit, this time to find Toby seated at the tiller, his silver hair shining like a burnished helm, and an expression of near bliss on his face. The pipe clenched in his teeth was flying a tiny pennant of blue smoke that trailed away with the wind. "Sorry to have flaked out on you like that," she apologized. "Can I get you some lunch?"

"Oh, not to worry, we had some. I did look in on you, but you were sleeping so soundly I didn't disturb you. With our very early start and all you've been through the past few days, I thought you needed the rest."

She sat down beside him in the cockpit. "How's it going?"

"Oh, a few minor glitches in the rigging, and the mizzen sail is not functioning quite right, but, all in all, she's behaving like the fine lady she is—we're making excellent time." Toby was evidently in high good humor and at peace with the world.

She looked around. "Where are we?"

"Well, if you look to port you can see Maui in the distance, and we've just passed Kahoolawe—that's the uninhabited target island. You can see Hawaii coming up dead ahead—there's a big plume of smoke over Mauna Loa—maybe Pele is acknowledging our arrival with an eruption." He grinned at her.

She looked forward as directed and let out a little gasp. Kaowa stood erect in the bow, gazing ahead, one hand steadying him on a forward stay, the other holding a beer bottle. He had shed his shirt and was naked to the waist, his bronze flesh gleaming in the sun. He had also shed his trousers and was now clad only in a long loin cloth. She peered at it. "Dear Lord! I think that's a genuine tapa-cloth man's skirt—a real museum piece! What a sight!"

"Yes, impressive isn't it?" Toby said softly. "Kaowa is going home—and he's going in royal style. Can't you just see him in one of those red and yellow feather capes and those amazing 'Greek' feather helmets, returning home in the prow of his war canoe, a ruddy great spear in his hand? Extraordinary those helmets—I wonder if Alexander's general Niarchos really did get this far with the Greek fleet and that's where they got the idea."

Penny slid him a sidelong glance, for it was evident that the enchanted spell of the islands had already reached out and grabbed Toby's soaring Celtic imagination in no uncertain measure. "Well Gladwyn certainly thought so, and made quite a case for it," she murmured diplomatically: she did not believe it for a moment herself.

"Why don't you get yourself some lunch and then come up on deck and get some sun?" he suggested. "There's a couple of those plastic mesh chaise longues in the main cabin. You could stretch out aft." He jerked his head. "Just keep your head down and watch out for the mizzen boom—the winds will change when we come alee of the big island."

"Can't I do something to help?" she enquired.

"Nothing *to* do—relax, enjoy!" he commanded.

She went and fixed herself a smoked-salmon sandwich and a salad, and settled for a glass of a Napa Valley Sauvignon Blanc, instead of the omnipresent beer. Then she dragged the chaise longue up to the afterdeck and wondered giddily, as the cobalt blue, white-foamed water slid by at a furious rate, if she were doing a very wise thing. However, by jamming the chaise lounge between the after hatch and the bow rail, she found she could keep it from sliding as the yacht pitched, and so made another trip below to emerge with her notebook and Giles' Menehune book.

"Demon for punishment aren't you?" Toby grinned as he saw her reading matter.

"Well, I thought I may have missed something useful," she murmured and settled down in the sun. But concentration was hard to come by, and after a while she let the book slide from her fingers and just lay there listening. Kaowa had deserted his position in the bow and had now taken the tiller from Toby, who was relaxing with yet another bottle of beer, as the two men conversed casually.

Kaowa was evidently relating the history of the big island, and one sentence jerked her out of her soporific state. ". . . then the great king refused the request of his chiefs to make human sacrifices to prolong his own life. 'I will go in my own good way,' he said, then touched noses with his greatest friends, the *haole* John Young and the chief Hoapili, and so died."

Penny sat up: she had forgotten all about Hoapili— could it be? She called out, "Kaowa—the *kahuna* Hapili— does he claim descent from Kamehameha's friend Hoapili, by any chance?"

The huge head swivelled around. "It is what *he* would like the ignorant to believe. But you should know, as well as I, that the *kahuna* class is hereditary, and that they were *never* of the aristocracy. Hoapili was a great chief, an *alii*—so, no, there is no connection."

She had been put in her place, but persevered. "And isn't your own name unusual? Wasn't that the name of Kamehameha's chief enemy and rival as king of the islands?"

Kaowa glowered. "True he was Kamehameha's chief opponent, but he was also a mighty chief endowed with great *mana*, so that in after generations the royal family honored him as such by retaining the name in their own line." He turned his back on her dismissively and continued his chronicle to Toby.

They were now abreast of the big island, as the great active cones of Kilaeua and Mauna Loa heaved up to the south, the dormant Mauna Kea more mistily to the east. They were passing the lesser bulk of the equally dormant Hualalai and were starting to bear inshore, so that the vivid colors of the great island reached out and captured her with all the impact of an Impressionist masterpiece:

the tender green of the coastal palms, the dark lush green of the tropical canyons, the daggers of blood red earth, the blackly glittering sands, and everywhere the stark grey-black tortured majesty of the towering lava cliffs. A land forged in the violence of Nature, she reflected, and shaped by the violence of Man. She was so captivated by it all that it was some time before she realized Toby was very much on the alert, standing at the port rail and with his binoculars trained on the coast. From time to time he would point and consult with the seated Kaowa, but she could only hear snatches of the conversation, for the wind was picking up and keening through the rigging. "There's Ke-ahole airstrip . . . first *heiau* beyond that . . . Kaloko fish ponds? . . . the twin *heiaus* Hale o Mono and Hale o Lono . . . burial cave . . . two entrances, one guarded by the great white shark. . . ."

What on earth was he on about now? she wondered sleepily, too lazily content to find out. She drowsed off again, and when she came to felt chilled to the bone, for the wind had sharpened and the sun was dipping towards the horizon. They had rounded a headland and were now headed into a bay at the end of which the crowded masts signalled journey's end—the haven of Kailua. Toby and Kaowa were both forward, struggling with the spinnaker which was behaving erratically. With a shiver she gathered up the chaise lounge and her belongings and went below to make herself a hot drink and put on a heavy sweater. By the increasing activity on deck, she deemed it prudent to stay where she was until the yacht slackened speed. The small engine coughed into action and they edged gingerly into the marina and then, even more gingerly, into a mooring slip, and the engine sounds died. At this point she deemed it safe to emerge, and found Kaowa on the pier securing the mooring lines, as Toby ran down the last sail.

Margot Arnold

No sooner was *The Dancing Lady* pinioned than she started her restless, relentless ticking from side to side, to which Penny's stomach promptly responded with a queasy qualm. To take her mind off it, she looked around her: the little town of Kailua had a cosy look as it nestled along the narrow strip between the ocean and the steeply soaring flanks of the dead volcano. It had none of the toweringly overbuilt slightly claustrophobic air of Honolulu, and, taking in its relatively small size, her hopes of finding out more about Freyer's strange trip there and a lead to the mysterious Hapili began to rise.

Toby had disappeared below, and when he emerged had added a decrepit windcheater and an old faded digging hat, pulled right down over his ears, to his ensemble: they made him look more like a beachcomber—and a slightly dim-witted one at that—than ever. Kaowa too had disappeared in his wake and reappeared dressed in Western garb once more. The men held a brief conference and Toby ambled up to her. "Dinner on shore?" he suggested. "I'm ravenous."

"Yes, fine!" she said, hoping dry land under her feet would take care of her increasing queasiness.

"Good, then let's go. Kaowa will take care of the marina business and stand watch on board. He says a good place to eat is . . ." Toby began, but was interrupted by a shrill cry from the dock, "*Dancing Lady*, ahoy there!"

They looked down in surprise to see a tall, fair, slightly horse-faced woman, impeccably, if improbably, clad in English twill jodhpurs and a tweed riding jacket, and even more improbably clutching a couple of orchid leis. She was looking up at them and behind her loomed a slightly taller, dark-haired man, with a long, saturnine face fixed in a permanent frown. "Can you tell me where I might find Sir Tobias Glendower?" The accent was English and cultured.

Toby recoiled a little. "What do you want him for?" he enquired.

"That is none of your business," she snapped. "Will you tell him Mildred Payson of the Payson estates is here, and wishes to speak with him—at once, please!"

"I'm afraid it is my business," Toby said mildly. "Since I am he. What do you want?"

Her eyes widened in shock and she gulped, but collected herself quickly. "Oh, Sir Tobias, I'm afraid I didn't recognize you! We've been expecting you. We're the Paysons—great friends of Giles Shaw—and *so* grateful for what you are doing for him. This is my brother Gregory. . . ." The dark man gave them a gloomy nod. ". . . and my other brother Philip is back at the ranch awaiting you. We wish to extend you our hospitality while you are here, and simply won't take *no* for an answer!" She surged on board without further ado, and with a girlish giggle looped one of the leis over Toby's unwitting head, "Aloha to our beautiful island home!" She turned to Penny, "And you *must* be the Doctor Spring of whom we've heard so much from Giles." The other lei was dropped over Penny's dishevelled head. "Welcome! We've come to take you back to dinner and do *so* hope you will honor us with your company. No need to dress up or anything, come as you are—we're *terribly* informal, you know."

After the initial surprise, Penny's mind had moved into high gear. There was no way in hell Giles could have had a hand in this, which meant that their departure from Honolulu had been watched and their destination disclosed. There had to be far more to the Paysons than met the eye. She glanced over at Toby and was interested to see him in wordless communication with the silent Kaowa, who had given him a slight nod. To give him a little extra time she answered in an equally gushing tone, "Well, that is really extremely kind of you, Miss Payson—we had no idea we were expected, Giles made no mention of it when I saw him yesterday . . ." for a second there was a flicker of alarm in the tall woman's pale blue eyes. "But, as to your invitation, well, that's up to Sir Tobias. He's the captain of our sight-seeing trip around the islands, so his word is our law at the moment."

"Oh, *do* say yes," she pleaded. "All the facilities of the estate will be entirely at your disposal—we can talk of it over dinner. We would be so *honored*. In fact if you'd *stay* with us we'd be overjoyed to have such a distinguished compatriot as our guest."

He gave Penny an inscrutable look, then said blandly, "That is most thoughtful of you, Miss Payson. Yes, indeed, we'd be most happy to dine with you. If you'll just excuse for a moment, while I change my jacket?"

"Me too," Penny muttered, and dived after him down the companionway. "What do you think?" she hissed, as they hastily scrambled into more respectable clothes. "We've obviously been watched!"

"Of that I am well aware," Toby rumbled. "An interesting development—very. It may just be that the mountain, or at least part of it, has come to Mahomet. Let's play along."

Chapter 8

Mildred Payson had been so urgently persuasive that they had taken along overnight bags; a fortunate happenstance, as it turned out, although what transpired was none of Penny's doing or planning. Things had started off badly when Mildred had said in her penetrating voice and within easy earshot of Kaowa, "I hope you have brought any valuables you may have along—these Polynesians are terrible thieves, you know. You have to keep *everything* locked up—so tiresome!"

Toby had looked murderous but had not dignified her statement with a reply, instead he ostentatiously handed over the keys of the boat to Kaowa and had said meaningfully. "If you need to go off on business of your own, my friend, I am sure you will find a kinsman who will keep an eye on things in my absence—feel free to do so."

Kaowa grinned his understanding. "You may count on it." And the last they saw of him was his massive figure making for a pay phone on the pier.

Mildred had compounded her error on the longish drive north on the Waimea road, by constantly interlarding her chatter with "We, English . . ." always to the detriment of whosoever she was contrasting them with. Penny, sitting in the front passenger seat by the silent Gregory, who was driving, waited tensely for the inevitable explosion.

At one "We, English" too many, Toby burst forth. "Madame," he said icily. "Neither of us is English. I am Welsh, therefore a Briton; Dr. Spring is an American, so am I to assume these derogatory remarks of yours are aimed at us in particular or just the non-English in general?"

It was too dark by now to see the expression on Mildred's face, but by the sudden thunderstruck silence, Penny, quietly hugging herself in glee, knew that the barb had penetrated Mildred's thick skin: however, by her gabbled answer, it evidently had not penetrated very far. "Why, of *course* not, Sir Tobias," she gulped. "How could you even think such a thing! Why—British, English, it's all the same thing, isn't it?"

Toby let out an outraged snort, but did not deign to reply.

"And Dr. Spring *must* be of English descent with a name like that!" Mildred went on desperately.

"It's my married name," Penny said sweetly, stirring the pot a little and omitting the fact that her maiden name of Thayer was equally English.

"*You* are married!" Mildred exclaimed in blank surprise. "Well, I assure you I was just speaking in general. I meant no offense, none at all!" But it effectively silenced her until they drew up before the large, sprawling Payson ranch house.

Philip Payson, who greeted them with almost boyish enthusiasm and immediately went into action as host at the drinks tray, served his purpose in lightening the strained atmosphere a little. He was the same height as Mildred, and also fair-haired and blue-eyed, but with a round, ingenuous face: they bore little resemblance to their dark-haired, dark-eyed elder brother, who quickly excused himself and departed to his study.

Under Philip's casual charm and his probing interest in the details of their voyage down, Toby thawed a little, but dinner was very late in arriving and Philip lavish in his provision of drinks, so that by the time the food did appear, Penny saw with a sinking heart that Toby was already very drunk; his eyes glazed like blue marbles, his face flushed and his speech very slow and deliberate. The long day plus so much alcohol on an empty stomach and on top of the considerable amount he had already consumed on the boat had caught up with him, and she realized it was only an effort of will that was keeping him upright during the long, rather elaborate dinner that followed. When they got to the coffee stage and Gregory, who had reappeared to preside as host, had got out the brandy decanter, she decided enough was enough, and got to her feet. "We've had a very long day and are very tired," she said firmly. "So if you will excuse us now? Come along, Toby."

Toby got slowly to his feet and staggered slightly as he gripped the back of his chair. She took him by the arm. "Need any help?" Philip said with a knowing smirk, which she did not particularly care for. "No, we're fine, thank you, and I do know the way to our rooms," she said sharply. "Good night."

"Just come down whenever you want," Mildred sang out. "Breakfast is a help-yourself affair—nostra casa, sua casa, you know!"

"Insufferable woman!" was Toby's only mumbled comment as Penny steered him into his room and over to the bed on to which he collapsed with a groan and was instantly unconscious. She took off his shoes, pulled a blanket over him and left it at that. With a sad shake of her head she reflected that neither of them was getting any younger, as she made her way to her own room and wearily climbed into bed.

It was not that she was tired—she had slept so much during the day that sleep was elusive—but she was strangely depressed and tense. Was it this house? Their hosts? she wondered, trying to sort out the few facts she had elicited from her dinner partner, the monosyllabic Gregory. There was strain here and tension—between brother and brother, brothers and sister. What was its nature and its cause? One more thing to find out, as well as the even more intriguing reason why the Paysons were so anxious to cultivate them.

One thing she had elicited from Gregory had interested her enormously. For all Mildred's "We, English" the Paysons had spent little of their lives, apart from their schooldays, in England itself. They were in essence refugees of the defunct British Empire. They had all been born in Tanzania to a wealthy, landowning father, and when that had become independent had fled to Southern Rhodesia, and it was only when that too had become independent as Zimbabwe that they had migrated to the islands, where they had been some eight years. So here was the African connection again: not a direct one, but definitely there.

But, as Toby had pointed out already, Africa was a big place, and it was stretching a point to link them with Van Norkirk who, by his very name, was a South African of Dutch Boer descent, which would seemingly put him beyond the pale of the Paysons almost paranoid "Englishness": the South African English hated the Boers and vice versa, so there appeared little likelihood of a meeting of such minds, still less of actual partnership. She just *had* to find out more about Van Norkirk, and decided then and there that, after tomorrow, she would leave Toby to take care of this end of things and head out for Hilo by herself. Her mind made up, she settled into sleep.

She was up early, and descended to find the dining room deserted, although one place had already been used. Before breakfasting herself, she decided on a quiet reconnoiter to get the feel of the place, and peeked into all the main rooms, including Gregory's study: there were a few good English antique pieces, but the majority of the furnishing was modern American and lacked distinction in both style and taste. The house in general had an unloved look to it. What did catch her eye were the only Polynesian things in evidence—in the main small objets d'art like elaborately inlaid kava bowls, shark-tooth clubs and boar-tusk bracelets, all of which were of the finest quality, and she wondered how the Paysons had come by them. The only other things she found of interest were two framed pictures. One was a portrait which, by its likeness to Gregory, she took to be the father of the line. He was painted in the standard garb of African safari, clutching a large rifle and standing with one foot on the carcass of a lion. Although his long saturnine face was very like Gregory's, there was more of a rakehell look to him, and the smug smirk on his face was unpleasantly reminiscent of Philip's: not a man she would have cared to have known, she thought. She passed on to the other, which was a dated photograph of the whole family, with a teenaged Gregory standing behind his seated father, who had Mildred on his knee, and with the baby Philip on his mother's lap; his mother being, predictably, fair and with the same faintly horsey features of her daughter.

Penny did some quick sums in her head and her eyes widened in surprise: all the Paysons were a lot older than they looked. Gregory had to be in his mid-fifties, Mildred at least in her mid-forties and Philip just over forty. He, in particular, looked a good ten years younger than that.

She returned to the dining room to find a remarkably bright-eyed and robust-looking Toby tucking into a plate of scrambled eggs and bacon with evident appetite. He waved a piece of toast, thickly spread with dark English marmalade, at her and said brightly. "Help yourself—at least the breakfast is damn good! And I've found out where we are."

Marvelling at his recuperative powers, she helped herself from the silver chafing dishes that stood on a massive teak sideboard, and commented, "So was dinner last night, but I don't suppose you remember that."

"No, not a thing," he admitted cheerfully, as she sat down beside him and reached for the coffee pot. He put out a restraining hand. "I shouldn't—it's terrible. Try the tea—it's very good."

She tried the tea, which was. "Alright, where are we?"

"Just east of the Hawaii Belt road that runs from Kailua to Waimea and Parker ranch country, in a valley between two of the ancient lava flows from Hualalai. The ranch runs mainly to the north and east, but not as far as the coast, so far as I can make out. I found a handy plan of it in the back hallway."

"Oh, so you've been snooping too," she put in.

He ignored that and went on. "They appear to have two others as well. One is on the flanks of Mauna Loa near Na'aelu and the other on the Wailuku river in South Hilo.

"On Freyer's shaded area?" she said eagerly.

He shook his head. "No, just off it. His map begins just to the north of it."

"I've decided to be polite and stay for today and then head for Hilo tomorrow. Can you handle things here?"

"Good idea." For some reason he seemed almost relieved. "Yes, I'll hang on here for a bit—give Kaowa some time to amass information."

Their tête-à-tête was interrupted by the arrival of Mildred, clad in a fresh outfit of tailored riding clothes and looking a little frazzled in the morning light. "My, you're early birds!" she exclaimed, casting a quick eye over the table. "Gregory's been and gone I see. I don't think Philip has even surfaced yet." She collected some toast and bacon and sat down opposite them. "Do you ride?" she asked.

"Only under extreme duress and if no other transport is available," Penny said cheerfully.

Mildred looked shocked. "And you, Sir Tobias?"

"I have ridden on occasion," he admitted with no great enthusiasm.

She was crestfallen. "This is a horse ranch," she said mournfully. "All-purpose—we raise and breed them. I love horses. . . ." she shot a belligerent look at Penny. "I find them more interesting and a lot pleasanter to be with than most people."

"And are your other two estates also horse ranches?" Toby enquired.

She looked at him in surprise. "Oh, so you know about those! No, the one in K'au is mixed—a bit of everything. Gregory has a manager down there. The one in South Hilo is mainly beef cattle for the local Hilo market, but Philip runs a few horses there too—not that he knows much about them."

"So that one is Philip's?" Penny put in to keep the flow going.

Mildred gave a shrill, angry laugh. "Oh, no, they are all Gregory's—everything is *Gregory's*." She stopped short, belatedly aware of the bitterness of her tone, and tried to pass it off with another little laugh. "Primogeniture and all that. Gregory is the firstborn of the first marriage. He got everything—most of it was his mother's, you see. Our poor Mummy only left *us* enough to keep us in riding boots. We live on Gregory's bounty."

Which explained one hell of a lot, Penny thought, as

Mildred rushed on. "Philip manages Wailuku for Gregory—not that he does much managing." She finished her tea with an angry gulp.

Toby carefully wiped his mouth and put down his napkin. Under the table his bony knee pressed meaningfully into Penny's, in what she interpreted as a "get lost" signal by what followed. "This is such a beautiful spot. I was wondering, Miss Payson—or may I call you Mildred?— if I could impose on you to show me around?"

Mildred's face lit up. "Why, I'd be *delighted* to show you anything you like. I am entirely at your disposal." And looked as if she meant every word of it.

"I am particularly interested in the antiquities of this historical area," he went on pompously. "More especially the *heaius* of the region."

Her face fell. "Er—*heaius?*" she said dubiously. "I'm afraid I don't know anything about them. What are they?"

"The sacred temple enclosures of the ancient Hawaiians—there are many around here associated with the great king Kamehameha."

"Oh, him!—yes, I've heard of *him*," she muttered. "Well, I'm afraid I don't know where they are."

"Ah, but *I* do," he soothed. "Perhaps if I showed you on a map, we could explore them together, after you've shown me the ranch?"

"All of us?" she queried pointedly.

"Oh, not me!" Penny said, taking her cue. "I'm feeling far too lazy for tramping around looking at *heaius*. I'll just poke around the ranch on my own, if that's all right with you." *Heaius?*—what the *hell* was Toby up to?

Mildred was transparently relieved. "Oh of *course!*" she breathed. "Make yourself completely at home, and I am sure Philip will take you anywhere you want to go. If you want to shop, he could even run you back to Kailua. But be sure to be back by six tonight. We're holding an old-fashioned luau in your honor—dances and everything!" Her face was alight with pleasure.

"Somebody taking my name in vain?" enquired Philip, who had come soft-footed into the room behind her. "Whatever she's told you about me, don't believe a word of it." He grinned over at Penny.

Mildred swung around. "Oh, there you are! Sir Tobias and I are going to look over the ranch, and I was telling Dr. Spring you would look after her."

"Delighted I'm sure. You don't mind if I have my breakfast first, I hope?" There was a slight sarcastic edge on his voice.

"Take your time," Penny murmured. "I'll join you and have another cup of that excellent tea."

Mildred positively bustled Toby out of the room, as Philip returned with a heaped-up plate, which he proceeded to wolf down greedily. "So what do you want to do?" he enquired between mouthfuls.

She had been thinking about that, and a trip to Kailua did seem a good idea: she wanted to get an urgent message to Kaowa. "Well, if you're not too busy, I was wondering if you'd run me into Kailua some time today?"

"We'll have to wait till Gregory gets back," he said. "He's got the other car today, because the damn 'copter is on the fritz."

Her interest quickened. "Oh, so you run a helicopter?"

"Only way to go in the islands," he said. "Particularly with the spreads as far apart as ours. We really need two, but Gregory's too mean to get another. He hogs ours most of the time." He sounded like a petulant small boy.

"So you can fly it too?"

"We all can—even Mildred, when you can get her off a horse," he snorted. "Damn nuisance it being out of whack. Means I'll have to drive back to Hilo tomorrow."

Better and better! Penny thought. "May I cadge a ride from you then? I'm off to Hilo tomorrow myself."

He looked startled. "Leaving so soon? You only just got here."

"I have some people I must see in Hilo. Sir Tobias can pick me up there in the boat later."

"Ship," he corrected absently. "I know everyone who is worth knowing in Hilo—who are you visiting?"

"I doubt whether my friends would fall into that category," she said dryly. "They're native Hawaiians—people I met doing fieldwork in the islands."

"Oh!" he said blankly. "Not friends of Giles?"

"No." She looked hard at him. "You know Giles well?"

"He's a great chap," he hedged. "Good party man—what a head on him!"

"I've been wondering how he let you know we were coming," she said, and was startled by his answer.

He looked surprised. "He didn't. Mildred saw it in the paper—got all excited."

"The paper!" she echoed in amazement, a horrible qualm of doubt shaking her.

He got up and rummaged in a pile of papers that lay untidily on a side table. "See—here," he pointed.

She read the item with a sinking heart and silently cursed Brad Field whose name was on the byline. "The distinguished criminological team of Sir Tobias Glendower and Dr. Penelope Spring of Oxford University, the recent discoverers of the bizarre 'Menehune' murder and friends of Dr. Giles Shaw, currently under arrest for the murder, are off to the Big Island on the yacht of millionaire-industrialist Benedict Lefau, *The Dancing Lady*. A reliable source says they are headed for Kailua. We wish them good hunting on this latest caper."

"What a load of rubbish!" she exclaimed weakly, her

doubts now in raging flood. "We're just here on vacation."
Was that all there was to the Payson's interest? she
thought. The evidently man-hungry Mildred doing a little
"lion" hunting like dear old Dad and capturing them as
prizes?

Philip was looking at her searchingly. "You mean you
are not here to get old Giles off the hook?"

"No, I've done all I can for him already," she blustered.
"He's got the best attorney in the islands, and I have
complete faith in the efficiency of Hawaii Five-O."

He cocked his head, "I think I hear the car. Gregory
must be back. I'll nab it before he gets away again." He
rushed out.

Still boiling with fury at Brad, she went up and collected
her totebag and a jacket, and came back to find Philip
looking somewhat ruffled. "He says he'll have to have it
back by one, so it won't give us a lot of time in Kailua.
Do you still want to go?

"Yes, if you don't mind. I need some things from the
boat."

"Nothing better to do here," he grumbled. "Damn 'copter won't be fixed for two more days."

He drove at a reckless speed into Kailua and dropped
her off at the marina, instructing her to meet him there
again at noon, before speeding away again. She made her
way to *The Dancing Lady*, still ticking restlessly at her
moorings, and was halfway up the gangplank before she
realized it was blocked by a massive figure, but that it
was not Kaowa's. This man was a mere six feet tall, and
so extremely broad that he appeared much shorter. "I'm
Dr. Spring," she said firmly, "and I'm after Kaowa. You
are a kinsman?"

The man unblocked the gangway and stood aside. "I
am his cousin Kuali," he said. "I guard the ship. Kaowa
is not here."

"Can you find him for me?"

"Kaowa is not in Kailua." Kuali was evidently a man of few words. "I give him message when he return."

Penny sighed: it was not turning out to be her day. "I'll write the message down, and you give it to him as soon as you can. It is very important."

He nodded and she went down to the cabin, packed some more clothes in a bag for the Hilo trip and hastily scribbled a note. "Find out everything you can about the Paysons and the Payson estates—financial status, how they are thought of locally, and any connection with Norpark enterprises. Also movements of their helicopter, particularly any recent trips to Oahu. This is *urgent*." She added as an afterthought the address and number of Mama Luali. "You can leave messages for me here. Pass info on to Sir Tobias also, he will be staying at the Payson ranch," and gave that number. As she sealed and addressed it to Kaowa she wondered bleakly if she was sending him off on a wild goose chase.

She said goodbye to the impassive Kuali, then wandered into town and made a few minor purchases to make her shopping expedition plausible. Philip was late at the rendezvous, and when he arrived had obviously been patronizing a local bar. He drove back even more recklessly, so she was quietly thankful when they got to the ranch.

There was no sign of Toby or Mildred, so she wandered vaguely around the ranch, watching the preparations for the luau—the fire pit being dug and lined with taro leaves, the straw mats being placed around the dancing area, the old fashioned torch-holders being stuck in the perimeter around it. Tiring of this after a while, she had a quick lunch—again a help-yourself affair—in the deserted dining room and, thoroughly depressed by the turn of events, went off to take a nap.

The nap did nothing for her depression but renewed

her energy, so she dressed up in a Tahitian muu-muu that she had mercifully packed against the possibility of just such an occasion as this, and floated down to see what was going on. Her descent coincided with the return of the explorers; Mildred animated, Toby looking somewhat strained—which, after a whole day in the company of Mildred, was understandable. But there was also about him an aura of quiet satisfaction, so it looked as if the trip had not been in vain.

Mildred, now openly proprietorial, bustled him away to get ready for the luau, and she reappeared before he did, clad in an elaborate muu-muu, a hibiscus flower tucked coyly behind one of her pale ears, so that Penny had no chance of a private word with him before they were joined by a surprisingly affable Gregory and a spruced-up Philip, who had a gleam of impish glee in his pale eyes.

The luau got underway as light dimmed and the vivid stars came out on the velvet blue-black of the night sky. The festive air and the excellent feast that followed served to raise her drooping spirits. The Paysons had gone all out on it, for not only was there the inevitable whole roast pig, but also *laulau,* pork, salmon and beef roasted delectably together; *pipikaila,* the Hawaiian dried beef that tasted like venison; a mixed vegetable dish of *limu* and *poi;* and the luscious *haupid* made from coconut cream for dessert.

Happily replete, she settled down to enjoy the dances. She had always preferred the more active and violent male fire dances and spear dances to the langurous strains of the hula, and since the majority of the ranch hands were male Polynesians they made a very impressive showing against the flaring torches that surrounded them. The music changed to the softer lilt of the hula, and the few female dancers—whom she assumed were recruited from the household servants—appeared in the inevitable ti-grass skirts and leis. They were headed by an enormously fat woman, who stationed herself in front of Toby and played exclusively to him, her hands and body gestures conveying their openly erotic message that had the Polynesian onlookers in gales of laughter. Toby's face was a study in furious embarrassment, as the enormous hips waggled in front of him, the woman's grass skirt almost brushing his nose, as he sat cross-legged on the ground, pinned down, with no possibility of escape. Mildred was looking daggers at the placidly-smiling hula dancer, and Penny, peering beyond her, saw Philip smirking with satisfaction and deduced that he was behind this little ploy.

She was glancing idly around the amused crowd, wondering how she could break up this little game before Toby exploded or passed out from sheer embarrassment, when she froze, all the doubts that had assailed her during the day dissipated. In the full light of one of the flaring torches lounged a tall young Polynesian: it was the man she had seen leaving the Freyer's house on the day of the break-in.

A sense of suffocating excitement welled up in her and she reacted quickly. She snatched the mini-camera with which Toby, in good tourist fashion, had snapped flash photos of the festivities all evening, aimed it at her quarry and got off a couple of quick snaps. She dug Toby in the ribs. "Quick!" she hissed. "Ask Mildred who that young man is, standing by the third torch from the left. Quickly, before he moves."

Toby tore his horrified gaze from the gyrating mass of flesh in front of him and leaned over to Mildred. After a little he turned back. "She says he is Manua, one of their horse–handlers. Why?"

The young man had thrown up his head suddenly, like some wild animal scenting the wind and sensing danger.

He looked quickly around and then faded beyond the lighted circle like a shadow into the darkness beyond. She managed to get off one more profile shot as he went.

"It's the man who broke into the Freyer house," she whispered. "I'm certain of it." She handed him back the camera. "Get those films developed as soon as you can and send his photos to Lyons—soonest! It's our first real lead. Can you follow up on this alone, or would you like me to put off my Hilo trip?"

"No, you go along," he said quietly. "Kaowa and I can handle this."

"But we don't know where he is!" she protested.

Toby looked at her with a little smile. "I do," he murmured. "He's here now and will be waiting for me in my room when I get back. Kaowa is a man of many friends and many parts."

Chapter 9

This time it was Philip who so overindulged at the luau that, after a noisy belligerent interlude where he had to be restrained from fighting one of the bigger Polynesian ranch hands, he passed out cold; in the ensuing embarrassed retreat of the Paysons bearing off his body, Penny and Toby managed to slip away unnoticed to rendezvous with Kaowa.

His news was more titillating than substantive and amounted to this: he had established that Hapili had definitely been in Kailua two days after the break-ins and Kaowa had followed his trail to a small village just outside of Mahai'ula on the coast a little to the north-west of the Payson ranch. There it had petered out: Hapili was not there and the villagers either did not know or would not say where he was, although Kaowa had the definite impression that some of them knew more than they were telling but were too intimidated by the *kahuna's* sinister reputation to speak. Hapili, in short, could be anywhere; he could even have returned to Oahu. Nor would anyone say what his business in the village had been. It was a dead end.

Kaowa listened in enigmatic silence as Penny recounted her identification of Manua, but roused himself when she repeated the gist of the note she had left for him but which, naturally, he had not as yet seen. "Yes, all that I can do," he rumbled, after an enquiring glance at Toby. "I will take all these matters in hand. It may take some time, but I will be in touch." And he took a silent-footed departure through the darkened house.

As soon as he had gone Penny tackled Toby. "Now perhaps you'll tell me what all this *heaiu* business is about," she said with some asperity. "Why all the mystery? And why this sudden sweetness and light with Mildred, who is not exactly your cup of tea?"

"I'd really rather not say at this point," he said maddeningly. "Because so far I can't make any sense to it at all, considering Freyer's background and interests. I'll just say this, I *think* I have located the area of Freyer's second sketch–map—the *heaius* were guidelines to it, but I still have to locate a couple of other things to be sure. Mildred, ghastly though she may be, does know the local terrain and will save me a lot of time. One thing you could do for me before you go is give me Griselda Freyer's telephone numbers. I really must contact her. I have the feeling there is something she knows about her father's doings that she hasn't said or doesn't even realize is important."

"You can't do that from here!" she exclaimed. "The Paysons may not be any too bright, but they'd soon tumble to the investigation if you contact the dead man's daughter."

Toby looked at her with scorn. "I have absolutely no intention of doing so! Kaowa has relatives in Kalaoa, just to the north of here, and they have a telephone. Anyway, as soon as I get the information I'm after, I'll cut out of here and get back to *The Dancing Lady*."

Margot Arnold

"Then how on earth am I to contact you?" Penny fussed. "Maybe I shouldn't go, maybe we should stick together and leave Hilo for later."

"No!" He was definite. "It is very important now that you get on to Van Norkirk and see what is going on over there. After all, this may all be pure moonshine and have nothing to do with anything. I have this Mama Luali's number—I'll leave word there where I can be reached."

"This morning I'd have sworn it *was* moonshine—but after tonight and seeing Manua . . . " Penny shook her head. "Well, there just *has* to be a link. When you think of it, the Paysons fit very well into our hypothetical picture of the murderer. All of them seem a bit thick, there's an African connection *and* they all fly a helicopter—but what conceivable tie could they have with Freyer or Hapili? And what conceivable *motive,* either for his murder or for pinning it on Giles?"

"Unless there's a link between one of them and Van Norkirk and he put them up to it," Toby said. "But there's no use speculating at this point, we just don't have enough information. Let's call it a night—you'll need all your wits about you for Hilo."

"I suppose so," she said, making for the door. "I hope dear Mildred, insane with jealous rage, isn't lurking outside with an ax. One thing for sure, she's got her sights trained on you."

Toby groaned feebly as she cautiously let herself out.

Mildred was so relieved to see her go the next morning that she was positively gushing over breakfast. "It's been such a *short* visit—you simply must come back and stay with us again *anytime.* We'll look after Toby and keep him amused while you are gone, you can be sure of that."

Always a firm believer in keeping an option open, Penny replied in kind. "Well, I'd *love* to if it is at all possible.

Such a beautiful place, and I found the luau last night just fascinating!"

"Wasn't it fun?" Mildred enthused, then her face clouded. "Of course, trust Philip to go too far—but that's so typical of him!"

Philip, when he eventually appeared and they got off to a tardy start, was evidently in the grip of a ferocious hangover. He snarled at both Gregory and Mildred, and when he got behind the wheel drove in a morose silence. It suited Penny well enough, for she had a lot to think about and was in no mood for polite chit-chat. They drove north towards Waimea, passing through the little town of Kaluoa that Toby had mentioned, but before they got to Waimea—the heart of the Parker Ranch country—turned off on to a secondary road at Saddle Road junction and bore south again, first through the cattle ranges of the huge Parker ranch and then around the intimidating bulk of Mauna Kea, on the top of which she could make out the University of Hawaii's observatory.

The road was twisting and precipitous, but it did nothing to slow down Philip's reckless driving and they ate up the sixty-mile stretch in very short order. As they came into the outskirts of Hilo, he broke his silence with a weary sigh. "This is where I would normally turn off to the ranch, but I suppose you're headed for downtown Hilo. Where are you going?"

"I'm heading for the Hukilau on Banyan Drive, but if that's too much trouble, just drop me at the first car-rental place or taxi stand we come to and I'll take it from there. It has been most kind of you to take me this far."

Her pacific answer mollified him, because he gave a shaky laugh and said. "No, no trouble at all—I have to go into town anyway. 'Fraid I'm a bit under the weather this morning—you mustn't mind me." And when he deposited her and her baggage in front of the Hukilau, leaned out the window and said. "If this place doesn't suit you, you're welcome to stay out at the ranch. Come and visit me anyway, and I'll show you around."

"Thank you very much, I'll certainly do that—but I'll call first," Penny said and waved him cheerfully off as he zoomed away.

She booked in without any difficulty, explored the large complex of rooms that were wrapped around a lush flower garden, a swimming pool and an even bigger fish pond, and found she could rent a car right there. While it was being arranged she retreated to her comfortable room that overlooked the quiet waters of the fish pond, sank into the plush lounge chair provided and applied herself to the telephone directory.

Norpark Corporation offices were listed, but there was no home listing for Van Norkirk, so she deduced an unlisted number. She would just have to beard him at the office. But, first things first, she called Mama Luali's number and was a bit nonplussed when she was answered not by Mama Luali herself but by a daughter, who announced her name was Gladys and seemed a little wary.

While Gladys was away from the phone consulting her mother, Penny searched her memory. Mama Luali had been a much-married woman and she recalled that one of the early husbands had been an ardent Evangelical Christian of some kind and had foresworn the old ways and the old names—Gladys had to be one of his offspring, and she vaguely remembered a slim, teenaged girl lurking behind her mother's ample form, as Penny had listened to and reasoned with the strong-minded woman. Gladys came back to the phone—this time a lot more affable. "Yes, my mother would like to see you very much, Penny Spring. When can you come?"

"At once, if it is convenient."

"Yes, that will be all right," and Gladys went into some complicated instructions as to how to reach them to the north of Hilo between Kawai Nui and Pepe'ekeo on the coast. Right in the area of Freyer's map, Penny reflected, as she copied down the instructions and, thanking Gladys, went out to collect her car.

As she drove along the coast on the belt road, she recalled with some amusement her involvement with the redoubtable 'Shark' woman. Mama Luali took her totemic duties very seriously and, at the time of their first meeting, had been in deep trouble with the Honolulu authorities for carrying them out. Every day she would go to the ocean and throw into it an offering of food for "her" kinsmen, the sharks. Unfortunately, this was in the harbor of Honolulu, and the powers-that-were took a very dim view of anything or anyone that attracted sharks to those thronged waters: they were all set to arrest Mama Luali and throw her in jail as a public menace. On her side, Mama Luali was adamant that it was part of her religious duties and that what they were proposing was unconstitutional: she was not about to stop.

It had taken the young and earnest anthropologist many hours of cajoling and persuasion before a compromise had been reached. The authorities had agreed to drop all charges if Mama Luali would relocate. Penny had persuaded one of Mama's older sons, a fisherman now on the Big Island, to take her in. Mama Luali, between husbands at the time, was happy to return to the island of her birth. And so it had been arranged to everyone's relief. Mama Luali had been so grateful to Penny that not only had she bestowed on her priceless information about totemic practices on the island, but had sworn eternal friendship. They had indeed kept in contact for many years, though the erosion of time and distance had finally snapped the link. Penny hoped fervently it was a link that could be restored.

She reflected, as she turned off onto the appropriate dirt road, that Mama Luali had certainly never stopped her offerings to the sharks, so that by this time the waters of the neighborhood were probably teeming with them! With some difficulty she located the tiny, but neatly-kept, cement-block house, set among a huddle of such houses, many of them not as well kept and almost shanty-like in appearance, but they were set on a headland with a glorious view of the ocean, far below the lava cliffs, and with the lush dark canyons of Mauna Kea soaring up behind the settlement. It was typical of the many all–Polynesian settlements that were all that was left to the native Hawaiians of their own land, and she realized with a sinking heart that it would be swept away like chaff in the wind if a big corporation like Van Norkirk's gained possession of the land for development. It had happened many times before, it could happen again.

The door opened to reveal the figure of a large, fat woman, whom Penny initially took for Mama Luali but turned out to be Gladys, who, instead of inviting her in, took her around to the back of the house where, on a tiny lanai, a shrunken figure sat on a plastic chair, staring out to sea: time had enlarged Gladys, diminished her mother.

Where had the years flown? Penny thought in dismay, looking at the frail form of the old woman sitting in the chair, but was thankful to see the dark eyes were still bright with intelligence in the furrowed, shrunken face.

"It has been a long time, Penny Spring," the old woman said in a husky voice.

"Too long, Mama Luali," Penny said with a catch in her

throat. "But it is good to see you." The years rolled away, and for some reason a picture of the young Giles, laughing, his red hair flaming in the sun, his arm protectively around his dark-haired, adored and adoring Emily, flashed into her mind, and she felt tears prick her eyes.

"What brings you back?" Mama Luali had always been forthright.

Penny sank into another plastic chair that Gladys had unfolded before disappearing into the house. "I come to beg help from an old friend, to get vital information I need to help another old friend," she said.

"No need to beg, I will help if I can," the old woman said simply.

"Well, it's like this . . . " Penny began, and related a bare and precise outline of the problem. When she had finished she was startled when Mama Luali let out a high-pitched cackle of laughter. "A fight about Menehunes! Poor little things, it is ill to meddle with them. Luck they bring, and we need all the help we can get." She jerked her head towards Mauna Kea. "In the canyons they live, harming no one who harms them not, and asking little. What's a few shrimp after all? It's their favorite food so it draws them from the forest. Why should we begrudge it to them?"

Penny looked at her in dismay: maybe the old woman's marbles had shifted a little after all, "Er—you believe in them?"

Mama Luali looked at her slyly. "The fishermen often leave shrimp for them and the shrimp are always taken—and there are marks in the sand of feet like no other feet. These I have seen with my own eyes. So if this *haole* Shaw says he has seen them, I for one will not call him a liar."

Penny, in desperation, tried to bring the conversation

back to a more rational level. "But this man Freyer, was he ever around here asking questions about them?"

The old woman shook her head. "Not here. You are the first *haole* here for a long time."

"No one has been here trying to buy land? Men from the Norpark corporation in Hilo for instance?"

Mama Luali shrugged. "I do not concern myself with such things, I have better things to think of in the time I have left. Gladys might know." She raised her voice in an eldritch shriek. "Gladys, come here! You are needed."

Her daughter lumbered around the corner, an expression of alarm on her dark face. "What is it, mother?"

"Penny Spring wants to know what's going on around here—answer her questions, if you can. I know nothing, since you keep everything from me," her mother said with a flash of aged spite.

Penny repeated her question and Gladys' brow furrowed in thought. "I know nothing of this corporation you speak of. No one has been *here*. But I did hear . . . well, there's this man Paea Young—a successful man who drives a big car—he's been buying up some land along the belt highway, and he's been in some of the villages too. Some of them have found it wiser to sell to him."

"How do you mean—wiser?" Penny said quickly.

"The headman of one village chased him out. Some time later his fishing boat was burnt and his nets all destroyed."

"What do you know of this Paea Young?"

"He's more *haole* than Hawaiian—a white father, a half-white mother. Her Polynesian half was of a good line, an *alii*."

Penny was thinking hard: Brad Field had established that Van Norkirk had used locals in Africa for his land-grab there. This could be the same pattern—and with strong-arm tactics beginning. "If he bought up all the land along the highway he could limit your access to it and isolate you, couldn't he?" she said thoughtfully.

Gladys' chins went up. "We would always have the ocean," she said defiantly. "He could never keep us from that."

"Where is this Paea Young to be found?"

"Hilo—I think." Gladys' tone was doubtful.

"Should I approach him or would it be best to leave it to Kaowa?" Penny murmured, thinking aloud.

Gladys pounced on the name, her eyes brightening. "You *know* Kaowa, our nationalist leader in Honolulu?"

"Yes, he's here with us—helping us. In fact he will be calling here with messages for me." Penny said quickly. "All this is very urgent, you see."

Gladys bloomed like an oversized flower. "Well, in *that* case I'll spread the word in the area," she said graciously. "I will find out all I can and let you know. How can I contact you?"

Penny gave her extension at the hotel and turned back to take her leave of Mama Luali, only to find the old lady had dozed off in her chair. As she walked back with Gladys to the car, she said, "I would very much like to do something for your mother. I did not bring anything with me this time, but if you would only tell me what she would like or needs, I'll bring it the next time."

Gladys' head went up proudly. "We have sufficient and she needs nothing. It has been a pleasure for her to see an old friend, for her time is very near now. If you help our leader to help us, that will be reward enough."

In the face of this firm dismissal, there seemed nothing more to be said, so Penny took her leave and got into the car. As she drove back to the main highway and turned toward Hilo, she felt that at least some progress had been made and another link in this tangled chain found. Her next objective would be to beard the lion in his den; she had to see Van Norkirk and get the measure of the man. A faint smile played on her lips: Mama Luali had just given her an idea that might get under his skin without showing too much of her own hand. She could hardly wait to try it out.

Chapter 10

"Wait" turned out to be the operative word. She got back to Hilo only to find the office of Norpark Corporation closed for the day, so she had to wait until opening hours on the next. Then, after she had fought her way past various personnel in the outer office, she won her way into the inner office to be faced by a surly and dour-faced male secretary. He became even more dour-faced when she asked for an appointment with Van Norkirk, but refused to state her business other than to say it was on a personal matter. "Well, you can't see him today," he barked.

"Why not?" she demanded.

"Because he's not here—he's in Oahu on business."

"Since when? And when will he be back?" she said quickly.

"Since yesterday—not that that is any business of yours," came the crushing rejoinder. "He should be back tomorrow."

"Well then I wish to make an appointment for tomorrow. My business *is* important," she insisted.

"Mr. Van Norkirk is a very busy man, and if you won't

say what you want to see him about I can't give you much of his time," he grumbled, looking at the appointment schedule on his desk. "You could see him between two-thirty and two-forty-five A.M. tomorrow."

"That will do. I am sure when he hears what I have to say he'll want to talk longer than that," she said sweetly. "You had better write it down—I should hate to be over-looked. The name is Spring, Dr. Penelope Spring." She watched as he scribbled it impatiently into the book.

As she made her way back through the outer office another thought came to her, and she approached the most amiable-looking secretary she could see. "I wonder if you could tell me in which office I might find Paea Young?" she asked smoothly. "I have an appointment with Mr. Van Norkirk for tomorrow, but it may save some time if I talk with Mr. Young today."

The girl looked at her blankly. "No one of that name has an office here—you must be mistaken."

"But he does work for Mr. Van Norkirk?"

"I don't know," the girl faltered. "I've never heard of him."

Penny's heart sank. "Oh, and just one other thing—I'd like to send a gift to Mr. Van Norkirk at his home. Could you let me have his address?"

The girl's face closed up. "I'm afraid we are not allowed to give that information—you'll have to get it from his private secretary. I'm sorry."

Stymied again! "Of course. I'll do that tomorrow when I come in," Penny said, and beat a hasty retreat.

She bent her steps to the public library and applied herself to the phone directory once more: Paea Young was listed, so she set off to hunt him down. His office, which apparently was housed in the front of his house, was in a rather run-down section of Hilo, and its shabby appearance belied Gladys Luali's description of a successful man.

Worse, from Penny's point of view, it was firmly shut, and although she walked around the house banging hopefully on all the doors it was to no avail: nor was there any sign of the big car Gladys had mentioned. "I'm getting nowhere," she muttered angrily to herself, getting back into her own car. "Mercury must be in retrograde or something—the whole damn planetary system must be in retrograde."

She drove aimlessly around, trying to decide what to do next, but, apart from noting that Hilo had grown enormously since her last visit, and that in its tendency to soar upwards it was beginning to resemble a miniature Honolulu, nothing tempted her to stop, nor did any bright ideas surface, so she retreated to the hotel. There she had a large lunch to console herself, and after a despondent stroll through the flower garden sought her room for a post-prandial nap.

She had scarcely got inside the door when the phone rang. It was Gladys, who reported with near-reverence in her voice that Kaowa had called and would Penny call him at once at the number she had been given. Penny thanked her and said, "Oh, and Gladys, if he or anyone else calls for me, you can give them this number. I don't want you and your mother bothered."

"Oh, it's no trouble," Gladys assured her. "It's a pleasure. But I will give them your hotel number."

With a lift in her spirits Penny dialed the number given and to her relief Kaowa's deep bass answered. She listened intently and with growing interest as he rumbled on, marvelling at the vast network of informants he must have at his disposal to have got so much, so quickly.

What he had to say was rivetting: the Paysons had been living at a continuing loss ever since their arrival in Hawaii eight years ago. The bulk of their capital—Gregory's capital—had gone into buying the three ranches, but of those

113

only the one in K'au had ever shown a profit, but even this in no way counterbalanced the losses on the other two, particularly Philip's, which was heavily in the red.

Gregory had been forced to mortgage over the past two years to keep things going—not yet up to the limit, but if things continued the way they were he soon would be. On top of this was the fact that the younger Paysons were noted as big spenders. Mildred had lost a packet in trying to breed and run a string of racehorses. This had been halted by Gregory, reportedly with much acrimony on both sides. Philip, for his part, was very lackadaisical in his management of Wailuku ranch, to the point that in a recent and public row Gregory had been heard to threaten to sell it out from under him. In addition to this, Philip had a weakness for any kind of gamble and Gregory had been forced more than once to pick up his outstanding markers. In short, the Paysons, despite their affluent life-style, were in trouble. On the movements of their helicopter Kaowa still had no information but, he concluded, he was working on it, and how was she getting on?

"Nowhere near as well as you've been doing," Penny confessed. "You've done wonders! Van Norkirk is in Oahu, so I can't see him until tomorrow. There is one thing though . . ." and she related the doings of Paea Young. "Is that of any help to you?" she queried, at the end.

"It could be. I'll get right on it." Kaowa sounded concerned. "And, Dr. Spring, if there is a link here between him and Van Norkirk, be careful! If they are already using strong-arm tactics on my people, they would not hesitate to intimidate an off-islander and a woman at that."

She smiled faintly at his unconscious chauvinism. "I am not easily intimidated."

"Then in this case you should be," he growled. "I've seen enough of this kind of thing to know how rough they can get. If there's a land-grab going on, they'll not

let a lone individual hamper them. Take my advice, at
the first sign of any trouble get out. Don't hang around—
they tend to move quickly."

"How's Toby getting on?" she said, not wishing to pursue the subject.

"He's planning to return to the yacht tomorrow," Kaowa's tone was guarded. "He hopes to finish up at the
ranch today. He'll either be in touch with you at the hotel
number you've given me, or you can reach him at this
Kailua number . . ." and gave her yet another number to
add to her growing list. "And you can always get a message
to me here," he concluded.

"Many thanks, Kaowa, you're a marvel," she said. "I
wish I were half as successful."

"There's a great deal at stake." Again there was an odd
note in his voice. "Perhaps more than any of us realized."
And he took his leave.

After she had cradled the phone she sat mulling over
what she had learned. Now she wished she had paid more
attention to the silent member of the Payson family, who
was beginning to loom large as a likely suspect. There was
a connection between the Payson ranch and Freyer
through Manua, Gregory's employee. There could easily
be a connection between Gregory, with a worse-than-
useless ranch on his hands in this area and the land-hungry
Van Norkirk. Anything that harmed Van Norkirk and his
plans could equally well harm the beleaguered Gregory—
so both Freyer and Giles could be seen as obstacles to be
removed. It could easily be the motive, but . . . she
sighed heavily, thinking it was still all pure speculation.
She *had* to find proof, had to find a link. . . . And where
the *hell* did Hapili fit into all this? She paced around the
room in an agony of frustration, willing away the hours
until she could get into action.

For want of anything better to do, she called Paea

Young's number, but there was no response; not even an answering machine. Then a bright idea struck her and she called Hilo airport—it was worth a try. She put her query and was bounced around through several extensions before ending up in the right department, where a puzzled voice answered her question. "I'm afraid you've been misinformed, madam. Mr. Van Norkirk does keep his Cessna here, but he has a landing pad for his helicopter on his estate and only uses our facilities for that when he comes in on it to use the Cessna. We have no idea of its movements."

"Oh, how silly of me!" she exclaimed. "Of course, I should have remembered that! I was asking because I was planning to meet him when he returned from Oahu tomorrow, so I'll just have to go out there, won't I? Thank you so much—there's just one other thing. It's been some time since I've been in Hilo and so much building has gone on that I'm no longer sure where I should turn off for the estate. Could you help me?"

There was a slight hesitation at the other end. "I'm afraid I can't tell you exactly, madam, but Lahue Point is not difficult to find. I'm sure you can get directions when you get there."

"Quite right—I'll do that. Thank you *so* much," she gushed, and hanging up in triumph grabbed for a map of the island. She found Lahue Point just north of Hilo Bay and hard by Hanoli'i Cove. Afire with new purpose, she bustled out to scout the enemy's terrain.

An enquiry from a Japanese who kept a small wayside store in the area put her on the right road, but a slow drive past the high-walled, iron-gated estate, in which she could just see the red-tiled roof of the house peeking through the trees, showed her that at least from this side Van Norkirk's citadel was impenetrable without an "Open Sesame" of some kind to get past the gate. She drove on down the road, which ended in an overlook at the cliff edge, and peered hopefully down. Sure enough, at the base of the cliff was a small landing stage, a power boat bobbing on one side, a small yacht on the other. There had to be a way up from the beach to the estate. She could see no means of descending the cliff nearby, so drove around to the cove, parked the car, and set out for a leisurely stroll along the beach. She plodded doggedly on through the yielding sand until the dock came in sight, and scanned the cliff face; a precipitous staircase soared to the heights above, but it was enclosed on both sides by a high wire-mesh fence and ended in another iron gate topped with intimidating spikes. She tried the gate: it was locked. Van Norkirk was evidently a man who knew how to guard his privacy.

However, on looking up the cliff, she could see where a recent rockfall had left a heap of small boulders that formed a pile against one side of the fence. A scramble to the top of those and it would be easy enough to scale the fence and drop down on the staircase. It was nothing she fancied doing, but if worse came to worst, it was something to bear in mind. Distant voices on the stairway sent her scurrying back the way she had come and, regaining the car, she drove wearily home, feeling that she had done all she could for the day.

Well before the appointed hour she was back at the office, and was greeted by the sullen secretary with the news that Van Norkirk was still at lunch and she was too early. "I'll wait," she said firmly and plumped down in one of the luxurious blue leather chairs that flanked a magazine-strewn table in the inner office. In her keyed-up state time dragged; two-thirty came and went, then two-forty-five, with no signs of her elusive quarry. In a few minutes she was joined by a dark-suited man with a briefcase, who settled gloomily into another chair after an appraising glance at her. The phone buzzed and was quickly answered by the secretary, whose name according to the nameplate on his desk was Dirk Botha, and therefore a fellow–countryman of his boss, she deduced. Botha listened intently, uttered some soft words in Afrikaans and hung up.

He came over to her, a phony smirk of apology on his dour features. "I'm afraid something has come up at the estate and Mr. Van Norkirk will not be in again today. You'll have to make another appointment." He wheeled on the seated man. "Mr. Wheeler, Mr. Van Norkirk has authorized Mr. Foster to act for him in your concern. You can see him right away—second door on the right as you go out."

The man got up and stumped away muttering under his breath, "Fine way to do business, I must say. . . ." Penny also rose and followed Botha back to his desk. "Well?" she challenged, trying to fight down her rising temper. "When can I see him?"

Botha looked smugly at her. "The same time, day after tomorrow is the best I can do," he purred.

"That's preposterous!" she flared. "I can't hang around Hilo forever, waiting for a few minutes of Van Norkirk's time! I have to see him before that."

"Since you refuse to state the nature of your business there is no reason for him to see you at all," he fired back. "I told you he was a very busy man. Now, do you want that appointment or not? If not, the door is behind you. Good day!"

Penny collected herself with an effort. "Certainly. Put me down for it, and you can tell Van Norkirk that it will be very much in his own interest not to break *that* appointment." But as she in turn stamped out she knew that she had no intention of waiting that long.

Still fuming, she drove toward her second target, the

equally elusive Paea Young. Parked in front of his house was a large late-model silver Oldsmobile, flashing fire in the afternoon sun. Her small face grimly set in determination, she sailed into the office without knocking. A sandy-haired man, his close-set blue eyes widening in surprise, looked up at her from behind a large desk piled with grid-maps. Only the faintly dusky color of his skin betrayed his strain of native blood—otherwise he looked like a seedy Scotsman. Penny took a deep breath. "Mr. Young?" she stated. "I've been looking for you for two days and, as my time in the area is very limited, I hope you will be able to spare me a few minutes on a matter of business."

Looking even more surprised, he waved her to a straight wooden chair on the other side of the desk. "Certainly. What can I do for you?" In contrast to his seedy appearance his voice was a rich, melodious baritone.

"Well, I want to buy a property for my retirement home—I'd like at least an acre plot. I want it somewhere in the area between Onomea and Pepe'ekeo—the nearer the coast the better, of course. I understand you have been buying up properties in that area, so wonder if you would show me a selection of them, perhaps today? I really am in a great hurry."

His eyes narrowed. "I'm afraid you've been misinformed. There are no single properties for sale—that's a Polynesian area, you know. It would not be suitable for you. I can't help you."

"Oh, I know about the natives, but it's where I *want* to be," she cried. "I've just come from the Norpark Corporation and they assured me you could help. Mr. Van Norkirk said . . ."

"He would never have sent anyone to . . ." Young began, then stopped short, belatedly aware of his admission. His thin mouth clamped shut. "You've been totally misled," he went on. "I do not handle property there. I cannot help you."

But she had learned what she needed to know. She got up looking suitably crestfallen, "Well, I don't understand this at all," she fussed. "I was assured . . . but if *you* won't help me I'm sure there are others that will." And she left quickly.

Paea Young watched slit-eyed until she was safely back in her car, then he swiftly reached for the phone. . . .

As she drove toward her next objective, she thought she could safely leave the rest of Paea Young's dubious affairs to Kaowa and his supporters, but she was still bent on seeing Van Norkirk and was not about to wait any longer. She knew she was taking a risky gamble—a gamble that Toby, for one, would thoroughly deplore—but decided in the interests of saving precious time it was well worth the risk involved.

She parked the car in Haoli'i Cove, walked back along the beach, scaled the rock slide and dropped awkwardly over the wire-mesh fence. She walked down the staircase to the gate and found to her relief that it had a lock that could be opened from the inside without a key. It was also bolted, top and bottom. She slipped the bolts, opened the gate wide and then turned, her escape route open if needed, to toil up the steep stairway.

As she puffed up it, she was busy planning her strategy; with any luck she could work her way around to the front of the house through the screening trees and by applying at the front door could make her unorthodox arrival seem at least semi-innocent. At the top however, as she clung to the fence post getting her breath back, her luck ran out, for, appearing out of a bank of shrubs, came a husky Hawaiian leading a mean–looking Doberman on a short leash. They both bared their teeth at her. "Stay right where you are, lady," the guard growled. "You're trespassing. How the hell did you get in?"

Penny looked at him in astonishment. "I'm not trespassing—I'm here to see Mr. Van Norkirk. He was unable to keep an appointment with me earlier today at his office, so I came to see him here instead. Kindly direct me to him."

"How the hell did you get in?" the guard repeated on a rising note.

"Why, through the gate of course! It was open," she twittered, pointing downward. "See! I came along the beach—it's such a lovely day."

The guard saw the open gate and went slack-jawed with amazement. "How the hell . . . ?" he muttered, and shook his head in disbelief. "You'd better come along with me, and no tricks mind, or I'll let the dog go."

He marched her smartly towards the house, but she had time to observe the general layout of the grounds and to see the helicopter standing on its concrete pad at some remove from the house. She wished she knew more about such things, but all helicopters looked alike to her, and of the one that had soared over her head that fateful morning of the murder she only held a faint image. They rounded the corner of the large house and came upon a quiet domestic scene; by the side of a kidney-shaped swimming pool a nubile blonde clad in a string bikini basked on a chaise longue; beside her at an umbrella-shaded metal table a man sat working on some papers, a tall glass in his free hand. They both looked up at the intruders in some surprise.

"I found this woman on the grounds, Mr. Van Norkirk," the Hawaiian said. "She claims she had an appointment with you downtown and was coming to see you here instead. Came up the back way from the beach—the gate was open, but I don't know how that happened. Did you expect her?"

Van Norkirk looked at Penny for a few long seconds. "No," he said softly. "I did not expect her, but now that she's here I'd like to hear what the hell she thinks she's doing." He shifted his head slightly and said to the blonde, "Get lost, Linda." She got up with a becoming pout and sauntered languidly into the house; both men watched her swaying hips with appreciation, while Penny watched Van Norkirk. A man in his mid-forties, she estimated, and all wire and whipcord, his fair hair thinning and receding so that his high forehead overbalanced the rest of his long, lean face. He emanated a restless energy. He turned back to her. "Well?" he challenged, "Who the hell are you and what do you want?"

Here goes! she thought, and launched into her act. "My name is Dr. Penelope Spring, president of the World Association for the Preservation of the Menehunes. I am taking up the cudgels on behalf of Dr. Giles Shaw, our local champion, now in jail for a murder he did not commit, and for the Menehunes. I thought it only fair to warn you, since you appear to have vested interests in that area, that we intend to mount the expedition he had planned to find the Menehunes, backed by television and press coverage, and that nothing and no one is going to stop us. We would appreciate your support, naturally, but, failing that, we will not brook any further interference from you or your henchmen."

For a second she thought there was a flicker of concern in the dark, intelligent eyes fixed upon her, but then it was gone. He leaned back in his chair with a snort of disgust. "Just as I thought—a king-size nut. Get her out of here, Keali!"

"Wait!" she cried, as the Hawaiian grasped her arm and started to tow her away. "Hear me out! The police know of your connection with Freyer. They know you were paying him off to discredit Shaw. They know the Norpark Corporation paid for the expensive car in which the poor man drove to his death. They are on to you and what you are up to, Mr. Van Norkirk, and so are we. And I warn you that we intend to petition the legislature to have that area declared a National Reserve, so that it can be secure for all time for its present inhabitants. Doubtless the police will also have some interesting questions to ask about your involvement in all this."

This time she had got through to him and his slitted, angry eyes took on a dangerous look. He rose out of his chair, planted both fists on the table and leaned towards her. "And I warn *you* that I brook no interference in my affairs," he said with quiet venom. "You come bursting in here with all these slanderous accusations and stupid threats! My answer is—don't take me on, lady, or you'll live to regret it. Now, Keali, show her out, and make sure the beach gate is secured behind her and that nothing like this ever happens again—or I'll have your head for it." He turned on his heel and headed swiftly for the house.

She shook off the Hawaiian's hand. "Keep off me!" she snarled. "I can find my own way out and I've no intention of being pushed down those steps. There are plenty of people who know I'm here—so don't try anything!" Surprisingly, the Hawaiian backed off and followed behind her as she cautiously descended the stairway to regain the beach. Even more surprisingly, after he had locked and bolted the gate behind her, he called in a mild voice, "He means it, lady—don't come back! It's for your own good, believe me." Which left her wondering how faithful a Van Norkirk employee he was.

As she plodded back to the car, she pondered as to what she had accomplished by all this. At least she now had the measure of the man and this, in a way, did nothing to raise her spirits, for there was no doubt that Van Norkirk was a man of quick intelligence, and she just could not see him committing a murder as unlikely and as stupid as Freyer's. She was certain Van Norkirk was the kind of man whose enemies would disappear without trace. He might still be behind it all, she supposed, but proving that would be well-nigh impossible. She climbed back into the car with a weary sigh: tomorrow she would take another crack at Paea Young, see Gladys and Mama Luali one more time and ask them about Hapili, and then she would head back to Kailua and Toby.

She decided on an early dinner and an early night, and ate absentmindedly at a seafood restaurant on Hilo Bay, while she ran over everything again. She added a farewell visit to Philip at his ranch to her list of things to do on the morrow and drove back to the hotel.

There were two messages waiting for her at the desk, one to call Toby, another from Kaowa. She hastened up to her room to put in the calls, opened the door and stopped appalled on the threshold. All her clothes were scattered about the room—they had been slashed to ribbons. A white card lay by the telephone with a simple, typewritten message. "You next?" it read.

Chapter 11

Despite the fact that Toby Glendower came of the purest
Welsh lineage which, as his fanatic Celtic father had oft
proclaimed to the world, was untinged by a single drop
of English blood, the simile most applied to him, by
friends and foes equally, likened him to an English bulldog. And in that they were not too wide of the mark: like
the bulldog Toby was slow to arouse, but once he had
taken his tenacious grip on any problem nothing short of
death would shake him loose from it. In the course of his
long and distinguished career this had occasioned the despair and downfall of many a careless scholar and, more
recently, of sundry careless murderers. But in this present
instance he found himself in a terrible quandary, afraid
that the wild, imaginative surmise that had come to him
as he had pored over the maps in the Bishop Museum,
and which every little bit of evidence he had picked up
since was driving him inexorably towards, was so bizarre
that it matched Shaw's preposterous Menehune claims.
He did not *want* to believe it, but his tenacious streak
was forcing him along this obscure path, and it was this

basic ambivalence in himself that made him testy as he finally made contact with Griselda Freyer.

"Miss Freyer," he trumpeted, "I am sorry if this is painful to you, but I simply have to know more about your father's interests and activities. I will try to be as concise as possible in my questions, but I beg you to give them all deep thought. First, was your father an expert on or particularly interested in the great king Kamehameha? Especially about his death and burial? Did he write any papers or do any research along those lines?"

After a pause Griselda's voice came thinly over the phone. "Why no, as I think I explained to Dr. Spring, that wasn't his field at all. He was primarily an urban anthropologist. Of course he did know a lot about the king in a general way, but no, he never published anything about him."

Toby grew even testier. "Then was he closely associated with any colleague here or elsewhere in the world who *was* an expert? Think, Miss Freyer, think!—this is very important."

There was a longer pause. "Well, no," she said faintly. "Unless . . . well there was old Mr. Donelson, but I don't think. . . ."

Toby pounced. "Who and where is he?"

"I'm afraid he's dead," she faltered. "He was an eccentric old man who used to play chess with my father, but he wasn't a scholar or connected with the university. He was a fanatic about Kamehameha—had spent most of his life assembling notes for this great work on him that never got written. He died about six months ago and left all his papers and collection to the University of Hawaii, and named my father as his literary custodian and executor."

"Your father had these papers in his office?" Toby said eagerly. "They are still intact?"

"No, they were not in his office," she said, evidently

deeply puzzled by his eagerness. "After he'd looked through them, my father put them in the University Archives for storage until he had more time to give to them."

"And when was this?" he demanded.

"About four months ago." She had finally caught his drift. "You think they may have something to do with my father's subsequent involvement with Hapili, who first appeared at that time?"

"Indeed I do."

"Then I could check to see if he had recently looked at them. The archives keep a register of consultations. Would that help?"

"Yes. In fact I would like you to do more than that." Toby cleared his throat. "If your father has been consulting them recently, I would like you to do the following. As your father's heir I imagine that the custodianship of the papers now falls upon you—I would like you to request the archives to release them to you on a temporary basis, and then fly with them down here. I will pay all expenses."

A dismayed gasp came over the line. "But, Sir Tobias, there are boxes and boxes of them! And I can't possibly get away at a moment's notice! Couldn't you just tell me what to look for and I'll get back to you when and if I find it?"

"I cannot tell you because I do not know myself," he boomed impatiently, but came to a quick decision. "If you can't come here, then I'll have to come to you. I'm calling now from a little place north of the Payson ranch where I've been staying, so I'll have to return there, pick up some things and then try and get a flight out by some means from Ke'ahole airport today. Could you get the papers back to your house by tonight? I will come there as soon as I get in. If I can't make it by tonight, I'll know in the next hour or so and I'll phone you again. If you *don't* hear from me, it means go ahead."

"Yes, I can do that if it will help," she agreed. "But can't you tell me what this is all about?"

"If my theory is correct, it will explain the break-ins after your father's death and the second sketch-map you found in his car. Since nothing meaningful except one map folder was stolen from *him*, I think the thieves were after something that may well be contained in those boxes in the archives. I may be quite wrong, but the acquaintance of Hapili with your father started shortly after those boxes came into his possession, so there may be a connection there. I am afraid that's all I can say at this point."

"Well, alright—I'll bring them to the house right after work, unless I hear from you to the contrary," she said distantly, and rang off.

Toby scribbled an explanatory note to Kaowa, currently off trying to make contact with the ranch-hand Manua, who appeared to be as elusive as the absent Hapili. Then he tried to contact Penny, but to his annoyance she was out, so he left a message for her to contact him and hoped she would do so before his precipitate departure. "Never around when you need her, and always underfoot when you don't," he grumbled to himself as he drove back to the Payson ranch.

There he burst in upon the Paysons at lunch. "I'm afraid something has come up about *The Dancing Lady* and I have to get back to Oahu at once to take care of it for Mr. Lefau," he lied cheerfully. "I was wondering if you had any timetables for Ke'ahole airport handy? I should try and get off as soon as possible."

Mildred looked at him in utter dismay, but Gregory patted his lips carefully with his napkin and said with quiet decision. "Unless you have an aversion to helicopters, Sir Tobias, perhaps I can help you out. I was planning to go to Oahu myself this afternoon. I could take you—my helicopter is functioning again. Otherwise it would take you much longer—the Ke'ahole flights are not all that frequent."

Before Toby could say anything, Mildred, after a startled glance at Gregory, piped up. "Oh, and don't forget I'm coming too—arrangements for horses for the gymkhana, remember?"

Her brother looked at her in some surprise. "I thought that had been taken care of?"

"Not entirely." She slid a coy glance at Toby. "What fun if we all fly together!"

Damnation take the silly woman! Toby thought miserably, but it was too tempting an offer to refuse. "That's most kind of you—yes, if I can get a lift up with you. I'll just throw a few things in a bag as I don't know when I'll get through up there, so I'll find my own way back."

"Oh, but you *will* be coming back here surely, Toby?" Mildred shrilled anxiously.

In the circumstances it seemed churlish to say he would return directly to the yacht. "Well, you've already been so kind, I hate to impose further on your hospitality," he hedged.

"Oh, but you *must* come back, we do so enjoy having you here!" She turned to her brother. "Tell him, Gregory, tell him he's like one of the family already and must stay a little longer!"

"You are welcome to stay with us as long as you please, we enjoy your company," her brother said obediently, leaving Toby no option but to say he'd return.

Before they took off an hour later, Toby surreptitiously slipped down to Gregory's study and tried again to contact Penny, still with no result. A trickle of unease went up his spine: knowing her propensity for getting into trouble, he did not like this continuing silence on her part. Still, he consoled himself, she *had* been in touch with Kaowa, so she had to be all right.

On the flight up he tried to draw his host out about the helicopter, but Gregory as pilot was as uncommunicative as Gregory as driver, and after a series of his monosyllabic replies Toby gave up on it and fixed his attention firmly on the panorama of the islands passing beneath them, and himself became monosyllabic as Mildred, in the back seat, leaned forward and tried to draw him into her bright chit-chat. He had even more difficulty after they had landed at Honolulu airport in shaking off the Paysons, who seemed bent on staying with him. He was on the verge of becoming extremely rude to them when providence stepped in, and they were hailed by an acquaintance just as they emerged from the terminal. With a gabbled farewell, he managed to make his escape by diving into a taxi, leaving them looking forlornly after him.

He had made such a rapid trip that he half-expected not to find anyone in when he got to the Freyer home, but his tentative knock was immediately answered by a startled-looking Griselda. She ushered him into the bright little living room with profuse apologies at her state of unreadiness, but his attention was already fixed on the ten cardboard cartons that stood piled up in the center of the room.

"I was going to arrange them in my father's study," she said in a faint voice, as he immediately dived into the box on the top of the pile. "I thought you'd be more comfortable in there—I'd no idea you'd be here so soon."

"No, this is fine, just fine," he said absently, piling the contents of the box on to the coffee table and starting to leaf quickly through the papers.

"Is there anything I can do to help?" she asked.

"No, no, just do whatever it is you usually do," he muttered. "Don't mind me—this may take some time."

"Anything you need?" she queried, backing slowly away.

"Couple of empty folders, maybe? Mind if I smoke?" he rumbled.

"Er—no. I'll get you an ashtray," she said, and disappeared.

Totally absorbed he worked on, scarcely conscious of her return with the folders and a large ashtray. After a glance at the blue cloud now entirely surrounding him, she surreptitiously opened a window and left him to it.

The hours rolled by, and on the fifth box he drew in his breath sharply—he had come upon the original of the sketch-map and pinned to it were several other papers. There was an Hawaiian family tree, which for the moment meant nothing to him, and a series of yellowing photographs of Hawaiian petroglyphs. He extracted all of them and put them into the empty folder, and going back through the box added other papers to the second folder, before proceeding onwards. From time to time he would add something to a folder, but his momentum never slowed, as the pile of boxes diminished. It was only when he was on the last box that he became dimly aware that night had fallen; lights were now all on and Griselda had rejoined him and was hovering uncertainly over his shoulder. "Er, I wondered if you'd like to take a break while I get us some dinner. You must be tired," she said timidly.

Toby straightened up, glanced at his watch and was amazed to see it was already after eight o'clock. "Most kind of you, Miss Freyer," he muttered. "But I insist on taking you out to dinner. Just let me finish this last box and then we'll go. You choose the place, and I'm afraid we'll have to take your car. Will that be convenient for you?"

Griselda blushed. "Yes, if you insist—I'll go and get ready then."

Twenty minutes later he piled the contents of the last box back into it and stood up with a satisfied sigh. "Finished," he announced to the girl who was seated in an armchair watching him intently.

"Did you find anything?" she asked.

"Enough to convince me that my theory may be correct," he said smugly. "Though what it all means will require a lot more study." He tucked the two folders lovingly under his arm. "Shall we go? If I show you some of the things over dinner, maybe you'll be able to throw more light on them."

Over dinner he tried to tear his mind away from the siren lure of the folders, but found it heavy going. Griselda appeared equally distracted, to the point that he enquired. "Were you expecting someone else to be here? If so, I'd be delighted to have them join us."

Again the easy color flooded her cheeks and she said in some confusion, "Er, no, not really. It's so late he's probably been and gone, but this is where Brad Field usually eats dinner. We've been coming here quite often."

"Oh!" Toby's tone was hollow; he was not enthused at the idea of a reporter being around his precious folders.

Griselda pulled herself together. "Do tell me what you've found, Sir Tobias. I've been so worried about all this and I would like to help."

Toby pushed aside the remnants of his dinner, reached for the top folder and extracted the sketch map and its attendant papers. "Well, I am pretty certain I have located the area of this map," he said, tapping it with a long, lean finger. "Even your father's map, which is much less detailed than this one, had some features on it that have led me to this conclusion. You see this long line at the top? I believe that to be Ke'ahole airfield. Here is Wawaloli beach with a *heiau* marked just to the south of it. This mark indicates the Kaloka fish pond, and to the south of that again two more *heiaus*, those are Hale o Mono and

Hale o Lono. And tradition has it that somewhere in that area lies the burial place of the great king Kamehameha." He paused and looked at her. "I think that what we have here is a treasure-hunter's map—that someone is after the burial cave of the king with its attendant treasure."

As she looked at him in blank astonishment, he pushed the petroglyph photos towards her. "Do you know anything about these things? I am sure they must be markers of some kind."

She stared at them but shook her head vigorously. "But . . ." she faltered. "You think my father was involved in a treasure hunt? How on earth could that be? What could it have to do with Dr. Shaw or the Menehune controversy?"

"That's just it—probably nothing," Toby said firmly. "It's a second and separate strand. Let me put a hypothetical reconstruction to you. Your father was initially engaged in the Menehune controversy with Dr. Shaw. He is approached by the Van Norkirk syndicate who also has interests of its own in seeing the feud settled and who then hires him." Seeing her start to bridle at this, he added hastily. "Since their views coincided with his own your father saw nothing wrong with that, and indeed was doing an excellent job of making Dr. Shaw look ridiculous. Then, suddenly, a *kahuna,* Hapili, approaches him, just about the time he comes into the possession of the life's work of a man whose sole interest was the great king. Equally suddenly your father, who has Giles Shaw on the run, is anxious to get the matter settled. Why? Because now he is involved in this other affair—which, if valid, could be the greatest archaeological discovery ever made in the islands." He stopped and looked enquiringly at her.

"But it still makes no sense to me!" she cried. "Why murder him? And what about the helicopter and the bizarre murder method? What proof have you? It still seems to me that Dr. Shaw had the best motive, opportunity and everything else."

"We still don't have all the pieces or all the actors identified, and in fact your father's murder might indeed have been a setback to the treasure hunters, hence the break-ins," Toby said patiently. "They were looking for something which they did not find; something presumably that was in Donelson's boxes in the archives. Since a map folder *is* missing it is possible they may also now have a copy of this map," he tapped it again. "You see we *have* found the perpetrator of that first break-in and right in this same area. Dr. Spring identified him and we are now hunting for him. . . ." And he went on to tell her about Manua.

Griselda still looked doubtful, so he decided not to press the point. Instead he handed her the genealogical tree, which was written in a very crabbed and indecipherable hand. "Does this mean anything to you? Do you recall your father and Mr. Donelson ever discussing genealogy?"

She shrugged helplessly. "I never paid much attention—the old man used to ramble on so." She squinted at the chart. "It's very hard to make out, isn't it?" Then she suddenly let out a soft exclamation.

"What is it?" Toby demanded.

She pointed to a word at the top of the chart. "I think that word is *kahu*."

"Well?" he prompted. "I'm afraid I know very little Hawaiian. What does it mean?"

"*Kahu* means a hereditary caretaker," she said faintly. "They were usually recruited from the ranks of the lesser *alii*. It was their duty to guard and look after the tombs of the grand *alii*. It was a very sacred and secret duty." They looked at each other in sudden wild surmise.

"My God!" Toby muttered. "This may be the key—I'll have to get it to Kaowa as soon as I can." He signalled for

134

the check, stowed the papers carefully away and became all brisk efficiency. "Now, if you will ferry me back to your house, and I'll call up the hotel nearest the airport and stay there for the night. I should be able to get an early morning flight out. This has been a tremendous help, Miss Freyer, I am most grateful."

"Not at all," she said dazedly. "I'm glad to have been of help, even though it's—well—so mind-boggling."

They drove back to the house in absorbed silence, but as they got out of the car, Toby said, "I would urge you to take the papers back to the archives tomorrow. It will be safer. If we have further need of them, I'll consult them there."

"Yes, I'll certainly do that. I could not bear any more trouble," she said, letting them into the house and switching on the lights. "You can telephone from my father's study." She preceded him into the living room, then recoiled violently; the room looked as if it had been hit by a snowstorm, for every single one of the boxes had been emptied of their contents and the papers were scattered ankle-deep over the entire floor.

"It's happening again!" Griselda choked out. "Oh God! The window . . . I forgot to shut the window." And she slumped quietly at his feet in a dead faint.

Chapter 12

It did not help matters when Griselda, on reviving from her faint, went into a fit of hysterical sobbing. To have to cope with a woman was bad enough, but a crying woman to Toby was an abomination before the Lord and he had not the faintest idea how to deal with the situation. His efforts at consolation consisted of a tentative thump or two on her quivering shoulders and stern exhortations to "Brace up—no real harm has been done," mixed with fervent craven pleas to "please stop crying." "Come!" he exhorted, as the storm seemed to be subsiding a little, "let's clear up this mess. We can do it in no time—none of the boxes was in order anyway, and I am certain I already have all the vital stuff in the folders." And, suiting the action to the word, he began to shovel the contents of the boxes haphazardly back into them.

Griselda, slumped in a small disconsolate heap on the floor, made no effort to join him, but after a while the sobs died away and there was much nose blowing and throat clearing, then she said in a nasal quivering voice, "Someone must have been watching the house all this time—I can't stand it any more, I really can't—I'm so afraid." Her voice started to rise into hysteria again.

"It may not be as bad as that," he said quickly, trying to head off another outburst. "Who knew at the university, apart from yourself and the archivist, that you were bringing the Donelson collection home? Someone there may have seen you putting the boxes into your car."

"No one is around—it's still vacation time," she hiccuped. "Brad helped me load them into the car and then followed me in his and helped unload them this end. It took no time at all."

"*Field* knew?" he queried sharply.

"Why yes, but . . ." she looked up at him with a sudden blaze of anger. "You're not thinking *Brad* did this?—that's ridiculous! Why on earth should he?"

Toby retreated before her anger. "No, no—there are many other possibilities," he muttered. Two likely ones he did not care to think about as yet. "Anyway . . ." he dumped a handful of papers into a box and closed the lid. "That's the last of it. It's late and you'd better get into bed after all this upset, and I'll be on my way. No sense in notifying the police this late, you can call them in the morning."

She surged to her feet and held out her hands imploringly to him. "Oh, *no!* Please don't leave me! I can't face it alone, I really can't. Please stay here for the night. You can have my father's room—it's all ready. *Please!* And I don't want the police around again. They don't do anything except tramp around and make messes, and they'll say it was all my fault for leaving the window open."

Toby was panic-stricken. "Well—er—aren't there some friends I could take you to for the night?" he gobbled. "Someone you could stay with until you've settled down?"

"No one, no one at all—even the Eberts are away," she

choked and more tears started to trickle down her cheeks.

"Alright, I'll stay," he said in desperation. "Please get hold of yourself and calm down! Do you have any sedatives here?" She shook her head. "Any brandy?" This time she nodded and pointed mutely to a decanter standing on an end table with four glasses arranged neatly around it. He poured her a hefty slug of it, then poured himself an even heftier one: he badly needed it.

Her brandy finished and her point won, Griselda calmed down and became the perfect hostess—she showed him around, they checked to see everything was shut and locked, and then with a pathetic little smile of gratitude she retreated to her room. Left to his own devices, Toby helped himself to another glass of brandy and retreated gloomily to his room, a prey to dismal thoughts.

Storing the precious files under his pillow, he climbed into bed and turned off the light, but tossed and turned restlessly as a host of new possibilities—all of them unpleasant—flooded his mind. Only two other people had known about his proposed consultation of the Donelson papers—Kaowa and Brad Field. On the time and distance factor alone he felt he could safely rule out Kaowa, even granting his extensive network of helpers on the islands, and that left Field, who, up to this point, he had not even considered as part of the case at all.

Now, when he thought about it, Field's activities could be viewed in a more sinister light. He had been very early on the scene after the murder. According to Penny, who was never wrong about such things, he had made a dead set at the girl and had been close by her ever since. He had tracked *them* down with an incredible speed and, now it occurred to him, had provided them with all the information that had sent Penny hareing off on Van Norkirk's trail. Had that been deliberate obfuscation to draw them away from the real crux of the case: Freyer's witting or unwitting possession of materials pertinent to the treasure hunt? The reporter, he felt, would bear further investigation.

But, if it wasn't Field, there was another uneasy possibility: the Paysons, either one or both of them. And, if so, it meant that they *were* involved in this up to their necks. Had they been on to what he was up to from the start, and their easy hospitality merely a front? They had been very loath to let him go, and it would not have required too much effort or guesswork to track his taxi ride to the Freyer residence. He wondered if he had underestimated them and their seeming lack of intelligence.

The final possibility was the one he least liked. That Griselda Freyer was right and the house had been under constant unseen surveillance. And there the most likely candidate was the elusive and sinister Hapili. If so she could be in some danger. What on earth was to be done about the poor wretched girl? On this unhappy thought he finally fell asleep.

The haunted look in Griselda's pansy brown eyes and the dark circles under them finally decided him, as he faced her across the breakfast table. His dominating thought was to get the folders to safe haven and into the custody of Kaowa and his kin, but he obviously had to look after this girl. He cleared his throat. "I think, Miss Freyer, that this should be our order of business. First, we take the boxes back to the archives. Second, you make whatever arrangements have to be made for you to take an indefinite vacation, and third, that we return together to the big island as soon as possible. Until you are over this present upset, I think it would be wiser and safer if you came with me. You can stay on *The Dancing Lady*, where you'll be well-guarded, and Dr. Spring should be back by now to keep you company." Toby fervently hoped this was true.

Griselda's eyes lit up. "Oh, yes! May I really come with you? That would be wonderful! I'm sure I can arrange it with the university. And I really don't want to go back to the police again."

"Good! Then let's get on with it," he said briskly.

While Griselda signed all the boxes backed into the archives, he took a quick look at the consultation register and jotted down the dates when Freyer had looked at them. He noted with interest that one of the dates co-incided with his well–publicized fistfight with Shaw and the latest one was on the day prior to the murder. Mulling over this, he followed her back to Freyer's office, but as soon as they were there she said pointedly, "I'm going to have to do some calling around to arrange for my absence and it may take some time. Why don't you take the opportunity to explore the campus? It really is worth seeing."

"I should call the airport," he said, somewhat surprised at this brisk brush-off.

"Oh, I can do that. Two returns on the earliest flight to Ke'ahole?" She took a flight schedule from the desk and consulted it and the clock. "To be on the safe side I think the one-thirty flight out would be the earliest feasible one, and should I ask for a car at the other end?"

"Just a one-way ticket for me. Tell them I'll pay in cash at the airport. And yes, get a car. I'm going to have to make a couple of stops on the way to Kailua."

"I should be through in an hour. If you could be back here by then, we'll go back to the house, pack and get out to the airport." She was all business.

"Alright." He ambled off, pondering on this remarkable change of manner, but then the workings of the female mind had always been an enigma to him, he concluded with a resigned sigh. He wandered around the lush campus, puffing on his pipe and arranging his next priorities in his mind. Coming across an office that advertised a copying machine available for students, he wandered into it and after acquiring a load of change from the sleepy-looking student in attendance, occupied himself by making copies of all the papers in the two folders he had stashed in his briefcase. This done, he acquired a large manila envelope and some stamps from the young man, then wrote a note in his precise, neat script to Inspector Lyons to the effect that these were copies of vital documents in the Freyer/Shaw case and should be guarded zealously by Hawaii Five–O, that he would shortly be in touch with them with due clarification of same, but that one or two matters still remained to be clarified on the big island. "Never hurts to play it safe," he murmured to himself as he mailed the package. "And that should pique their curiosity a bit. Should soften them up for step number two." And he headed back for his rendezvous with Griselda.

He caught her just as she was emerging from the office, her eyes bright and a pink flush on her cheeks. She was looking extremely pleased with herself. "All set," she announced. "We'll just have time to drop by the house and get out to the airport to pick up our tickets."

Later, as they drove out to the airport, she enquired casually, "Where are we stopping after we land?"

"First at a little place called Kalaoa on the Belt Road. I have to see Kaowa and fill him in on all this," Toby mumbled.

"Oh, yes, Brad told me about him. Did you know he was a graduate of the University?" she interrupted. "He has a law degree."

141

"No, I didn't know that." But it came as no surprise to him, he had already realized that Benjamin Kaowa was a man of many parts.

"And after that?" she prompted.

"I'll have to stop by the Payson ranch where I've been staying and pick up my things—they were expecting me back there."

"Oh, dear, I'm afraid I am being an awful nuisance to you." She looked at him with troubled eyes. "But I do so appreciate this."

"I was intending to get back to the yacht shortly anyway," he soothed. "I'll probably be taking it around to Hilo, where I can drop you and Dr. Spring off, and then Kaowa and I will be heading back to Honolulu. I should have enough by then to persuade Lyons to release Giles Shaw."

She looked at him in astonishment. "Really?"

He nodded. "Really," but did not elaborate.

Once they were airborne, he extracted the Hawaiian genealogy from the folder and started painstakingly to transcribe it into a readable form. Griselda watched with interest and occasionally would offer a suggestion about the form of a name. The suggestions were all so sensible that Toby began to look at her with a growing respect. "Do you know why these particular names are underlined in the chart?" he asked, pointing at the line of descent on the extreme left of it.

"Yes, well, I think this designates the senior line—first son of a first son etcetera, which is so important to the Hawaiians. The underlined names are undoubtedly the ones the actual *kahu* descended to. Those other lines are junior lines from second and third sons, and so on, and so would not be eligible if the senior line continued. If it died out then the most senior branch of the second son would take over, and so on. . . ."

"The chart only seems to go down to the 1940s," Toby murmured. "There's a whole generation since then. I wonder why he didn't bring it up to date."

"Poor old Mr. Donelson was a bit scrambled," Griselda admitted. "He was not a trained scholar—more like a magpie. He'd gather bits here and there, but he'd never really *finish* anything."

"Tell me more about this *kahu* system," he encouraged. "Would the secrets about the burial places be only known to one person, or would the family in general know about it?"

"I don't know a great deal," Griselda confessed. "But it was generally *only* the *kahu* who knew, although I've read in some books where other family members have followed the *kahu* and found out, and then have been sworn to secrecy with the most awful *kapus*—taboos— put on them."

"And this still goes on?" Toby was very interested.

"I think there has been a certain amount of breakdown—after all, there aren't many purebred Hawaiians around anymore, and the mixed bloods don't tend to take it so seriously. There has been much tomb robbing in the islands," Griselda said somberly.

"But no one has ever found the tomb of Kamehameha." He was equally somber.

"It has been tried often enough," she said quickly. "A man called Julian Rodman went after it in the 1940s—I read his account. He tried to find the great cave of Hale'iliili from the ocean, but got nowhere. And there have been many others."

They were interrupted by the landing announcement, and in the bustle of landing and picking up the rental car the subject was dropped. To his profound irritation, Toby found that, due to the lay of the land, the quickest way to get to either Kalaoa or the Payson ranch was by driving down the coast highway almost into Kailua in order to pick up the Belt road going north again. "In that case, while we're in Kailua, I'd best check on the yacht and I can drop you and your bags off. Maybe Dr. Spring and Kaowa are already there," he told Griselda hopefully.

His luck was at least partly in, for when they arrived at *The Dancing Lady* the unmistakable bulk of Kaowa could be seen in converse with two other Hawaiians over whom he towered. Toby and Kaowa's surprise and delight at seeing each other was mutual, and after introductions had been made and Griselda safely stowed below decks with instructions "to make herself at home," Toby hastened back to Kaowa with explanations. "Another break-in at the Freyer house and the girl was so upset by it that I thought it best to bring her here—she may be useful. Dr. Spring can look after her so she won't get in our way. Any word from her?" He tried not to sound as worried as he felt.

Kaowa's answer did nothing to calm him. "No, not a word. And she has checked out of the hotel in Hilo. That I found out when I tried to reach her there."

"Then she must be back at the Payson ranch. Did you try there?" Toby said anxiously.

"I tried, but was told you and the Paysons had all gone to Oahu. I thought I would go in person yesterday evening, in case she had showed up by then—I was anxious to see her." Kaowa paused. "It is certainly not evident, but the Paysons now have a very tight patrol system on the ranch. I was stopped before I ever got near the house itself." A faint grin appeared on the rocklike face. "I did convince my brethren not to throw me out or take me on, and though they would not let me near the house they did become most cooperative. She is not there and there have been no calls. The one certain thing I did find out is not good. Manua has disappeared. He left the day after the luau and has not been seen on the ranch again. What is worse, he took nothing with him—I checked his things in the bunkhouse myself and confirmed this. I do not like it at all, for I had just found out his connection with Paea Young, about whom Dr. Spring was so excited. Their mothers were sisters."

"Who the hell is he?" Toby said, his fears in full flood.

Kaowa told him concisely. "And what of your news?" he concluded.

"Important, but it'll have to wait. I'm going out to the Paysons, I have to find out what's happened to Dr. Spring. Keep an eye on the girl for me, will you, until I get back?"

But it was not to be that simple. When he informed Griselda of the situation, she grew very agitated and begged to go with him, growing tearful in the process. Not wishing another hysterical scene, he succumbed to this threat and once more they were on the road heading north together.

Toby had quick confirmation of Kaowa's experience, for as he got out to open the main gate leading from the side road to the ranch house, two burly ranch hands appeared out of the bushes, one of them armed with a rifle. When they saw who he was, they nodded affably after a curious glance at Griselda in the car and faded back into the bushes again. He drove up to the gravel expanse in front of the house just in time to see Mildred cantering towards him on a large bay horse, an expression of delight on her long, thin face. The delight faded to anxious enquiry as she spotted Griselda.

"Why, Toby, back already? How nice!" she exclaimed, dismounting from the horse and coming over to the car.

His anxiety made him brusque. "Yes, I'm afraid there is a change in plans. This is Miss Griselda Freyer, Miss Mildred Payson." The women nodded coolly at each other as he hurried on. "On top of all the other great shocks she has had, there was a most unfortunate break-in at Miss Freyer's house last night, so I thought it safer to bring her down to the yacht. I've come to collect my things and Dr. Spring, if she is back."

"I'm afraid she isn't," Mildred said uneasily.

"Then have you heard from her?"

"Er—not directly." Mildred turned a concerned face up to him. "We did have a call from Phillip this morning about her. I'm afraid something very unfortunate has happened. . . ."

Chapter 13

After the first appalled shock at the vicious destruction of her belongings had subsided a little, Penny went into action. This time, she told herself grimly, she was going to do the sensible thing and take Kaowa's advice: she would get out of here first and regroup in safer surroundings. The sheer speed with which Van Norkirk had reacted—if indeed this was the handiwork of his minions—shook her to the core. She reached for the phone, but after a short reflection pocketed the card with its typewritten threat. The management would undoubtedly call the police, and to explain the card would lead her into complications and delays that she did not wish to face.

The management came and saw and were duly shocked. The police came and saw and, after ascertaining that nothing had actually been stolen and that the door had not been forced, deduced that some sneak thief had entered from the balcony, whose doors had been unlocked, and finding nothing of value had vented his spleen on her belongings. Did she know of anyone who held a grudge against her?

"Not really," she said. "I am chiefly here as a tourist, although I have just returned from a rather unpleasant business discussion with Mr. Van Norkirk at his Lahue Point estate." She dropped this in to see their reaction, but by the way they recoiled at the very mention of his name, it was evident that this was nothing they wanted to pursue. They departed, shrugging their collective shoulders and muttering "vandals," leaving her with the manager. He repeated his shock and concern, and added tentatively that the hotel was covered by insurance for damage to a guest's property, and in this case he would be most happy to recompense her at once and in cash rather than have any unpleasant publicity for the hotel. "I assure you we have not had an incident like this for a very long time," he said earnestly. "I will, of course, change your room to a higher floor or to a suite, if you prefer it, with no extra charge."

Apart from the nuisance value of losing her clothes, there was nothing she really valued save the Tahitian muu muu, that ironically enough had been a present from Emily Shaw in the long ago, and which now lay in colorful shreds on the bed. "In the circumstances I feel I had best move on," she murmured. "This has been quite a shock. But I would appreciate it if the hotel would compensate me for the articles I will have to replace before resuming my travels. What sum did you have in mind?"

The manager ran a practiced eye over the remnants and named a sum that seemed overly generous to her but which she quickly accepted, and they departed to his office where he produced the cash and, unexpectedly, two suitcases to replace the ones that had been slashed to ribbons. She cheerfully signed a waiver absolving the hotel of any further responsibility, loaded her empty cases into the car, and set off to do some quick shopping for the vital necessities she would need until she got back to the rest of her belongings on the yacht.

As she diligently shopped in the few stores that remained open, for the shades of night were now falling, her mind was busy as to where she should seek safe haven. If Van Norkirk really meant business and was after her, she really did not want to hang around Hilo. On the other hand, she did not fancy the long tortuous drive around Mauna Kea in the dark to reach the Payson ranch. She toyed with the idea of seeking shelter at Mama Luali's, but quickly abandoned that: the last thing she wanted was to draw trouble upon them, and she had no idea if Van Norkirk would go to the lengths of having her followed. It seemed to leave her but one alternative: to seek shelter with Philip Payson for the night, and then head back to Kailua and the yacht in the morning after a farewell stop at the Paysons. If Philip was to be believed, he and Van Norkirk belonged to the same social circle, and she could not see Van Norkirk going to the lengths of having her pursued to the home of a friend or even an acquaintance. It was worth a try.

She sought a phone and called the Wailuku ranch. The phone was answered by a soft, melodious woman's voice which, by its liquid vowels, signalled a native of the islands. Philip Payson was not at home but was expected back later in the evening, could she take a message? Penny explained at some length who she was and asked if she could come over.

"Oh, yes," the voice cooed. "Mr Payson has spoken of you. Come, by all means—he will be most pleased that you visit him."

"Um—I was wondering if I might even beg a bed for the night, if it is not too inconvenient? I'll be going back to his brother's ranch tomorrow, and since you are on the

way, as it were, I thought it may save me some time."
The voice assured her that she was sure that would be
fine with Mr. Payson and that she would see to it right
away. "You know where to turn off?" she asked.

Delighted with her success, Penny assured her she
would find it and would be right along. She went and
gassed up the car, consulted her map and headed hopefully for the Wailuku ranch. She found it easily, and took
this for a good omen. The ranch house itself was small
and somewhat run-down—a far cry from Gregory's elaborate establishment—but her ring at the door was
promptly answered by a young and lovely Hawaiian girl,
clad in a beautiful, if scant, muu muu, who announced
her name was Lalai, and who ushered her into the house
and up to a bright bedroom. Penny followed, eyeing the
girl's nubile figure with appreciation and reflecting that
Philip's English ethnocentricity obviously did not extend
to his female companions.

"Please make yourself at home," the girl murmured.
"There is a drinks tray I have prepared in the living room
for Phil . . . er . . . Mr. Payson. Can I get you anything
to eat?"

"No, I have eaten, thank you, but I would like to use
your phone, if I may? I'd like to call my friend who is
staying with Mr. Payson's brother," Penny said.

"The English lord?—he is not there," the girl said
quickly. "Philip told me. They are all gone to Oahu in the
helicopter."

Penny felt a jolt of surprise. "Any idea why?"

The girl shrugged. "Mr Payson might know. You could
ask him. He should be home soon—very soon. There is
nothing I can get you?"

"No, nothing, Lalai, you have been most kind—I'll just
go down and have a drink and wait for Mr. Payson."

"Make yourself at home," the girl repeated and disappeared.

Penny went down to the nondescript living room that, nonetheless, was very clean and showed little loving touches, like huge bowls of fresh flowers, that was in marked contrast to the unloved air of Gregory's home. She helped herself to a drink, which she felt she needed after her hectic day, pondered briefly on Toby's unexpected flight to Oahu, then looked around for something to do. There wasn't a book or a magazine in sight, so she decided to explore the house.

She found the dining room had an unused look to it, but on her second try hit pay dirt when she opened the door on a room as large as the living room and which was evidently Philip's study. Here the furnishings, though out-of-date, were almost sumptuous. From one wall the head of a large maned lion loomed beneath a pair of ivory tusks, balanced on the other wall by a huge African buffalo head, flanked by outsize horns of kudu, impala and oryx. Beneath them was an old-fashioned glass–fronted mahogany gun case with an assemblage of high-powered hunting rifles: one of them was missing, and she wondered if that explained Philip's absence. Balancing that was another glass–fronted case that housed a mounted collection of bows and arrows and native spears. She peered in and recognized a Bushman and a Pygmy set, complete with their little gourd poison-pots, but there were several others she could not identify and she noticed with quickening interest that one had an attachment for a poison-pot but that the pot itself was missing. She tried the door of the case for a closer look, but it was locked.

Behind the huge mahogany desk and its matching red leather chair was an open bookcase in which reposed a rather pathetic little collection of objects that, unlike the rest of the contents of the room, she surmised were Philip's own and only contribution to the Payson heritage. There was a small silver trophy for hurdling, bearing the arms of a lesser English public school; a framed photo of a cricket team with the same arms, with the young Philip resplendent as captain in a First XI blazer. There was a larger silver trophy for marksmanship—this one with the insignia of a Southern Rhodesian gun club on it, and another framed picture of Philip and his father, safari-clad and grinning proudly at the camera over the carcasses of two rhino. On the bottom shelf was a battered cricket bat inscribed with a lot of names and a moth-eaten cap with the insignia of a Rhodesian cricket club.

Penny looked at the things with a sad twinge of sympathy. She understood all the practical reasons behind the rigid clinging of most European countries to the rule of primogeniture, where everything was lavished on and descended to the oldest son, but she had never accepted it emotionally. It seemed to her most unfair, and she had always been thankful that this particular cultural seed had never found root or flourished in America. Here with the Paysons it was so obvious: Gregory had gone to Eton, that most prestigious of English public schools, but there had been no Eton for Philip. Gregory, however precarious his circumstances now, lived in the grand old style; Philip lived humbly, even if he did have the added consolation of an attractive native mistress. And if Philip was something less than satisfactory as a man of the world she could easily see why.

She came out of her reverie with a guilty start at the sound of a car drawing up outside: that had to be Philip and she felt, after her unheralded arrival, it would not do to be found snooping around his private sanctum. She looked frantically around for some reading matter and spotted a small bookcase by the door cluttered with a hodge podge of books and magazines. Grabbing a couple at random from the top of the pile, she scuttled back to the living room and found she had acquired a *Soldier of Fortune* magazine and a very old issue of *Time*. She hastily opened the *Time* magazine, fixed herself another drink and waited expectantly.

It seemed, however, that Philip was in no hurry to greet his unexpected guest, for she heard a low murmur of voices issuing from somewhere in the back of the house, then his booted footsteps going into the study, where he remained for a while before she heard him come out and cross towards the living room. He came in, clad in riding togs that appeared to be regulation wear for the Paysons, and greeted her breezily. "Hello! Quite a surprise. Tired of *poi* and Polynesians already? Anyway, welcome to what you have undoubtedly noticed already is my very humble home. Just overnight is it, or are you settling in for a spell?"

As usual his manner was an irritating compound of arrogance and smugness, but Penny with her newfound insight did not allow herself to be irked by it. "Oh, just overnight. I'll be off to Kailua first thing, but I do appreciate you putting me up at such short notice. I did not fancy the drive back in the dark, and I had rather a nasty shock today, so I wanted to get out of Hilo."

"Oh? Trouble?" he said casually, fixing himself a drink and sitting down in an easy chair opposite to her.

"Yes. Very upsetting," she said, and related the incident at the hotel, omitting the threat of the card. She noticed he was only listening with half an ear and appeared keyed up with some intense inner excitement that was almost gleeful. At the end of her account he threw back his head and laughed; his laugh was a high, almost vacant-minded, boyish giggle and added to his general air of immaturity. "Good God, it sounds as if you really got across one of

153

your Polynesian pals—can't trust them an inch, you know. Good idea to come here, they'd know better than to try any of their nasty little tricks around me. I'd soon show 'em!" He was like a boastful child.

Penny decided to fish a little. "I somehow don't think it was like that at all," she murmured. "Tell me, do you happen to number a man called Van Norkirk among your Hilo acquaintances?"

Philip gaped at her. "Piet Van Norkirk? Too rich for my blood and I'm not rich enough for his on all counts. He knows Gregory quite well—these landed gents stick together. Know him vaguely, of course. Why? What's he got to do with it?"

"Just that when I met him in Hilo he did not seem at all pleased that I was around," she said blandly, and left it at that.

This seemed to unsettle him. "Well, you must be all in after a nasty shock like that, want to call it a night? I'm ready to turn in myself—it's been a long day." He got up. She gulped the last of her drink and got up too, but he followed her out to the stairs and then said in an almost wheedling tone, "Now that you're here, don't rush off first thing. Let me show you around the place and we'll have lunch, then maybe you could take me with you as far as Gregory's? I'm going to try and get the helicopter out of him, and he always makes such a business out of it if I come in my own car. If he thinks I'm without transport and he'll be stuck with me for a few days he may let me have it right off."

"I'd be glad to take you, but I thought they all went to Oahu in it," Penny said.

He looked at her with narrowed eyes. "How did you know that?"

"Lalai told me when I arrived. Any idea why they went?"

"None. Probably kowtowing to your hoity-toity friend," he returned. "Lord, how they love a title! And I gather he's loaded as well."

She forbore to bristle. "Well, I'll bid you goodnight and see you in the morning." And she sought her room, reflecting that Philip was a man with whom it was very hard to stay in sympathy for any length of time.

The next morning found him a very insistent host. He towed her over every inch of the ranch and managed to extend the tour until lunchtime. After lunch he insisted on showing her over the house, and when they got to the study he went on at some length about its contents. "My sole inheritance from dear old Dad," he said sarcastically. "He never did have much time for Gregory, who couldn't do any of the things *he* enjoyed doing well. *I* was his favorite because I did and enjoyed it too. We had some great times." There was a note of yearning in his voice that disappeared as he went on. "Not that it made one fuck of difference when it came to the will, of course. He should not have died when he did. We should never have left Africa to come to this God-forsaken place. Jesus, if I had any money I'd be back like a shot to South Africa—only decent country left for a white man in the whole world! With enough lolly you can live like a king there still." The yearning was back.

"I notice you have a most interesting collection of bows and arrows," Penny murmured. "I can identify a few of them, but what are the others?"

He looked at her blankly as she indicated the case, hoping he would open it. "Oh, Dad picked them up here and there—they're from all over. I don't know beans about them." He passed rather hurriedly on to the gun case. "Some fine pieces here—not that one gets any real hunting in this benighted place!" But Penny noted with interest that the gun rack was now full, so wherever Philip

155

had been yesterday he evidently *had* been on the hunt. She was beginning to feel restive and a glance at her watch confirmed it was already after three. "Er—yes—most interesting," she muttered. "But don't you think we should be on our way? It's getting rather late."

"Oh, alright. There are just one or two bits of business I have to take care of, if you'll excuse me for a little?" Philip said. "Why don't you fix yourself a drink and then we'll be off. Got some calls I must make."

Penny brought her things down and stowed them in the car, then for lack of anything better to do did help herself to a drink. She had finished it, without further sign from Philip, and was beginning to get thoroughly annoyed, when he finally appeared, cheerfully oblivious, and said, with a phony American accent, "Let's get this show on the road, babe."

As they went out to the car he held out his hand for the keys. "I know this road like the back of my hand. I'll drive."

"No you won't," Penny snapped. "This is a rental car and I don't have third-party insurance. If you want to come you're welcome, but *I'm* doing the driving." Two trips with him had been hard enough on her nerves and she was in no mood for a third trial.

He looked taken aback. "Well, all right," he mumbled and got meekly into the passenger seat, where he proceeded to sulk in silence. They had reached the most tortuous part of the road, when all her attention was firmly fixed on negotiating its sinuous bends, when the earth beneath them suddenly trembled and there was a long drawn-out rumble that sounded like the firing of a gigantic cannon. Philip jumped and exclaimed, "What the hell is that!"

She slowed to a crawl and looked frantically around.

"Good Lord! Look over there!" An enormous dark pall hung over Mauna Loa, its underbelly illuminated by an ominous fiery red, as a central column of 'grey rose swiftly above it into the clear air. "Mauna Loa is erupting!"

He peered out then grinned over at her. "Ringside seat for Pele's fireworks—not every tourist gets to see that, you know! She must be angry about something. I'll probably have to give Greg a helping hand when we get there. This sort of thing drives the horses crazy. Won't do my cattle a whole heap of good either." But he did not seem overly concerned.

She speeded up again, but in a short while had to turn on the windshield wipers as a fine ash started to settle on the windows. And she was duly relieved when they got to the belt road and turned south on the smoother, easier highway. Philip was watching the fiery cloud with all the fascination of a small boy, and she was thankful for his silent absorption. As they gained the ranch and drew up before the house, it was to see Mildred standing on the front steps, shouting orders at a group of ranch hands. Spotting her brother, she came racing up to the car. "Oh, I'm so glad you're here, Philip! Everything has gone crazy. First the damned accident and Gregory and Toby going off in the most terrible tizz—as if it matters if some stupid ranch hand gets drunk and falls off a cliff! And then this eruption as soon as they went, and I'm left to cope with everything. It's really too much!" Her voice was shrill with anger and she shot a furious look at Penny. "Please go and see they do what they should to calm the horses, Philip!"

"Righto!" he got out with alacrity. "Bit of excitement, eh? Thanks for the lift, Dr. Spring—don't suppose I'll be seeing you again, so all the best!"

Mildred started to follow him, then turned back for a

moment. "You'd better go in the house until things settle down. You'll find the other girl there—Miss Freyer." And she hurried off.

Griselda here? Penny hurried into the house and came upon Griselda, a worried expression on her face, gazing out of the window. The girl turned to her with relief. "Oh, I'm so glad you are alright and are here. Sir Tobias has been terribly worried."

"But where is he and why are you here? What's going on?" Penny cried.

"Just after we arrived this afternoon he went tearing off again with Mr. Payson when the news came in," Griselda faltered. "A body was sighted at the foot of a cliff. It's Manua—he's dead."

Chapter 14

Mercifully, Penny and Griselda were left completely alone, as the sky darkened with the spreading ash from the volcano and with approaching night. A rattled servant had appeared to close all the windows and shutters against the encroaching ash, plunging them into premature night, but huddled together on a couch in the cosy circle of a reading light, Griselda related all that had transpired since Penny's departure to Hilo.

Penny listened in appalled silence, and it was only after Griselda had faltered to a close that she roused herself. "I can scarcely credit it—a hunt for Kamehameha's treasure? It sounds even more bizarre than the Menehunes!"

"That's what I thought," Griselda murmured, "But Sir Tobias seems so certain about the sketch-map and everything, and then with this new break-in it does seem to be connected somehow with old Mr. Donelson's papers. But how Dr. Shaw fits into any of this or how my father was involved, I really don't see at all. Brad feels the same way."

"You told Brad Field about all this?" Penny queried sharply.

Griselda colored. "Why, yes. I had to let him know where I was going or he'd have been frantic with worry. And of course he wanted to know why, so naturally I told him."

"That was not very wise," Penny was blunt. "It will probably be spread all over the papers tomorrow in highly sensational and totally inaccurate form."

Griselda's chin went up defiantly. "Oh no, it won't. Brad agrees with me that the less said about this the better for the moment. He's promised he won't say anything of it unless I give him the go-ahead. *I* trust him even if you don't."

Penny nearly said "More fool you," but restrained herself with an effort. There was no sense in antagonizing the smitten and ingenuous girl, but some rapid thought had brought her to the same conclusion Toby had already arrived at—that Brad might be more involved in all this than had first appeared. The thought that he may have sent her off deliberately on a false trail to Van Norkirk and his land deals enraged her even further, after all she had been through. "So what is his theory? Does he think Dr. Shaw is guilty then?" She tried to keep the sarcastic edge off her voice.

"No, he doesn't," Griselda said to her surprise. "He doesn't think that at all, but he doesn't really have a theory either. He just thinks Van Norkirk has to be involved in some way."

"But there is absolutely no connection between Van Norkirk and all this other new business!" Penny cried.

"Oh, but there is—and you found it!" Griselda said, looking at her wide-eyed. "A very important connection—especially in view of what has just happened."

Penny gaped at her. "I did? Then you tell me."

"Paea Young—I don't even know who he is, except that he's connected in some way with Van Norkirk. He and

Manua were related—first cousins—and you know how important that is here," Griselda said with some asperity. "Kaowa told Sir Tobias that just before we came on here. You identified Manua as the man who broke into my house, then he was missing, and now Manua is *dead*."

For a few moments Penny was literally speechless as the new facts churned in her overloaded memory bank. She felt she was about to blow a fuse. "Where is Kaowa?" she said at length.

"Back at the yacht with two other men. I've no idea who *they* are."

"I've got to talk to Kaowa," Penny said with decision, and jumped up. "There is no sense in us hanging around here. Let's go back to Kailua right now."

"But what about Sir Tobias? He's been so anxious about you," Griselda remonstrated. "Shouldn't we wait for him?"

"Oh, God knows what he's up to or how long he will be—he'll catch up with us eventually," Penny said impatiently. "Everything is starting to make less and less sense, and if I don't straighten out some of it I'll go crazy."

But her zeal for escape was cut short when Griselda held up a restraining hand. "Listen! I think I hear the helicopter—they must be back. There's no sense in dashing off now before we have heard what's happened."

Penny subsided back on the couch and tried to quiet her heart as the sound of the engine died. There was a couple of minutes of nerve-stretching silence until the sound of footsteps echoed in the hall and a man's angry voice could be heard. The door was flung open and Toby came in, closely followed by Gregory Payson.

There was a flash of exquisite relief on Toby's face as he spotted her, then his expression settled back into a sphinx-like calm, although she could tell by the rigid set of his head that he was very angry. His anger was nothing compared to his companion's, for Gregory Payson was a transformed man; his long face livid with rage, his eyes flashing, his fists clenched. "I repeat," he roared, "I think your interference in this matter is completely unwarranted and insufferable. You had absolutely no right or reason to turn a very simple matter into some cheap sensation that will have the ranch in an uproar and police poking into our affairs. I consider it a gross breach of hospitality!"

Toby was totally unmoved by this tirade. "The constable agreed with me that Manua was dead before he ever went off that cliff. There was *no* blood to speak of, and had he been killed in the fall, the rocks beneath would have been covered with it. What he really died of has to be established by an autopsy, but he certainly did not fall off that cliff—he was thrown off it. And that points to murder. I'm sorry if this upsets you, but facts are facts."

"The policeman was just an ignorant Hawaiian, for God's sake!" Gregory cried. "It would not even have occurred to him if you hadn't interfered. It would have been put down as an accident and that would have been that!" He was so concentrated on Toby that he completely ignored the two startled women.

"Murder *is* murder," Toby murmured. "Or is that also of no consequence to you because of its inconvenience?"

"There's no *proof* it was murder," Gregory yelled. "It was a damned accident I tell you!"

"If that is so, which *I* very much doubt, then an autopsy will prove it and you will have nothing further to worry about, will you? Except for the small fact that the man had apparently been missing for at least three days and that you did nothing about it, even though your foreman had informed you of this," Toby went on implacably.

"These damned Hawaiians are always wandering off for no apparent reason—it meant nothing, I didn't even give it a thought." Gregory strode over to a side table and poured himself a drink from a decanter, his tall frame quivering.

Penny raised her eyebrows at Toby, who responded with a slight shake of his head, as he went on. "But in the circumstances, now I see that Dr. Spring has rejoined us safely, we can collect our things and relieve you of our burdensome presence."

Gregory became belatedly aware of his audience and with a vast effort got himself under control. "Oh, so you're back Dr. Spring. Philip did inform us you had been in some kind of trouble in Hilo. Did he bring you here?" This thought did not seem to please him either.

"I brought him," Penny said sweetly. "He thought you might need some help after the eruption."

"Then who the hell is looking after things at Waikulu?" Gregory demanded. "That damned native tart of his? Why doesn't he mind his own affairs and leave me to manage mine!" The hate was almost palpable in its intensity.

And it was on this unhappy note that Mildred and Philip entered on the scene, dirt-streaked from the omnipresent ash and looking very tired. "Everything is under control," Philip announced curtly. "Lucky I arrived when I did. You barreling off like that, leaving Mildred to cope with everything, was pretty hard on her, Greg."

There was a brief snarling match between the three siblings which climaxed with Mildred shrilling, "You're not usually so concerned about your employees, Gregory. What were you trying to do—impress our guests as lord of the manor? How bad was it, anyway, and who was involved? You dashed off so quickly I never did hear that."

Gregory gave an angry snort. "It was Manua—fool fell off a cliff, though our *distinguished* guest here," he jerked his head towards Toby, "will have it otherwise and has got the police all riled up to investigate it as a murder. He. . . ." Gregory broke off as their eyes were drawn to

163

Philip, who had gone a ghastly white and staggered as if he had been hit. For a second Penny thought he was going to pass out, but he slumped into a chair and gazed at his brother with dazed, bewildered eyes. "But it *can't* be Manua, it simply can't," he whispered through dry lips. "I don't understand—there must be some mistake."

"What the hell is the matter with you, don't you think I can recognize one of my own hands?" Gregory snarled. "Anyway why the great concern? Don't tell me Manua was one of your little playmates too!"

But this barb went unheeded as Philip continued to gaze at him in shocked disbelief. He shook his head dazedly from side to side, then looked pleadingly at his sister. "Not Manua!" he repeated.

Mildred was staring at him, an enigmatic look on her lean, strained face. Suddenly she wheeled on them. "Philip has always been very sensitive—he gets upset easily. You'll have to excuse us." And with amazing strength hauled his unresisting figure out of the chair and pushed him forcibly out of the room.

Toby, though as surprised as everyone else at this little scene, was the first to recover. "Well, we must be going and leave you to sort out your affairs," he said with a hint of irony. "I'll just pick up my things and we'll be out of your way."

A perplexed Gregory looked at him. "Yes, well in the circumstances perhaps that would be best."

"Our thanks for your generous hospitality," Penny said sweetly, and led their orderly retreat. When they got outside, where the ash-rain appeared to be dissipating in the brisk wind that had sprung up, she turned to Griselda. "Do you think you can face driving Toby's car back to Kailua? I simply have to talk to him, and I think that's the most sensible way of coping with the two cars. We can turn one of them in when we get back to town."

The girl agreed with a relieved alacrity and they set off in convoy towards the Belt Road, with Penny behind the wheel of the second car. "Now," she said, as they left the Payson ranch, "Will you go first or shall I? I feel as if I'm going to pop—none of this makes sense anymore. We seem to be going around in a circle."

"I think we are too," Toby said surprisingly. "But it is a circle with Freyer right in the centre of it, and with two more bits of information I think I'll have enough to get Giles Shaw out of prison, if not entirely off the hook. But you go first. . . ."

Her account took most of the journey, and he listened in absorbed silence, except when she fished in her pocket and pulled out the card with its threat. " 'You next?' " he rumbled. "The nerve of it! Thank God you had enough sense for once to get out of there. That's all I'd need— you with your throat cut."

"Thanks a lot!" she grinned. "But what beats me is the *speed* with which Van Norkirk moved."

"If it *was* Van Norkirk," Toby interrupted. "There is another possibility which, in light of what has just happened, might make more sense."

"You mean Paea Young? Yes, that had occurred to me too. I thought I was pretty convincing, but if he did see through my act . . . " she murmured. "God, I'm confused! Do you honestly believe this stuff about the treasure hunt?"

"Indeed I do," he sighed. "By the way, do you have any idea what might be in the treasure cave? I mean apart from the usual Polynesian paraphenalia buried with a king?"

"As a matter of fact I do," she said briskly. "But I may point out that that 'Polynesian paraphenalia,' as you put it, would itself be worth a king's ransom today—feather cloaks, *kahilis*, feather helmets, the king's war implements of every kind, and the war canoes all stuffed full of the cream of Polynesian craftsmanship of the time. But apart from all that there was bullion. Tradition has it that Kamehameha was worth about a million dollars in silver and gold coins and ingots he'd hijacked from Spanish galleons en route from Mexico to the Phillipines. That's all more or less a matter of record."

"Enough to whet any man's greed," Toby murmured. "And I think that is why Freyer died and Shaw was framed."

"I don't get your drift."

He settled back in his seat, leaned his head back against the headrest and closed his eyes. "Suppose it went like this. While Freyer was embattled with Shaw he unexpectedly comes into possession of an eccentric old man's papers to which he pays scant attention because he is embroiled in this other affair. Then he is approached and told of something in those papers that piques his interest."

"Hapili?" she queried and he nodded.

"He is hesitant at first, but starts to check these things out—hence the trip, maybe two trips, to Kailua and the Kona area. What he finds convinces him that there is something in it, so he becomes anxious to settle the Menehune affair." He paused and appeared to go off on a tangent. "How would you have assessed Freyer's character prior to all this?"

"Well, as I told you before—a good enough scholar, but a bit of a stuffed shirt. In his own field he did some good honest work. Ambitious, but not overly so, nor very materialistic—that's why the Porsche struck me as so odd," she returned. "And you've seen his home—he obviously wasn't into high living!"

Toby nodded. "Exactly! So what would you expect the reaction of such a man to be to what might prove the archaeological find of the century?"

"I think I see where you're heading," Penny said. "As a scholar he would be more interested in the kudos attached to such a find, with his name trumpeted around the world as its discoverer, than in the monetary worth of the treasure itself." A sudden thought struck her. "Do you think he may have let Giles in on this in some way? Because of his archaeological expertise?"

"I'm just guessing, but yes, from some hints I've found, I think he may have hinted, even boasted, about it to Giles—hence that punch-up that neither of them would talk about. The very fact that he had the sketch-map with him at the meeting indicates to me that if they had made an *official* truce brought about under your eyes, he would have borne Giles away with him and confided in him some more."

"And that one of his unseen partners who *was* only interested in the treasure, was not about to risk that and so brought about that incredible murder?" Penny drew the car up in the marina parking lot and stared out over the ocean. "But then the murderer had moved prematurely before they had all the necessary pieces to *find* the treasure, hence all the break-ins. Which brings us back to Manua and Hapili—one of whom seems to have dropped off the face of the earth and the other has been killed, probably murdered."

"And to the Paysons, Paea Young and possibly Van Norkirk," Toby muttered, gazing in horrified dismay at *The Dancing Lady*, whose sparkling white hull and sails had become a dingy gray under the rain of ash. "And with the outside possibility that our young reporter is not as innocent as he seems."

"Yes, the minute Griselda told me of that break-in it did occur to me," Penny said mildly. "But, you know, I find it hard to believe he's involved—he's just not the type and I would swear his interest in the languishing

Griselda is a hundred percent genuine. There is too much he does not fit into—the African poison for one, the source of which, as I told you, I may have found at Philip's place."

"Oh yes, we always come back to the Paysons," Toby's tone was somber. "The trouble is, which one? Or are they all in on it?"

"From what we've seen of them can you honestly see them acting as a *group?*" she said, climbing out of the car.

"With that much money involved I can quite easily," came the answer as Toby got out and stalked off towards the yacht.

They found the native population of *The Dancing Lady* had been increased by one, and that a very old shrivelled man squatted by Kaowa on the deck, as the latter directed his helpers in preliminary cleanup operations of the omnipresent ash. Kaowa greeted Toby with evident relief and indicated the old man. "I have found someone who can complete the genealogy you gave me. You will find it of great interest."

He produced the copy from his jeans pocket, handed it to Toby, indicated a starting point with one massive finger and nodded at the old man who started to chant in a high-pitched voice. It was a minute or two before Penny tuned in on the recitation of names and dates, and she felt a little thrill as she realized they were listening to one of the "specialists" of the native Hawaiian culture—a clan genealogist. She listened intently, but the names meant nothing to her until two familiar ones caught her ear— "Paea" and "Manua." The chant ended as abruptly as it had begun and Kaowa looked expectantly at Toby.

"Well, er, very interesting—but what exactly am I to gather from all this?" Toby said, a little at a loss.

"It means that both Paea and Manua came from the cadet branch of the house—from the line of third sons.

The senior branch is extinct and *kahuship* must now lie with the line of the second son, but they may have known some of the family tradition."

"I'm afraid I still don't understand," Toby said impatiently. "What family tradition?"

"It is the clan of the Keaweamahi I have recited," the old man said; his normal voice was surprisingly deep. "Keaweamahi, the friend and kinsman of Kamehameha. He who was made *kahu* of the king's burying place. Whose descendants now bear the sacred trust under *kapu* of death."

"So, much as I did not wish to believe you, you were right," Kaowa broke in. "Manua must have known something of the cave of Hale Iliili and disclosed it to a *haole*. But now we know of this we can get to him and put a stop to it before any further damage is done."

"I'm afraid it's a little late for that," Toby said heavily. "I come to tell you that Manua is dead—and that he too was murdered."

Chapter 15

It was evident to Penny that Manua's death was as great a shock to Kaowa as it had been to Philip Payson. Not that the reaction was outward and visible, but the big man had withdrawn himself instantly, like a turtle popping back into its carapace. That Toby was also aware of this was apparent as he spoke to his giant friend in his most mellifluous, cajoling voice, as the other Hawaiians gazed concernedly at their leader. "You've done marvels so far, so can you discover from your sources the results of the autopsy as quickly as possible? It is the last vital bit of information I have to have before we head back to Honolulu to get Giles Shaw free. I am almost certain I can do it now."

Kaowa's face was blank, but he nodded, grunted and took a massive departure surrounded by his entourage. "Well that certainly shook him up," Toby said thoughtfully.

"So I noticed," Penny said. "I hope we're doing the right thing confiding in him so much."

"What options do we have?" he demanded. "And where *is* that wretched girl with my car?"

"Just what I was wondering myself," Penny was uneasy. "I hope she's all right."

But as if in answer to their thoughts Griselda's voice floated out of the night. "Is that you, Dr. Spring? May I come up? I didn't know what you wanted done with the car, so I parked it three cars down from yours." She arrived on deck, clutching the keys which she handed to Toby. She too looked strained and anxious.

"Any trouble with it?" Penny queried.

"No, none." Griselda almost snapped her reply. "But do you think we might have dinner soon? I am absolutely famished."

Toby pocketed the keys. "Yes, why don't you two get something going? There's plenty of stuff on board. I have to go and make a few arrangements." And he hurried off before Penny could ask any questions.

They had eaten and Griselda had already retired to the forward cabin, pleading a headache and extreme fatigue, before he again appeared, looking totally absorbed. "Well?" Penny demanded, slapping down a plate of warmed-over dinner before him and filling a beaker with wine; this he immediately gulped down and helped himself to another

"Well what?" he growled, absentmindedly shovelling down the food.

"What the hell is going on now, that's what," she snapped back. The restless motion of *The Dancing Lady* was already getting to her and she was feeling both queasy and irritated.

"I'm taking the yacht back to Honolulu tomorrow first thing. For one thing I've got to get it away from all this damned ash and get it cleaned up—the Lefaus will be here in a week and it will take almost that long to get her shipshape again."

171

"You mean we are leaving just as things are hotting up!" she said in exasperation.

"I am. You're not. I need you here to keep an eye on things. I've arranged a meeting with Lyons and, with any luck, when I return I will have Giles Shaw with me." He was terse. "Maybe we can then get some much-needed answers out of him."

"Well thanks a bunch! And where am I supposed to go, pray tell? And what about Griselda?"

"It's safer if she stays with you—I've fixed it up that you can both go and stay with Kaowa's maternal aunt in Kalaoa. That should be safe enough and comfortable enough—her husband is a retired naval commander on a full disability pension, so they are well-to-do by local standards. Know anything about Hawaiian petroglyphs?"

The rapid change of subject left her gasping. "Some."

Toby dived into his briefcase and extracted the yellowing photos. "See what you make of these—I think they are markers of some kind."

"I'm no expert—since you'll be in Honolulu, take them to the Bishop Museum. Someone there will know more," she snapped, but took the photos and examined them curiously.

"I fully intend to," he retaliated, "I just wanted to see what you thought. They are numbered on the backs—one to three, and all marked *Iliili* you notice."

The first one featured a typical Hawaiian male "stick" figure with a spear in its hand. "Well, that's a man, a warrior, and there's a *kahili* behind him," she pointed to the feather standard. "That's usually an indication of royalty. And above it . . . " she peered more closely."
" . . . that looks like a star. Yes, the standard points to a star."

"Possibly the North Star?" he murmured.

"Maybe." She went on to the second, which showed a war canoe and something that looked like a crooked-legged centipede. "Ah yes, that's a 'marching men' symbol. And that war canoe looks odd—it seems to have too many paddles."

"Again possibly a number signal. I counted. There are sixteen of them. So it could be paces or yards or even miles. And again, if you think of a compass, the marching men appear to point north," he observed. "And number three?"

She knitted her brows. "I've never seen one like this before. The symbol at the bottom seems to be a hut and those dotted lines usually mean water. They are going upwards, so that might mean a spring. But what that thing above it is I have no idea."

"Could it be a cave?" he queried.

"*Could* be I suppose—or an oven, or even a female symbol. That circular spiral next to it is often where they would put the umbilical cord after a baby's birth," she murmured. "And then the *kahuna* would project the infant's horoscope."

"Well at least it's a start," he said with a weary sigh, returning the photos to their folder. "I've got to get some sleep. Tomorrow is likely to be hectic."

"Did you pick up any information on the eruption?" She was a little anxious.

"According to the harbor master, reports are that it isn't going to be a big one—more like a giant belch by Mauna Loa than an honest-to-God eruption. He thinks the worst is over."

"Thank the Lord for small mercies then," she said drily, as he tottered off, bearing the rest of the wine with him.

Supine, she found the motion of the yacht soothing and fell into a deep sleep from which she was awakened in the gray light of dawn by a commotion on deck, followed by some heavy thumps and the mutterings of several men. Unwilling to leave the cosy warmth of her bed, she decided to wait until Toby was all set to go, when he would presumably turn her out into the cold world, and so nestled down and drifted off again. When she next awoke it was full daylight, and there was still no sign of Toby, so she got up, showered, packed the rest of her things and went to find some much-needed coffee. She found her partner in the main cabin, red-eyed and looking extremely put out, absorbing a huge mug of black coffee. "Problems?" she queried. "Getting off to a late start?"

"You might say that," he said tightly. "I've been up since the small hours—getting Kaowa out of jail and sobered up. It appears that after he left us last night he went on one hell of a bender and ended up by taking one of the local bars apart. Luckily, it belonged to yet another kinsman who is not going to press charges, so I've managed to spring him. However . . ." he sighed heavily. "We're not going to make it back to Honolulu in time for me to see Lyons today, so I have had to put that off until tomorrow. I'll be leaving *The Dancing Lady* there and will fly back, probably tomorrow night. The delay has done one bit of good. The native constable who found Manua has managed to get me the preliminary report of the autopsy. It was murder all right. Manua's stomach was full of kava that had been strongly laced with a native poison, some toxic concoction made from the bark of the Kalaipahoa tree."

"*Native* poison," Penny broke in. "So that looks like Hapili—that poison was often used by the old-time *kahuna ana anas.* So he *must* be here somewhere."

"Not necessarily—he could be anywhere." Toby heaved another vast sigh. "Manua had been dead for at least twenty-four hours before the body was found. Even then its finding was a happy accident—two fishermen spotted it from their boat on the rocks below the cliff. Chances are it would have eventually been taken by the sea."

"Was it below the promontory of Hale Iliili?" she said quickly.

"No, a little further south, but the cliffs there are so steep that no one could ever have seen the body from the top of them. But while we're on the subject, tell me as much as you can about Hale Iliili while I finish this. Then you'd better get the girl and I'll be on my way," he fished in his pocket. "Here is the name and address of the people in Kalaoa. I'll phone you there when I get in."

She put it in her tote bag. "Oh, okay. Well, Hale Iliili means the House of Pebbles and was a sacred area centuries before Kamehameha's time. It was *kapu* to all but the great chiefs and it's where they used to come to lay battle plans in a great council house, the foundations of which are reportedly still there. One of the features of the place was an enormous spring, large enough to supply an army, and this was the only fresh water for miles. It also had a very narrow and well-protected beach, that again was the only good landing place in miles so, in short, the whole area was well protected from surprise attack. Reputedly, Kamehameha was interred in a great sea cave beneath this promontory and the sea entrance was blocked off and then guarded by a giant white shark 'kept in place,' as it were, by the ministrations of the 'Shark' people—I had this from Mama Luali, who is a 'Shark' woman. On the land side supposedly the main entrance to the cave was connected with the great spring, but that was filled in years ago by the *kahu* to prevent treasure seekers, although to carry out their sacred duties they would have had to have an alternative means of access."

"But surely, with all the people involved in getting the things into the cave in the first place, a lot of them must have *known* about all this? After all the Pharoahs of Egypt tried much the same thing with *their* tombs and a fat lot of good it did them," Toby put in. "They were all robbed within a generation or two of burial—sometimes sooner."

"Ah, but the Hawaiians did things a bit differently from the Egyptians," Penny said drily. "After the initial burial and sealing of the tomb had taken place, it was the first sacred duty of the *kahu* to slay all his helpers in order to guard the secret. They were always important people—aristocrats—so the murder of a few lackey commoners meant nothing to them."

"Good Lord!" Toby exclaimed, aghast.

"Added to this, of course, was the terrible tabu, the *pule ana'ana*, that was placed on the burial. The Hawaiians take such curses very seriously, and it is still the case with anyone with any degree of Hawaiian blood—very few would care to risk it. Even one of the same family as the interred can only enter his ancestral caves after specific rites of ablution. For instance, of all the Hawaiian kings only David Kalakaua ever had the courage to risk those tabus and go into the burial caves of his own family, and by all accounts it did not do him a whole heap of good. In fact . . ." Penny went on, warming to her subject, "I've been doing a bit of speculating on my own and I think I see where Hapili might fit into all this. So try this on for size. Suppose Manua, who is a half-blood or even less, had been indulging in a spot of tomb robbing in the area and then decides to go after the big prize—perhaps urged on by his white buyer . . . ."

"Who might also be his employer," Toby put in grimly.

Penny nodded agreement and continued, "But Manua is enough of a Hawaiian not to put himself at risk of the tabu, so demands the services of a *kahuna* who can at least alleviate the power of the *pule ana'ana*. So Hapili is brought in, clued in, helps out and now, apparently, feels himself strong enough to do without Manua, so does him in and is after the treasure himself or possibly with the original *haole* Mr. X, who doesn't care about the curse either."

"Makes sense," he agreed, but they were interrupted by the arrival of Griselda who, despite her long sleep, was still looking very pale and strained. Toby made a hasty exit and Penny poured the worn-looking girl some coffee, while she explained their ongoing plans. Griselda seemed preoccupied to the point of indifference, and it was only when Penny proposed some shopping in Kailua to supplement her diminished wardrobe before making their trip north that she brightened perceptibly.

Once more their baggage was unloaded from the yacht and into Penny's car by one of Kaowa's henchmen, while the other took off with Toby's car to return it to the rental agency. Kaowa himself was still stretched out on his sleeping bag in the bow, snoring lustily. Toby came to the rail as they went down the gangplank. "I'm taking Kai with me as well," he explained, as the burly Hawaiian boarded. "We need to make good time and Kaowa is still in no shape to be of much help. I'll be in touch when we get in and, for God's sake, lie low until I get back. Just one other thing—on your way up I'd like you to call in at the Paysons and tell them about the autopsy. I'll be interested in their reactions—particularly Gregory's. Oh, and you might also tell them that I fully expect to return with Giles Shaw and see how that grabs them."

"Will do," Penny said cheerfully, and steered Griselda

back to the car. They shopped diligently for the rest of the morning and it touched her heart to see what enjoyment the girl got out of such a simple female pleasure. It reminded her forcibly how restricted and isolated the girl's life had to have been up to this point, and she wondered grimly how Griselda was now going to cope with life alone, after so many years of subservience to a repressive father. At her urging, Griselda bought herself a couple of blouses and a sarong, and after much diligent trying on and anguished decision making, the delight the girl took in her purchases gave Penny's own spirits a much-needed lift. They had a leisurely lunch at an outdoor restaurant at Griselda's insistence, and Penny was further impressed by the almost hungry attention her young companion gave to the colorful, jostling throng of tourists. "Well, I hate to break this up," she said at length, "but I think we should be on our way."

"I suppose so," Griselda said reluctantly. "But this has been so nice. I wish we could just stay here."

"When things get settled down a bit, maybe we can come back," Penny comforted. "But for the moment I think we'd be better off out of the public eye."

Unexpectedly, Griselda volunteered to drive, and Penny, thinking it would keep her occupied, cheerfully agreed. Again they sped north and took the now familiar turn off to the Payson ranch. As they came up to the main gate, they found it firmly shut, and as Griselda stopped the car, Penny started to open her door, "I'll get the gate."

"No, let me," Griselda said and hopped out. She ran up to the iron gate, but as she put her hand on the latch Penny saw her look down at something in the bushes beside it and recoil sharply. Then she peered closer and with a shrill scream, covered her face with her hands and turned blindly away. Penny was out and running on the instant. She came to a halt, her heart thudding, as she spotted a huddled figure in the bushes, dust-covered and bloodied. She rolled it gently over to see a familiar face, blood running from its nose and battered lips. From behind her came the shrill hysterical voice of Griselda. "It's Brad," she shrieked. "They've killed him! He's dead because of me."

Chapter 16

Despite the extra pair of hands on board, *The Dancing Lady* did not make good time on the leg back to Honolulu. To the late start was added a series of minor glitches with the sails and rigging, more infuriating than disastrous, so it was very late when they edged into the Honolulu yacht marina. Toby debated whether to call Penny, then decided that she was probably long asleep and would not appreciate his tardy attention, so wearily turned in himself, his head full of his plans for the morrow.

Early awake he became a dynamo of action. He contacted the agent who had been looking after the yacht prior to their arrival, explained at length what alterations and repairs needed to be made in addition to the overall cleanup, and left the superintending of all this to the recovered but still withdrawn Kaowa. He then proceeded to phase two and what to him was an even more important task.

During his contacts with the police in many and varied parts of the world—some fortunate, some very much the opposite—he had come to the firm belief that to get them into action the best possible technique was to attack initially with as much ammunition as one possessed. In this case he felt he not only needed the ammunition but a very big gun indeed to help him in his quest, and with this object in mind phoned Giles' lawyer, the prestigious and palindromic Roger Rogers. He had expected opposition and a lively argument before gaining his end, and was pleasantly surprised when he got neither. Mr. Rogers would be happy to see him immediately and would certainly consider his proposition.

In the opulent surroundings of Rogers, Yokamura and Feldstein, as he shook hands with the diminutive lawyer, whose well-trained mane of gray hair was his most striking feature, Toby had no idea that he was profiting from the very success of the man who was not inaptly called the Melvin Belli of the islands. In his own profession Roger Rogers had been a phenomenal success, but with such success often comes an accompanying boredom. Rogers now only accepted cases that interested *him,* and from the first, the Menehune case had intrigued him since, on the face of it, it was hopeless and therefore a challenge. He did not much care for his client, whom he had found blandly obstructive, but he had become interested in the unlikely pair who were evidently so interested in freeing Giles Shaw, and so had investigated them in the reference books. There, it was not Toby's knighthood, wealth or outstanding achievements in his own field that had impressed him so, but the fact that he had been awarded the Order of Merit, which to Rogers was an even more impressive achievement than the Nobel Prize, being rarer. Any man who had been awarded this order by his queen deserved a hearing, he reflected, and that was why he was shaking the hand of this tall, stooped and spindly scholar with such enthusiasm.

To Toby's further surprise, Rogers produced a very tolerable bottle of St. Emilion—he had done his research well—and over it proceeded to listen to Toby's long and careful exposition with grave and avid attention. The claret and the exposition finished, Rogers leaned back in his green leather chair, nodded and said briskly, "Excellent, just excellent. Yes, indeed I will come with you to this interview with Lyons. Simply state your findings exactly as you have done to me and you can leave the rest to me. Inspector Lyons is not an easy nut to crack, but I think I can have Giles Shaw free before this day is out."

With this optimistic assessment they took off in Rogers' chauffeured Rolls Royce and were delivered with due pomp at Hawaii Five-0, where they were ushered into the presence of a wary-looking Inspector Lyons, who greeted them stiffly and waved them to chairs before seating himself on the other side of his large mahogany desk. "Now, Sir Tobias, perhaps you are ready to explain this rather extraordinary set of documents I received from you," he said, tapping the manila envelope on his desk. "Which, on the face of it, seems to have nothing whatever to do with the case."

"On the contrary, I am certain they are the key to Helmut Freyer's murder, and I will demonstrate this," Toby boomed, and for the second time launched into his exposition, during which Lyons' face became longer and grimmer.

"In light of all this new evidence, I demand the immediate release of my client . . ." Rogers began, but Lyons stayed him with an upraised hand. "One moment, please!" he turned his shrewd eyes on Toby. "Why, may I ask, did you not provide us with some of this information before now—about the helicopter, the car, the break-ins and the documents purportedly found in Freyer's car? Your actions could be construed as a deliberate obstruction of justice. You could be so charged."

Rogers opened his mouth, but Toby forestalled him.

"Nonsense!" he said stoutly. "Had we come to your earlier, without all this corroborative evidence, you would have dismissed it out of hand as an attempt by biased witnesses to get Shaw free. You *did* dismiss Dr. Spring's testimony about Manua's break-in at the Freyers', and presumably at the university also, as such. You laid it to Kaowa's door, but I have just proved to you conclusively that he could *not* have had a hand in this third break-in—he was in Hawaii and unaware of these particular developments."

"A break-in that was not even reported to the police," Lyons retaliated.

"I have explained that," Toby was almost testy. "Just as I have explained everything else. The fact is that you charged Shaw because he *appeared* to be the only one with motive, means and opportunity. Now I have shown you multiple motives and alternate means that could have led to the murder, and now there has been another connected murder in which Shaw could not possibly be involved."

"Oh, you most certainly have done that," Lyons agreed angrily. "But may I point out that if you had acted correctly and informed us of all this earlier, Manua, a key witness if all this is to be believed, could have been brought in and questioned. He would probably not now be dead."

"Oh, come off it, Lyons!" Rogers exploded. "This is put up or shut up time and you know it! I challenge you to bring Giles Shaw before a grand jury right here and now, and with all this I'll tear you to shreds. The very fact you haven't had him up before now indicates to me that you've gotten nowhere on the case and have nothing substantive. Your case is purely circumstantial. I'd make you a laughing stock!"

"Perhaps," Lyons murmured. "I am well aware of your reputation, Mr. Rogers." But he was gazing steadily at

Toby. "So what is your proposition, Sir Tobias? As I understand it you are accusing the *kahuna* Hapili and one or all of the Paysons—is that it?"

Toby's expression became wooden. "As to Hapili, yes. He has to be found, because I am virtually certain he is responsible for Manua's murder. As to the Paysons, I am not prepared to say. There is also the possibility of Van Norkirk's involvement through Paea Young. But in the face of the extraordinary poison used on Freyer—the possible source of which I have already indicated—I would say the greater likelihood rests on the Paysons, but from what I have seen of them I very much doubt that they were all involved. They are not a united family. Find Hapili and you will find your answer to that. We have tried and failed: we know he went to the big island and must have been there as late as three days ago when the murder of Manua occurred, but with the ease of communication between the islands he could be anywhere by now. Presumably with your greater powers and resources you should be able to track him down." He tried to keep the sarcastic edge off his voice.

"Oh yes, we shall certainly do that," Lyons assured him with grim amusement. "But what, might I ask, is your interest in all this now? What are your ongoing plans?"

"At first my only interest was in helping Dr. Spring liberate an innocent man," Toby boomed. "But now I have another, to me equally important, one: the safeguarding of King Kamehameha's treasure."

They looked at him in astonishment which deepened to utter amazement as he went on. "So there seems to me to be one perfectly obvious course of action—I must find the treasure first. This will ensure two things: one, it will then be squarely up to the state of Hawaii to ensure its future safety, and two, it should draw the murderers out of their protective cover if they know I am after it, and I intend that they do know of it. Manua's murder indicates to me that they no longer needed him—they know how to locate the burying place or think they do, so time is of the essence and I must return to Hawaii at once. It would be a help if Dr. Shaw could come with me, since he has greater knowledge of the local field."

Inspector Lyons got his voice back first. "Are you out of your mind! You propose to set yourself up as target for this supposed murderer or murderers, while hunting for a treasure that has baffled its seekers for two hundred years? Incredible! Impossible!"

There was a gleam of excitement in Roger Rogers eyes, as he leaned forward. "I should not be so hasty in my judgment, Inspector. May I point out that you are talking to the man who discovered the hiding place of Zadok's treasure in Israel, a feat that had baffled treasure seekers for almost two *thousand* years? If Sir Tobias goes after it, I for one believe he will find it. However, as to the other, I presume you will offer him some protection. He will be putting himself at great risk. If I could be of any use to him—which, alas, I could not—I would go with him myself." He sounded wistful.

"Be assured, Sir Tobias is not going to move one step from now on without a man of mine by his side," Lyons said tightly and pressed the intercom. "Ask Inspector Ching to come in," he barked and sat back.

The door opened to reveal a tall, wiry Chinese-American, whose dark eyes behind round glasses in his round face, that gave him a cherubic and marked resemblance to Toby, were alive with enquiry. "Inspector Charles Ching," Lyons said by way of introduction. "Chuck, this is Sir Tobias Glendower of Oxford University, to whose side you will be attached until further notice. He is not to make a single move without you. I'll fill you in later. And this is Mr. Rogers, Shaw's attorney, seeking his client's release in the light of new evidence."

Ching crossed to Toby's side, his hand outstretched, as behind him Rogers and Lyons started to argue over the details of Giles' release. "I am most honored to meet you," he announced. "My cousin in San Diego was a Rhodes scholar at your university and spoke most highly of you. He attended all your classes and seminars some fifteen years ago, so of course you will not remember him."

"I do not have that many Chinese students," Toby said mildly, taking the proferred hand. "So I do remember him very well—an excellent student as I recall. What is he doing now?"

"He is a neurosurgeon in San Diego, but is also much occupied in local archaeological doings," Charles said earnestly. "I too am most interested, but prefer the Classical world, though I have never had the great fortune to visit same."

Toby, whose heart was never far from the Athens of Pericles' time, warmed to him immediately, and for several minutes tuned out the heated wrangle that was now developing and happily talked shop with his appointed bodyguard. They were recalled rather sharply from the fifth century B.C. to the present by Inspector Lyons getting up and saying vehemently, " Sir Tobias, I have agreed to Dr. Shaw's provisional release, but be it clearly understood that if you intend to pursue this madcap idea of yours, he is on *no* account to accompany you. In the first place I am not as convinced as you are in his complete uninvolvement in all this . . . ." That makes two of us, Toby thought grimly. ". . . And in the second place, he too may be at risk and I cannot spare another man to guard him. So I am releasing him into Mr. Rogers' custody, and he will be equally responsible for seeing no such thing occurs. Is that understood?"

"Quite," Toby said promptly, reflecting that he could pump Giles Shaw just as well away from the scene of operations as on it, and that from what he had heard of the big Irishman he would be of dubious help anyway.

Lyons crossed to the door, signalling the end of the interview. "Just one other thing. I have no power to stop you making this reckless gesture, but I would point out that with Inspector Ching along you are also putting him at risk. Granted, that's his job and he is at risk every day, but again I urge you to let us handle the case from here on in. With this new information we should be able to rope in Hapili and to pinpoint the culprit."

"I've no doubt you could," Toby said impatiently. "But that will take *time*, and on this I'm afraid time has run out. If I cannot get ahead of the murderers, two things are bound to happen; a national treasure will be vandalized and you will have your entire native Hawaiian population in a state of ferment, but worse than that the story may break—I'm surprised it hasn't broken already, as a matter of fact. And then you will have an even uglier situation on your hands. I foresee the general public will swarm to the area just to see what is going on, maybe even to get a piece of the treasure hunt. The murderers do not *know* that their plans are now hopeless, that even if they find the treasure, they are not likely to get away with it, so it is highly likely other deaths may follow if they feel themselves threatened."

"I don't understand you—why should the story break? No one else knows of this, do they?"

"I'm afraid there is a complicating factor." Toby sighed heavily. "We have been dogged almost from the outset by a young reporter called Brad Field. He has ingratiated himself with Helmut Freyer's daughter, and I have the horrible suspicion that she has told him more about this than it is good for him to know. He may break silence at any moment, and even if he doesn't I'm afraid it would indicate to me he also may be involved in some way."

"Well I can muzzle him," Lyons said tightly. "I'll get right on to it. Now, if you will excuse us, I have to fill Inspector Ching in on all this. Will you wait downstairs?"

"I have to go to the Bishop Museum." Toby took an anguished look at his watch. "I was hoping to catch the four-thirty flight back to Ke'ahole. Couldn't the inspector meet me at the museum?" He looked enquiringly at the tall Chinese, who nodded.

"If you want to talk to Shaw, I suggest you take a later flight." Rogers broke his long and unusual silence. "With all the red tape involved, I doubt I shall have him free before three at the earliest. I'll start right away, but why don't you come back to the office about two and see how it's going?" His tone was heavy with meaning.

A little puzzled, Toby agreed and they left together, but parted company in the lobby, Rogers heading for the jail, while Toby took a cab to the museum.

There an intrigued Chris Bullard quickly corralled all the experts he could find, who duly pored over the photos. Their opinions on their meaning did not differ markedly from what Toby and Penny had already deduced, save one, who volunteered an experience of his own. "The time I came across something like this in connection with another burying place there were five markers," he said, "five being the Hawaiian sacred number, you see. Of course, that may just have been an isolated instance, or then again, you may have a couple missing from your set."

Toby's heart sank as Griselda's words on Donelson came back to him: "He never finished anything . . ." Perhaps he was not as close to the treasure as he had supposed.

Another expert vetoed Toby's idea that the sixteen paddles represented yards or miles, but opined it represented an Hawaiian frame of measurement, and after some complex sums on a scratch pad came up with a distance of 480 yards. "And due north from this petroglyph, I would say."

Yet another gave his opinion that a starting point for the markers could well be the old council house of the kings, which he had visited on one occasion. "It is the only visible remains on the Hale Iliili," he explained. "And I do recall there were several petroglyphic stones scattered around it."

A new sense of urgency grabbed Toby. "Well, my profound thanks, gentlemen," he said as he hastily gathered up the photos. "And it is understood that nothing is to be said of any of this until the murder investigation is concluded?" There was a subdued, if regretful, murmur of assent. He emerged from his conclave to find Inspector Ching gazing interestedly at the case of artifacts by the door, "I have a police car waiting,' he said with a broad smile. "All set?"

They sped back to Rogers' office, Toby now determined to get the earlier plane and forego the meeting with Shaw. Ching tactfully settled himself in the outer office, as Toby charged in on Rogers. The little lawyer was pacing excitedly around his office, and before Toby could say a word burst out. "Wait till you hear this! I got back to find an urgent message to call from Gregory Payson. I called him right back. He said he understood that Giles Shaw was about to be freed and was anxious that I extend to him an invitation to stay at the Payson ranch 'while he recuperates from his ghastly experience.' He was extremely pressing. I said I would relay the message to Shaw and would get back to him, but explained to him my position. He immediately invited me to come too!"

"But you can't be serious?" Toby exclaimed aghast. "You

can't possibly send Shaw into the lion's den like that—or yourself either, for that matter. Lyons, for one, would never stand for it!"

"Hear me out!" Rogers was almost hugging himself with glee. "I did get in touch with Lyons and it's all set. We are both going! They would never dare try anything with both of us there, and now I am all clued in I can keep an eye on the lot of them for you."

"But . . . but . . ." Toby spluttered. "What about your practice here, your other obligations?"

These were waved airily aside. "Nothing my partners can't handle," Rogers said cheerfully. "I'm all for it. I haven't had so much excitement in ages." He sobered a little. "Oh, there is one other thing though. Lyons got on to the *Hawaiian Gazette,* about Field? They told him he took off for the big island three days ago—on the track of a hot story, he said. They haven't had a word from him since and are getting a bit concerned. . . ."

"Dear God!" Toby groaned. "What now?"

Chapter 17

Griselda's hysterical screams had at least one good effect, for the corpse groaned and stirred feebly. Penny knelt and felt the artery in Brad's neck and found the pulse was strong and steady. "Shut up, Griselda!" she commanded sternly. "He's not dead, just knocked out. Here, come and give me a hand to get him into the car and off to a doctor."

The screams shut off like a tap. "He isn't?" Griselda quavered. "You're sure?"

"Of course I'm sure!" Penny snapped. "Now you take his feet and I'll take his head." Half-dragging the limp form—for Brad was surprisingly heavy—they managed to pour him into the back seat, and Griselda scrambled in beside him, cradling his head in her lap. Penny got behind the wheel, reversed and sped back to the Belt Road. In light of this she had abandoned all thought of seeing the Paysons until Brad was conscious and able to tell what had happened.

She looked up into the rearview mirror and saw Griselda was tenderly cleaning off the blood and dust from his battered face with a trembling hand. "Now," she said grimly, "suppose you tell me what the hell he was doing at the Payson ranch—or in Hawaii for that matter."

"I . . . he . . ." Griselda stammered and gulped. "Well, he said he might come down to see if I was getting on alright. He knew I was going with Sir Tobias. I tried to reach him yesterday, but he'd already left. I suppose he tried to find me in Kailua, then tried here. Oh, *why* did this have to happen? I'll never forgive myself, never. . . ."

The damn girl had probably told him everything, and he had been doing some private sleuthing on his own, Penny decided gloomily, as she sped into Kalaoa and into the nearest gas station to demand the whereabouts of a doctor. There was one right in town and, mercifully, in. Dr. McGregor, despite his name, turned out to be an Hawaiian of an almost equally imposing girth as Kaowa's, and on being summoned, lifted the semi-conscious Brad, who was aware enough to be smiling feebly up at Griselda, like the proverbial feather. He carried him into his examining room, where he firmly shut the door upon the two distracted women and went about his business.

He emerged some twenty minutes later and looked at them curiously. "How and where did this happen?"

"Is he alright?" "Can he talk?" Griselda and Penny burst out simultaneously.

"He's taken a bad beating but nothing's broken and there seems no major internal damage," the big doctor said. "A mild concussion and some bad bruises, but he's a very fit young man. I've patched him up and given him a shot, but he should be as good as new in a couple of days if he rests up. How did it happen?"

"We don't know," Penny said hastily. "We found him on the way to the Payson ranch and came directly here. May I talk to him?"

"Briefly. He'll be dozing off again with the shot I gave him. Maybe I can get particulars from the young lady here?" Dr. McGregor looked at Griselda's anxious face with appreciation.

Penny dove into the examination room before Griselda could protest, and bustled over to Brad. "How did this happen?" she demanded. "And what the hell were you doing there anyway?"

Brad smiled painfully at her. "Looking for Griselda—what else? I thought I'd better reconnoiter first, so I left my car outside the gates and walked on in. Got just about up to the house when these two Hawaiian goons jumped me and frisked me. Then a chap on horseback came along and they handed him my wallet and ID. He got off his horse, said that he'd show me what the Paysons thought of trespassers on their privacy—particularly 'jackals of the press' as he put it—and while they held me he proceeded to use me as a punching bag. I tried to tell him why I was there, but he just sneered. After a while the lights went out and I don't remember a thing." He closed his eyes and started to drift off.

"Did he say who he was? What did he look like?" Penny said, giving him a little shake.

"Tall, slim, glasses," he muttered.

"*Glasses!*" she echoed. "Fair or dark?"

"Fair," he murmured and was asleep.

She did not understand about the glasses, but on the face of it it had to be Philip—and found she was not overly surprised. Griselda poked her head in the door. "Dr. McGregor wants to talk to you. May I stay with Brad now?"

"He's asleep, but sure, you stay with him until I get things sorted out." Penny bustled out to an anxious conclave with the doctor. When she had explained the situation as best she could, he nodded. "Well, I'll need my examining room for my office hours, so I'll take him up to my bedroom—he can rest there for a bit until you can get things sorted out. If the Laolanis can't take him in, I'm sure someone else in town will."

"Isn't there a clinic or a hospital we could take him to?"

"Nothing closer than Kailua—and he really doesn't need it," he returned. "Just rest and peace and quiet."

"I'd better get over to the Laolanis then and see what can be done," she sighed. "I'll leave the girl here to keep an eye on him. Thanks, doctor, you've been very kind. I'll settle with you when I get back."

"No hurry," he grinned at her. "In this practice I'm quite used to waiting. Computerized medicine hasn't reached this far yet."

"You don't by any chance number the Paysons among your patients, do you?" she asked.

He shook his head. "No, never set eyes on them. My practice here is mainly among my own people and at the Parker ranch. My father was a foreman for Mr. Smart and the family paid for my medical studies. I'm sort of company doctor for them." He smiled faintly. "All I've heard about the Paysons is that they don't belong here and don't fit in, and after seeing this bit of their handiwork I can well see why."

Penny took herself off to the Laolanis, whom she found somewhat anxious at her late arrival. They were a very pleasant couple of late middle age, but she was quietly relieved to find that she and Griselda had been designated to a little house-keeping cottage, one of a small huddle of these that stood around the main house like chicks around a mother hen, and with which the Laolanis evidently augmented their income. "Do you happen to have another of them vacant?" she asked and explained about Brad. Duly horrified at her tale, they said they'd get one ready immediately and, much relieved, she zoomed back to the doctor's.

The comatose Brad was piled back into the car by

the doctor, Griselda in faithful attendance, and Penny saw them both into one cottage before making her way back to the other. There she sank exhausted into a rattan rocker on the porch and wondered what she should do next.

She did not much fancy a face-to-face encounter with the Paysons in light of what had just happened, but she still had to convey Toby's messages somehow; she knew he intended them to stir up the situation, but to what end she was not at all sure. For the present she would have to forego their reactions, she would just pass the messages. So decided, she made for a pay phone situated handily on the long verandah that ran around the main house and made her call.

Gregory came to the phone. "Dr Spring here," she said briskly. "Sir Tobias wanted me to convey to you a couple of messages. The first is that his conclusions were right; Manua was murdered. He was poisoned by a native poison and was dead before being thrown off the cliff. The *kahuna* Hapili is now being sought for this."

"Then I suppose I owe Sir Tobias an apology," but there was more relief than contrition in the deep voice. "No police have been here as yet, but I take it they will be."

"On that I have no idea. The second is that he has gone to Oahu to secure the release of Giles Shaw in light of new evidence, and hopes to return with him shortly."

His voice warmed. "Why that's splendid, just splendid! What a time the poor fellow has had. He must be an absolute wreck after being in prison like that. I hope he sues the shirts off those cloth-headed police."

She bit back the rejoinder that Giles' stay in prison had been entirely his own idea and his own fault, but said instead, "I would have delivered the messages in person, only having seen the shocking way you treat unexpected visitors I did not wish to take that risk."

"Risk?" Now the voice was puzzled. "I'm afraid I don't understand what you are talking about."

"Oh, come now, Mr. Payson!" she flared. "Miss Freyer and I came upon Brad Field of the *Hawaiian Gazette* beaten unconscious at your very gates. Mercifully, he is not badly injured, but according to him two of your employees held him while Philip used him as a punching bag. And I hope he sues you." She checked her rising temper, wishing she had not gone quite that far.

His voice was icy. "I have no knowledge of such an incident, and doubt very much that it is as you say, but if this man was trespassing on our property, Philip was quite within his rights to act as he did. I will look into this at once and so will bid you good day." The phone slammed down.

As Penny walked back to the cottage, she reflected that on some things at least the Paysons could show a united front. How far did that go? she wondered.

She dragged Griselda away from the still sleeping Brad to have some dinner at a small Hawaiian roadside restaurant, and was more relieved than anything when the girl opted to spend the night on the other bed in Brad's cottage in case he needed her. With a cottage all to herself, she fought off her weariness by sitting down and compiling a chart of all the relevant things she could think of connected with the case, with times, dates and events. When she had finished there were still a lot of queries on the chart, but the pattern that she saw there did nothing to lift her spirits. She was weary beyond belief and a glance at her watch showed her it was getting on for midnight and there was still no sign of a call from Toby. "Drat the silly man!" she mumbled. "Probably forgotten all about it," and stumbled off to bed.

She slept long and late, and when she rose took a long shower to clear her head, dressed and went off to see how the lovebirds were getting on. They were both still fast asleep, and, beyond a varicolored mask of bruises, Brad's color was good and his breathing normal, so she left them in peace and went to seek the Laolanis for word of her absent and absentminded partner. There was none, but they pressed coffee and breakfast upon her, and over it chattered merrily away to her about the recent happenings that had so evidently brought unexpected excitement into their quiet lives. Mrs. Laolani was obviously extremely proud of her giant nephew and his achievements, and she went on and on about the honor and glory he had brought to the family. After a surfeit of this Penny managed to get in a question about Manua, and the whole tenor of Mrs. Laolani's monologue changed, although it emerged they only knew of him through hearsay: a wastrel, that one; a drinker, a gambler, a womanizer—there was not a good word to be said about the dead Manua.

"Even pimped his own sister to a white man," the quiet Mr. Laolani suddenly put in with gruff disapproval. "And she but fifteen years old."

Penny looked at him in startled enquiry. "Yes, they say he lost her on a bet—more of his gambling, you see," Mrs. Laolani cut in, unwilling to lose the conversational ball. "And Lalai such a sweet, pretty girl too!"

A great flash of enlightenment came to Penny. "You mean the girl at Philip Payson's?" she exclaimed. "She's Manua's sister?"

"Yes, poor thing," Mrs. Laolani pursed her full lips in disapproval. "What a mercy she hasn't had a child by that wastrel—cut from the same cloth as Manua, that one. Don't know how his poor brother puts up with him, or with that hoity-toity sister either."

They were interrupted by the arrival of a starry-eyed Griselda who announced that Brad was awake and hungry, and where could she get some breakfast for him? More breakfast was provided by the motherly Mrs. Laolani, and Penny accompanied the tray-bearing Griselda back to the cottage, debating as she went how she was going to keep a rein on the ebullient young man now that he was back in circulation.

She was relieved and more than a little amused to see that this, at the moment, was not a problem. Griselda fussed around him, propping up his pillows, smoothing the covers, pouring his coffee and juice, and it was very evident that Brad was loving every minute of it. However, by the gusto with which he tucked into his food, it was equally evident that this "invalid-at-the-point-of-death" fantasy the two young people were playing out would not last all that long, despite the fact that they were both enjoying it to the hilt.

His breakfast devoured to the last crumb, Griselda rearranged Brad's pillows, into which he sank back with a convincing weary sigh, and she departed with the tray, leaving him alone with Penny. "Do you want to rest again or do you feel like talking?" she asked ironically.

"Oh, I'm fine," he said, looking a little guilty. "Let's talk. I'm anxious to know what's going on."

I'll bet you are, she thought, but countered. "Well, now that you are *compos mentis* again I'd like to hear more details of your encounter with the Paysons, and why you should have even thought Griselda might be there. The plan, after all, was to go on to Hilo in the yacht."

To her surprise he said earnestly. "But I did try there, I also tried Kailua—I practically tried the whole damned island, before it occurred to me she might have joined you at the Payson ranch. So I buzzed on up there . . ." and he went on to relate substantially what he had already told her, concluding with, ". . . I guess I was lucky at that. By all accounts the Paysons aren't always so tender with their visitors."

"How do you mean?" she demanded

"Well, I did a bit of digging into their African background and found out that they got out of Southern Rhodesia in the nick of time—just one step ahead of the posse, in fact."

Now Penny was intrigued. "How come?"

He inched himself up on his pillows. "As far as I can piece it together from newspaper reports, it went like this. Gregory went from the whites' 'Rhodesia is my home and no black government is going to intimidate me' die-hard position to a very hasty sale of his property. He packed up everything and the whole family took off with their goods and chattels in a gigantic overland safari to South Africa. That too hit the papers—you know the kind of thing 'Prominent white settler flees the black masses' and so on. Then one of the old servants on the farm blew the whistle—he led the new owner to a remote part of the plantation and quite literally said he knew where the bodies were buried. The police dug them up and there were half a dozen natives buried there—some had been shot, the others were too decomposed to tell. Anyway this caused an absolute furor. The new government—the Paysons had left just before the overall takeover—froze what few assets Gregory had left behind, and demanded his extradition from South Africa. Of course that got nowhere, but Gregory did issue a statement that the bodies were of a terrorist gang that had raided the farm with murder and mayhem in mind and had been driven off, but that he had not reported it due to the 'uneasy temper' of the times. The Zimbabwe government threatened vengeance, but by that time the Paysons had left South Africa to come here, so they were out of reach. Quite a story, eh? Come to think of it, I ought to have my head examined—barging in there unheralded when I knew all that. Love must be softening my brain."

"Quite," Penny said repressively. "And he gave no indication of who really did the massacre?"

"No, nothing more than I've told you, but if we are laying any bets I'd put my money on the guy who beat me up—a very nasty glint in his eye had he—what's his name? Philip?"

"Or maybe the whole lot of them," she said with a heavy sigh. "Well, you've given me more food for thought."

Griselda came in bearing a pitcher of guava juice, ice clinking invitingly within. "Time for your pain pills," she announced.

Penny got up. "Then I'll leave you to it—I must check to see if Toby has called, he's way overdue."

"But you haven't told me what's going on!" Brad protested.

"Later," she said and made a hurried exit.

On the way back to her cottage she ran into Mrs. Laolani, bearing an armful of assorted groceries. "I thought you might like these," the large woman confided. "I know how busy you are."

"Oh, that's extremely kind of you. Yes, come on in and I'll pay you for them," Penny said. "Any calls yet?"

"Not the one you were expecting, no." Mrs. Laolani followed her in and started to stow away the things in the tiny refrigerator and the cupboard above it, as Penny got the money from her purse. "But I did get a call from Benjamin. He says they'll all be returning by the six-thirty plane, so they'll be here tonight, though Dr. Shaw and the other man won't be staying here."

"Giles Shaw is out then!" Penny exclaimed.

"Yes. Isn't that good news? Benjamin was so happy. And to think last time he was here he stayed in this very cabin!"

"Kaowa?" Penny was puzzled.

"No, Dr. Shaw, of course."

A little cold hand clutched at Penny's heart. "Giles Shaw was here in North Kona? When?"

"Oh, it must have been about six or seven weeks ago."

"With Kaowa?" Penny persisted.

"No. Benjamin told him about our place of course, but he wasn't with him. He was alone—stayed, oh, three or four days. Such a pleasant man—quite a way with him he has!" Mrs. Laolani beamed in recollection.

"What was he doing here?" Penny felt her throat closing up.

"Just sightseeing I guess. He'd go off in his car every morning, didn't get back sometimes until evening. But always a cheerful word when he saw you." Mrs. Laolani gathered up her money and started to lumber out. "What a sweet young couple those two make, don't they? Makes one feel young again to see them. If there is anything else you need, just let me know."

"Thank you, I will. Thank you very much," Penny said absently, her gaze fixed on the careful charts she had made the night before—charts that she now knew were incomplete and possibly useless. She would have to do a massive rethink, and this time she would have to include the man they had just saved: the thought gave her no joy.

Chapter 18

A mini-conference was being held in the lobby of the airport where Toby, Ching and Kaowa awaited the arrival of Roger Rogers and the liberated Giles Shaw. "I am certain, if you give me a day or two," Ching was saying earnestly, "that I can persuade the local Hawaii authorities to give us all the extra backup we need—helicopters, walkie-talkies, even`extra men. It would be much safer than what you are proposing."

"No doubt, but we don't *have* any extra time," Toby said impatiently. "I am hoping that we are not already too late; that they have not made their move as yet. I intend to leave tomorrow first thing. Even if they are already there, it will take time for them to move the bullion that will probably be their first objective. I am hoping Kaowa will accompany me, but there is no need for you to put yourself at risk, Ching—after all, you know where I'll be."

"My orders are to stay with you, and that I intend to do no matter what," Ching said simply. "Besides, I am legally armed and that, too, might be useful."

"I do not like this idea, I do not like it at all," Kaowa growled.

Toby looked at him steadily. "I know you don't and why you don't and, believe me, my friend, if I could see any other alternative at this moment I would take it. But the plain fact is that your ancestor's burial place is about to be desecrated and plundered by men who care nothing for the old ways. You are a member of Kamehameha's family, so who better to enter the cave and ensure its future safety? Only you among us has that right, so I would like you to be there, but if you feel strongly against it, well then I'll go alone. I am not a plunderer, my only interest is to prevent what they have in mind to do."

Kaowa glared back at him and said nothing for a few long moments, then he rumbled. "No. I will go with you. You will need me. But it is a reckless man who dares to flout the *pule ana'ana*, which knows no race or creed. We all may die if we enter the cave and see what it is not for us to see."

"First we have to find it, and then, if we have got there ahead of them—well, then we may come up with some other means of protecting it," Toby said diplomatically. "What is the best way in to the Hale Iliili?"

"The best way is by sea and up the cliffs, which is difficult enough. The only access by road is just a rough cattle trail branching off the Mamalahoa Road, but that entails a hike of many miles over lava slopes before the promontory is reached," Kaowa said.

"Or by air," Toby was thoughtful. "As soon as we get to Ke'ahole I'll try and get a helicopter to drop us in there—yes, that would be best. I have already made a few phone calls from Rogers' office for some supplies we'll need—canteens, flashlights, ropes, bush knives and so on. They should be waiting for us at the Laolanis. Oh damn! I still haven't called Penny to tell her to expect them. Oh, well, it's a bit late for that now—she'll understand."

"Here they come," Ching said suddenly, and they wheeled to see Rogers and Shaw hurrying towards them: they made an incongruous pair, the small, neat, impeccably dressed lawyer and the tall, sloppily-dressed, wild-maned archaeologist. A great grin split Kaowa's rocklike face and he hurled himself towards the tall man. "Giles! It is great to see you—now all will be well." They hugged each other enthusiastically as Rogers came up to Toby and Ching, an amused smile on his face. "Well, one client safely delivered. You understand, Inspector, that we'll both be at the Payson ranch, but that I'll be in contact with you at the Laolanis, as I've discussed with Sir Tobias."

"As of tomorrow morning neither of us will be there," Toby put in. "You'll have to keep in contact with Dr. Spring, who'll be our anchorwoman."

"Oh, I see!" Rogers looked surprised. "You are going that soon?"

"I only hope it's soon enough," Toby replied, as Giles and Kaowa came up. He and Giles eyed each other warily, and there was a moment of strained silence before Giles said, "Well, Toby Glendower, I guess I owe you a lot. Rogers tells me you talked them out of going on with this nonsense."

"You owe far more to Penny Spring, who has been the prime mover in all this," Toby said coldly. "And I would hardly call two murders nonsense. You may be out but you are still scarcely in the clear, Dr. Shaw. We need to talk and I need some straight answers from you, so I suggest we sit together. Our flight has just been called."

Giles was eyeing Inspector Ching. "So that's the way it is," he said softly. "They've sent a watchdog with me—so it's not free I am at all, just on a longer leash."

"The inspector is with me," Toby replied. "Since Inspector Lyons feels with a murderer or murderers at large

I may be in some danger in what I'm proposing to do."

"And what is that?" Giles challenged.

"Why don't we talk about that on the plane?" Toby returned, and stalked off to the appointed gate.

They settled in their seats, Ching and Rogers behind them, Kaowa by himself in front. "So what can I tell you about me and me little Menehunes that you don't know already?" Giles said with an impish gleam.

"Nothing." Toby was abrupt. "To me your attempt to put a spoke in Van Norkirk's wheel over the land deal is a complete side issue, unless it does somehow impinge on this other matter. What I want to know is this—was the public row you had with Freyer anything to do with his search for Kamehameha's treasure? Did he approach you to help him?"

Giles was startled and silent, his eyes fixed appraisingly on Toby's. "Freyer was full of hot air—always trying to be important," he said at length. "He did mention something about it, but I thought he was just running off at the mouth as usual."

"Did he tell you he was after it and did he ask you to help? *Why* did you come to blows?" Toby pressed.

Again Giles pondered. "Yes, he said he had a clue to its whereabouts and suggested we call a truce. I told him only the stars of the heavens knew the resting place of Kamehameha and it would take a lot better man than he would ever be to find it. Flew at me like a wildcat he did, flailing away like a windmill. I had to knock him cold to defend myself."

"Did he mention anyone else in connection with this?" Toby was watching him keenly.

"He said something about the papers old Donelson had left him—another nut that one." Giles' reply was grudging.

"He did not mention the names Manua or Hapili?"

Giles shook his head. "No—who are they?" He seemed genuinely puzzled.

Toby changed tack. "So you turned him down—is that it?"

"I didn't take him seriously," Giles evaded.

"So how do you explain the fact that he brought a sketch-map of the Hale Iliili area with him to the Birthing Rocks for that fatal meeting?" Toby said softly.

"No idea—why don't you tell me." The answer came so quickly that Toby knew he was lying.

"Well, the way it looks to me is that Freyer hoped to come to some agreement with you over the Menehune business and was then going to show you something tangible to enlist your archaeological talents—talents that he lacked and needed to bring off the archaeological coup of both your careers. You may as well tell me, because it is too late for that, you know. I intend going after it myself tomorrow to prevent it falling into the hands of his murderers."

Giles Shaw threw back his head and let out a bellow of laughter in which there was no trace of mirth. "So that's it! It's after a few more laurels to stick in that heavy crown of yours, you are! Dear God, haven't you got enough of them already, man? There's many a fool has tried for Kamehameha's treasure before, and will again, no doubt."

Toby was unperturbed. "You haven't answered my question."

"Nor am I likely to, with Inspector Ching sitting back there with his big ears flapping at every word I say." There was an edge of angry contempt on Giles' voice. "What are they after now—another motive for me killing Freyer because their 'Menehune' motive couldn't be made to stick? Is this some kind of trick to make me commit myself? Like a puppet on a string they let me out just to jerk me

back, is that it? Whose side are you on anyway?" He was
getting progressively angrier.

"No, Manua's murder has put a whole new light on
Freyer's so, if you're not more deeply implicated in this
treasure hunt than you appear to be, you should shortly
be in the clear," Toby said tightly.

"This Manua has been murdered? Who was he anyway?" Giles calmed down perceptibly.

"He belonged to the *kahu* that looked after the burying
place. We think the *kahuna ana ana* Hapili is responsible—but I do not think he was acting alone in this."

"I see." A heavy silence fell as Giles chewed on this.

Toby broke it after a while. "Known the Paysons long?"

Giles roused himself. "Oh, five or six years. Rogers tells
me you were staying with them—veddy, veddy English,
aren't they? Are we going to be one big happy family?"

"No, I won't be going back there." Toby did not elaborate. "How did you meet them?"

"Bought a couple of horses from them," Giles said to
his surprise. "Emily and I used to like to ride, you know.
Had a nice place in Oahu with a couple of acres." He
sighed heavily. "I let it all go after she died—hadn't the
heart for it."

"So you don't know them all that well? I got the impression they were great friends of yours." Toby was casual.

"Oh yes, they were friends of mine—we hit it off right
from the start. Whenever Em and I went to the big island
they'd put us up. Very hospitable, and Gregory and Phil
are good drinking men. I stayed with them for quite a
while after Em died—Philip mostly. Very kind they were
then, very kind . . ." Giles trailed off sadly. "Of course
Mildred is a bit of a pain, and they aren't the swiftest lot,
but they were good to me—like taking me in now."

Toby hesitated. "Yes, well on that, don't be too san-
guine. In fact, although I am sure you'll be safe enough

since Rogers is along as well, keep a sharp eye out. The Paysons may have more of a vested interest in all this than you know—you see, Manua was one of their employees." Involved or uninvolved he thought he owed Giles this much.

Giles looked at him in astonishment as the seatbelt signs went on for landing. "You think the Paysons are involved in this treasure hunt nonsense? Impossible! They just haven't the brains for it. Philip is nothing but an overgrown schoolboy, and Gregory has let whatever brains he may have had go to seed in trying so hard to be the English country squire at far remove. As for Mildred, well she's a nonstarter in any field you care to name. No, I think you are way off base on this one."

"It is always dangerous to underestimate other people's intelligence," Toby murmured. "Under pressure—and I have reason to believe the Paysons are under many different kinds of pressure—it is amazing what any human being is capable of." He felt there was no more to be said. He had given Giles fair warning and if Giles did not wish to heed it, Toby did not much care.

Giles also seemed to feel there was nothing else to say, for he leaned forward in his seat, tapped Kaowa on the shoulder, and began an animated, low-voiced conversation with him until the plane touched down and rolled to a stop.

As they deplaned, Toby spotted Penny's small figure in the spectator's enclosure. She was shading her eyes against the westering sun and contriving to look anxious and extremely grumpy at one and the same time. His heart sank as his errors of omission came home to him, and he purposefully poked Giles and Rogers ahead of him so that she would greet them first. He was a little taken aback, as indeed was Giles, by the stiff way she greeted her liberated friend. By contrast she was markedly affable to Roger Rogers and the newly-introduced Charles Ching, while the bags were unloaded and claimed. Toby she ignored.

When they were collecting themselves for departure he edged up to her. "Er—sorry I didn't get in touch, but we got in so late yesterday and today has been so hectic I just did not have a moment. Did the things arrive?"

"In a steady stream all afternoon," she snapped. "You know I'm beginning to think my parents knew a thing or two when they named me Penelope—waiting around seems to have become my chief virtue. Unfortunately, I did not bring my loom along, so I can't spend my time undoing my weaving and waiting for something to happen like the original Penelope. For heaven's sake, let's go— I've got to talk to you *alone*. I certainly didn't expect you to return with a whole convention—can you dump them?"

"Bear with me a little longer," Toby said anxiously. "I have to stay on here and see if I can get hold of a helicopter for tomorrow, but I'll try and send the others off ahead. Why don't you go and have a drink or a snack while I make the arrangements? I'll be as quick as I can."

"I'll wait in the car," she growled and stamped off.

Giles and Rogers took off in a rental car with Ching and Kaowa as passengers, to be dropped off en route at the Laolani's. Toby sought out the only company that rented helicopters, and its operator and owner heard him out in silence. "Well, it's not my usual beat," he said at length. "I mostly take tourists over the Waimea canyon on a regular schedule. I *could* make it, but it would have to be early—say seven a.m.? You actually want to be left there? It's a pretty desolate area, you know—are you sure you know what you're doing?"

"Yes," Toby said, with a lot more certainty than he felt.

"Now then, we'd like to be dropped at the ruins of the old council house which reportedly are visible. Do you know them?"

The man shook his head. "No, but I can find them if they are. How about pick-up—or are you going to walk out?"

"No. I have no idea how much time we'll need in there, so I would like you to fly over the same place tomorrow evening. If we're not there, come back the following evening at the same time. Is that possible?"

The man looked at his flight schedule dubiously. "I have a five o'clock to Waimea, but I could squeeze you in just before dark. Say at six-thirty, but I won't be able to hang around for long, so *be* there."

"If at all possible, yes. But what about the next night, if we're not?"

"Okay—can do. Same time, same place. A special like this is going to cost, you know."

"Oh, that's all right—whatever it costs." Toby casually produced a gold American Express card that the man eyed with appreciation. "Er—what if you're not at the rendezvous point the second day?" he asked.

"Well, so then something will have gone wrong and you'd better yell for help," Toby said grimly. "Notify the local police and Inspector Lyons of Hawaii Five-O—just put the calls on my bill."

The man eyed him curiously. "This is a police matter?"

"In a way," Toby murmured. "A Hawaii Five-O inspector called Ching will be one of your passengers, as well as myself, Benjamin Kaowa and a bunch of equipment."

"Kaowa, the nationalist leader!" the man exclaimed.

"Yes—you know him?"

"Who doesn't?" the man countered, gathering up the card and scribbling out the invoice. "Well sir, you're all set—see you here tomorrow then at seven sharp. Must say it will make a change from Waimea canyon."

Relieved that at least one thing had gone off smoothly, Toby sought out his disgruntled partner. "The helicopter is all arranged for tomorrow," he said settling beside her. "So what's been happening?"

"You first," she said, putting the car in motion. "I need to know *everything* that happened in Oahu, particularly the deal on Giles. To say I was flabbergasted to hear he was going to the Paysons is the understatement of the year."

Toby told her in meticulous detail, concluding with, "Staying at the Paysons was Rogers' idea, and a good one if we are trying to bring things to a head. He'll be in touch with you, from the time we take off tomorrow until we get back, with details of their movements, so I'm afraid it will mean more hanging around for you, but it really can't be helped. With any luck we should be back tomorrow evening."

"Toby," she said in a muffled voice. "Don't go on with this—please! We've done what we set out to do—Giles is out of prison and the police are actively investigating. Let's leave it at that. Let's pack up, fly back to Oahu and get on with our vacation. It's up to the police now to take care of the rest of it. There is no sense and no need of your sticking your neck out further."

"Why this change of heart?" he asked quietly and saw her small hands tighten on the wheel until the knuckles whitened.

There was a long pause, then she said, "Because I think you may have been right in your very first assessment of all this and that I was entirely wrong. 'A whimsical murder by a whimsical man,' as I recall, were your very words. We may have just assisted at a gross miscarriage of justice, and all the rest of it—the Paysons, Van Norkirk and all—

may be so much moonshine. We've been led by the nose *into* all this. I think Giles may be as guilty as hell."

"Why?" he repeated, and she told him.

"Granted all that, he still could not have been involved in Manua's murder," Toby said at length.

"No, but Hapili could. What if he and Giles got together on this somewhere along the line and decided between them to cut Freyer out? What if we were *meant* to find Freyer's body and Giles soused like that? And then we'd have looked over the car with him, he'd have 'found' the maps—surprise, surprise! And things would have developed from there. Your speed in finding the police and bringing them back upset all that, hence all the subsequent break-ins by his partners, while he safely sat in prison waiting for the all clear—an 'all clear' brought about by Hapili as soon as Manua was expendable. It all makes a frightening sense to me. We've been used."

"Possibly," Toby murmured. "Although I do not agree with you entirely. I grant you Giles knew more about the treasure hunt than he has admitted, or probably ever will admit, but I still do not see him as a murderer. Whereas we know now, from young Field's discoveries, that one or all of the Paysons *undoubtedly* are. Anyway, we should know in the next twenty-four hours. I am committed now and intend to see this through no matter what. If the murderers are as desperate as I think they are, they will have to make their move. Wait any longer and then they may grab what they can get and lay low, and we may never know. I don't think either of us want that, do we?"

"I care one hell of a lot more about your obstinate, stringy neck than finding Kamehameha's treasure or bringing a murderer to book," she said gruffly. "Face it, Toby, we are getting too old for this kind of lark. Let's get out while we can."

"I'm sorry, my dear," he said mildly. "But I can't. I just can't."

"And that's your final word?"

"I'm afraid so."

She heaved a heavy sigh. "Oh hell, why do I even bother trying? Well, back to the waiting game. What time did you say you were leaving tomorrow?"

Chapter 19

"There it is!" Although Toby was senior by a good twenty years to the rest of his party, it was his trained eye that had picked out the outline of manmade walls in this savage terrain of brush and rock.

The pilot peered below, grunted acknowledgment and put the helicopter into a graceful downward spiral. To their left the calm face of the Pacific gleamed molten under the sun, already burning hotly despite the early hour. The helicopter settled on a tract of flat beaten earth that once had been the forecourt of this council house of kings, and the party went quickly and quietly about unloading the equipment. The pilot produced a bright-orange plastic ten-gallon jerrycan. "I'll leave this as a marker," he volunteered. "The light won't be as good when I get back this evening and this'll give us all something to aim for. Besides, it has water in it and if you do stay here for a couple of days you may find it useful."

"Good idea. Thanks. Then you'll be back around six-thirty?" Toby said.

"Better make that seven to be on the safe side. These Waimea trips sometimes run a bit late—but I'll be back for sure, and if you're not here will do the same tomorrow," the pilot said, climbing back into his seat. They crouched down as the rotors began to spin, and when the gaily-painted helicopter was once again airborne, watched it soar out of sight before turning back to their equipment.

A great silence fell, the air heavy, hot and still. No bird sang and nothing moved in the great thickets of guava and lantana that hedged them in on all sides. Kaowa moved uneasily, his head thrown back, scenting the air. "It is too quiet," he rumbled. "A bad sign—this is always how it is before an eruption." He took off the yachting cap he was wearing and wiped the sweat off his forehead with a massive forearm. Toby looked over at Ching, who was bareheaded. "You're going to fry without a hat," he said, fumbling in his knapsack. "Here, I brought an extra along, you'd better wear it." He produced an ancient linen digging hat that was bleached white from sheer age.

"Yes, thanks. I should have thought of that," Ching said, and put it on. With the hat shading his features, he and Toby looked like a matched pair.

"Before we load up, we'd better look for the first marker." Toby got out the old photo and showed it around. "I'm hoping it's somewhere around the perimeter of the council house." They split up, but it was barely a minute before a bellow came from Kaowa. "Here it is!"

They hurried to where he stood over a small triangular stone, its apex underlining the message of the *kahili* on it, for it pointed due north by Toby's pocket compass. "Well, here we go," he said, turning to the pile of knapsacks, ropes and canteens. Despite his outward calm he felt a mounting excitement that had set his pulse racing.

Kaowa, a large machete in hand, took the lead, Ching behind him and Toby bringing up the rear. Although the steady swing of Kaowa's machete slashed through the tough intertwined stems like butter, the lantana thicket through which they were headed was so dense that the going was slow, and after thirty minutes of this Kaowa stopped to mop his brow and take a swig from his canteen. Toby had noticed a narrow path bearing off to their right through the thicket. "There seems a track of sorts here," he observed mildly, taking a swig of water from his own canteen. "Would it be easier to follow that and see where it takes us?"

Kaowa gave a negative grunt. "By all accounts there are wild cattle here; strays from the local ranches. They make these tracks, but if those stones are in a definite pattern, following them won't help us any. We'd best keep on—we've come about 450 yards, so if that distance of 480 yards you told me about holds for all of them, we should be near the second." His arm took up its rhythmical swing and they toiled on in silence, their feet stirring up clouds of the omnipresent volcanic ash that coated the bushes to a scabrous grey-green.

"There!" said Ching suddenly, and pointed in excitement to his right. They crowded around the stone with the war canoe and the line of marching men. "It should be easier from here," Kaowa's voice held a strange note. He pointed silently beyond the stone to where a narrow path between dying, splintered branches could be made out. "Someone has been here before us—and not too long ago at that."

Toby felt a constriction in his chest. "So I see." He got out his own bush knife. "Maybe we should switch places now, and I can hack where necessary. The next stone should be 480 yards dead ahead." He looked up. "We seem to be heading for that ridge in front of us." He scanned it with his binoculars. "No sign of any movement, but there are one heck of a lot of cave openings in it."

"No, I lead," Kaowa said firmly and edging sideways into the narrow path began his chopping once more. They had gone about two hundred yards along the path when he stopped so suddenly that Ching collided with his massive back, and Toby barely stopped colliding with the policeman. "Did you see that?" Kaowa demanded, a tremor in his deep voice. He wheeled around, his eyes so wide that the whites all around his dark pupils were visible.

"No. What?" Toby demanded.

"A dog. It was a small white dog," Kaowa quavered. "It crossed our path."

Ching slid a sidelong warning glance at Toby. "Yes, I did see something white in the thicket, but it's all right, it has gone now," he said soothingly, but the big man seemed rooted to the spot. "Why don't we take a break?" Ching went on. "It's so hot, I could use a drink." Under cover of unscrewing his canteen and rattling it against the tin cup into which he was pouring it, he edged up to Toby, who was looking duly mystified by this turn of events. "The Hawaiians believe that the Goddess Pele sometimes appears in the guise of a small white dog," he murmured. "It is meant as a warning sign of great danger."

"I see. Did you see anything?" Toby murmured back. Ching glanced quickly at Kaowa's rigid back and shook his head slightly. Toby nodded and shouldered his way past Kaowa. "Time for me to spell you," he said briskly. "You've already done a lion's share and we're doing fine. It's not yet ten o'clock and it looks as if the brush is thinning out near the cliffs. Come on, we'll take a real breather at the next petroglyph." Ching followed him, and when they glanced back, Kaowa had roused from his stupor and was slowly following them, his head swivelling uneasily from side to side.

The trail suddenly opened out into a small clearing and there, in the center of a circle of larger stones, sat the third marker. Toby crouched over it looking around and up at the ridge, now looming above them, but of the symbols of the spring, hut or cave there was not a sign in the clearing. His high hopes began to sink and he began to search the whole circle in frantic haste for some other indication. A sudden exclamation from Ching, who also had been wandering around peering at the rocks, startled him, and he looked up. "Look!" said Ching, and pointed.

A little beyond the clearing and almost obscured by a tall guava bush stood a small, camouflaged army tent, its flaps secured. A low rumble came from Kaowa's throat, as Ching quietly unholstered his revolver and they approached on silent feet. After a quick glance at Toby, Ching said loudly, "Hawaii police. Come out with your hands up. I have the tent covered." There was no response, and only the beat of a distant helicopter's engine broke the absolute quiet.

At Ching's nod, Toby quickly undid the tent's fastenings and threw back the flap, shining his large flashlight into the dark interior—it was empty. They crowded in and took silent stock of the contents: a sleeping bag, a big knapsack, a portable radio, a jerrycan of water and an array of canned goods, neatly stacked against the back wall of the tent. Everything was covered by a fine layer of undisturbed ash.

"Doesn't look as if it's been used for days," Toby observed, as Ching knelt and began to take out the contents of the knapsack that disclosed an assortment of men's clothing. Suddenly Kaowa came out of his daze and pounced, as a small object fell out of the pocket of a pair of shabby blue jeans. It was a matchbook bearing the superscription "Bar Kahaka, Waikiki." "Hapili!" he growled, and pounced again as Ching produced an ugly-looking tiki in polished jadeite from the bottom of the bag. "Hapili for sure!"

"No wonder we couldn't find him, but it looks as if he's been and gone some time ago," Toby said grimly. "The big question is where."

They emerged from the stifling confines of the tent and looked helplessly around. A tumbled pile of boulders, fallen in long ages past from the looming ridge above them, heaped up to the left. "Give me your binoculars," commanded Kaowa, who now appeared back to normal. "I'll get up there and take a look around." He disappeared into the bushes, then reappeared, climbing with all the ease of a mountain goat until he had reached the top. His back braced against the topmost boulder, he did a slow 360 degree scan of the area, then swivelled back and looked west towards the ridge which had taken a sudden dogleg toward the south. After another suspenseful minute, he lowered the glasses and called down. "I think I see a bit of thatched roofing over there—just about a quarter of a mile, I estimate, and due west. And there seems to be some movement on the ground, but I can't make out what. Too small for a man." He started to clamber down.

"Well, it's worth a try." Toby again scanned the clearing. "There's certainly nothing here that indicates there's ever been a hut or a spring. Damnation! It looks as if there must be more than these three markers after all."

They shouldered their burdens and headed west, the heat and still air getting more oppressive by the minute. Kaowa had once again taken the lead, the thick bushes now giving place to the barren surface of a narrow lava flow. They had just reached the far edge of it and were about to plunge into more bushes when there came a loud flurry of wings, and a cloud of black and white myna birds suddenly rose, shrieking and chuckling, into the air dead ahead, and came swooping and circling over them. Kaowa

recoiled, then said grimly, "Mynas are carrion eaters—
there's something dead over there. Come on!" and broke
into a run as the mynas scolded above them.

They burst into another small clearing where the remains of a small mortuary hut sagged in ruin; sticking out
of the doorway were two bare brown legs—or what remained of them. Then the stench hit them. Kaowa reeled
back and turned away. After his first instinctive recoil,
Ching recovered himself, covered his mouth with a handkerchief and, walking over to the hut, peered inside. Toby
followed his example.

A middle-aged Hawaiian, clad only in an aged tapa-
cloth skirt and already badly decomposed, lay face up, his
head resting against the broken fragments of a brass-handled coffin. The body was so thickly covered with volcanic
dust that Toby was irresistibly reminded of the plaster
figures of Pompeii, contorted in their final death agonies:
but this body was no victim of volcanic fallout, the gaping
hole in what remained of its chest indicated that all too
clearly. "Looks as if he was shot at close quarters by a
high-powered rifle," Ching's voice came muffled through
the handkerchief. "Expanding bullet by the looks of it.
Dead for some days." He gingerly moved one of the
arms—underneath it the rotting floor matting showed no
sign of the ash. "Been here since before last week's eruption. Know who it is?"

Toby was looking grimly at the outline of a tiki that
hung on a leather cord around the body's neck. "I think
we are looking at what remains of Hapili," he said, as a
whole set of facts clicked into place in his mind and suddenly made sense. He turned to where Kaowa stood like
a lava monolith, his face frozen. "My friend, we need you.
I think it is Hapili, but only you can tell us for certain.
Please come—it will just be for a moment."

A quiver ran through the huge frame and Kaowa reluctantly came toward him, his eyes glazed. Toby handed him his handkerchief and turned away. As he did so, the sun glinted from something on the ground and he stooped and picked it up. "So that's it," he said sadly and, with the habit of years, slipped it into a glassine envelope produced from one of his sagging pockets. He wheeled around to see Kaowa nodding mutely at Ching, who said in a strangled voice, "This changes things I'm afraid. Let's get out of here and discuss it." He strode off towards the ridge, and perforce they followed, but in circling the back of the hut, Toby came upon the fourth marker: this time a line of marching men outlined in red and pointing west and another spiral "umbilical cord" engraving. He hurried after the others, and they came to a stop in another open space where the ghastly smell of rotting flesh was only a faint miasma in the heavy air.

"I'm afraid this murder takes precedence over everything. I have to get back as soon as possible to report it." Ching was now all policeman. "We must start out right away."

Toby's obstinate streak surged; now that they were so close he was not about to give up, but he temporized. "I'm not sure that's at all practical. How far is it from here to the Mamalahoa Road, Kaowa?"

"Between thirteen and fifteen miles," Kaowa rumbled.

"And over terrain like this it would take us a good five or six hours, I'd say, and we would still have to find transport to a phone after that. You'd never be able to get reinforcements in here before dark," Toby said earnestly. "It is now just about noon, the 'copter is due back at seven. Wouldn't it be better to wait for that? Then you could make your arrangements direct from Ke'ahole airport when we get in and you'd be all set for tomorrow morning at daybreak."

Ching pondered this. "You mentioned something about

the beach being the best way in, Kaowa? Perhaps we should go down there—it must be quite close—and we could signal a passing vessel."

Kaowa snorted. "A long shot, at best. That's a very difficult cove to get into, and on a day like this . . ." he looked up at the molten sky. "You'd never find a native fisherman out, and no *haole* could ever get in there without wrecking his boat."

"Then I suppose you are right. We'd best get back to the landing area and I can write out a preliminary report while we wait."

"But the pickup is hours away!" Toby exclaimed. "Why not go on now that we've come so far?"

"Go where?" Ching said. "We've run out of clues, haven't we?"

"No, I found the fourth marker back there at the hut. There should be one more, if my informant was correct, due west of the last," Toby explained rapidly. "If you want to stay here and rest, fine, but I'm going on."

"No, we had best stick together," Ching was resigned. "But if you don't find it we go back to the council house—okay?"

"Right," Toby agreed, and getting out his compass started to pace west. Another quarter of a mile brought them directly below the cliff face of the ridge, and it was Kaowa who spotted the marker. This time it was a huge spiral, outlined in red, inscribed on a boulder. "Now what?" Ching said impatiently.

Toby scanned the cliff face above that appeared riddled with the holes of lava tubes. Most were inaccessible, but he noticed a shelf of rock that formed a narrow pathway along the face thirty feet above them and off which gaped another series of holes. "I would wager that the entrance to one of those caves has a twin spiral to this one," he said. "And there's only one way to find out. I've got to get up there. Can you spot a route up to that shelf, Kaowa?" He handed him the binoculars.

Kaowa scanned the cliff face and suddenly grunted. "There to the left—footholds carved out of the rock—not easy." He handed the glasses back and pointed.

"No, but possible." Toby came to a sudden decision. "Let's have some food now, and then I'll tackle it. You also, Kaowa, if you feel up to it. No need for you to risk it, Ching. We'll leave all the kit here with you, except for the ropes, flashlights and canteens."

"You really think that's it?" Ching said with kindling enthusiasm. "No, I'll come too. No sense staying down here, kicking my heels and worrying."

They ate without appetite and in hurried silence, and while Toby was filling his already overloaded pockets with an assortment of things from his knapsack, Kaowa suddenly slipped off his shirt, strode over to the fifth marker, stepped up on the boulder, and emptied the entire contents of his canteen over his head. The water trickled in slow rivulets down his bronzed body, as he stood with his eyes closed, his lips moving silently. He stepped down, and without a word moved off towards the precarious staircase. As they reached the bottom of it, Ching murmured to Toby, "I don't have much of a head for heights. Mind if I go next? Then you can give me a boost if I get stuck."

"Go ahead. Just follow Kaowa's steps and don't look down. I'll be right behind you," Toby encouraged.

They mounted swiftly and started to inch along the narrow ledge, bracing their hands against the cliff face. Five cave openings were passed and Toby's hopes were beginning to fade, when Kaowa shouted, "The spiral!— here it is!" and half-turned toward him at the opening of the sixth lava tube.

Something whined through the air and Kaowa was

hurled off his feet, an expression of agonized surprise on his face, as a fusillade of shots raised thunderous echoes. Ching gave a choked cry, threw up his hands and crumpled. Kaowa's huge hand snatched him from toppling over the edge and dragged him inside the cave, as Toby instinctively flattened himself on the ledge and started to crawl toward its dark maw. A bullet ricocheted above his head and a flying splinter of rock carved a small gash in his forehead. He tumbled inside, blood streaming into his left eye.

"Bloody hell!" he groaned, as he pushed, while the crippled Kaowa pulled, the unconscious Ching out of the line of fire. "We've led the bastard right to it! He's got us pinned down." Secure in a niche away from the opening, he hastily tied his handkerchief in a rough bandage around his head to stem the blood, and turned to assess the damage. Kaowa's leg was bleeding freely, but the bullet had passed clear through the fleshy part of the calf and the bone was intact. It probably hurt like hell, but the damage was comparatively minor. He looked desperately around for something to bandage it with and stop the bleeding, but finding nothing, tore off his coat, then his shirt, and began to tear that into strips. He started to fashion a bandage, but Kaowa twitched it out of his fumbling fingers. "I can do that. See to Ching. He's worse off than I am."

Toby turned frantically to the policeman who lay, eyes closed and with blood dribbling out of the corners of his mouth. His eyes widened as he took stock of what had happened. Ching had been carrying his canteen slung on his back, and the bullet had hit dead square in the heart region, but had punched a hole in the canteen and been deflected. It had saved the inspector from instant death, but on its onward passage must have nicked a lung and he was hemorrhaging slightly: worse, there was no exit wound, which meant the bullet was still in him. On the plus side Toby found his pulse, though rapid, was strong. The bitter realization came to him that the bullet had been meant for him; that Ching, wearing his hat and of such similar build to himself, had been the prime target.

He wiped the blood out of Ching's mouth and propped him up against the wall to lessen the risk of his choking on his own blood. He then bandaged Ching's back as well as he could, cursing himself as he did so for his own stiff-necked obstinacy. He had been so obsessed by the hunt that it had never crossed his mind that the murderer would be this daring or could move so fast. He had led them into a trap from which, with two wounded men, there seemed small hope of escape. The murderer had only to wait them out, for they were trapped with no food and little water—his own canteen and what little remained in Ching's.

He settled himself against the wall to prevent Ching from slipping down and looked over at Kaowa. The big man was a greyish-green and sweating heavily, but from the way his eyes were roving wildly around, Toby surmised that it was not the pain of his wound but where he was that was affecting him so. For the first time he took stock of his immediate surroundings, although the cave was so dark that nothing was visible beyond the first ten feet. Within that compass were two coffins of solid Victorian manufacture, brass-handled and brass-plated. One was huge, the other, beyond it, smaller. At the head of the big one stood an assortment of antique spears and clubs and a feather *kahili*; at its foot a huge kava bowl of exquisite workmanship. Kaowa rolled an anguished eye at him. "My great-grandfather," he whispered huskily. "I recognize his name on the plate, and I know he kept to the old ways."

"It's all right, Kaowa," Toby said quietly, "You have a

right to be here, the *pule ana'ana* will not harm you. We'll get out of this, never fear."

"It seems to be working just fine this far," Kaowa growled. "Two of us out of action and a man with a rifle out there pinning us down."

"He might have us pinned down for the moment, but he can't get *at* us," Toby said firmly. The chaos of his mind was settling into a more normal, rational format, and he realized that, at worst, it was only a matter of holding out. But for how long? The helicopter pilot would come this evening and would go away again—little hope of attracting his attention from here. He'd return tomorrow evening, then blow the whistle and the police would come in in force. The murderer, he was fairly sure, had a helicopter at his disposal, so could come and go as he pleased, but would not dare to linger for any great length of time, for the finger of guilt would then be pointed directly at him, and he certainly would not linger once the police were called in. Say then, three days at the most—and there was always Penny who, knowing her, might not wait that long to take action. This thought comforted him.

However, now that the murderer had made his move, he just might try to finish them off, particularly if he had help, by a direct attack on the cave. Toby eyed Ching's revolver thoughtfully. Maybe it would be a good idea to let him know they were not entirely defenseless. "You any good with a gun?" he asked Kaowa, who had closed his eyes on his frightening surroundings and was no longer dripping with sweat. "No," Kaowa said, without opening them. "Are you?"

"I'm afraid not," Toby confessed. "However, I think I'll try something." He got out the gun, flipped the safety off, and edged to the opening, then propped his hat on the end of a flashlight and inched it into sight. An immediate fusillade answered his gesture, and when their echoes had faded, he put the gun at ground level in the opening and fired off a couple of rounds. "Just to let him know we're armed," he told Kaowa.

The sound of the shots had roused Ching who groaned faintly, his eyelids fluttering desperately to open. Toby looked at him and a new desperation seized him: for Kaowa and himself three days of privation would be survivable, but for Ching, seriously wounded and with the bullet still in him, it might be a death sentence. He had to do something more. He had to find another way out and get help.

He fumbled in his overburdened pockets and brought out the small first-aid kit he always carried with him on expeditions. "I have a couple of morphine tablets here," he told Kaowa. "I'm going to try and get one of them into Ching to knock him out. The bleeding seems to have stopped, but the less he moves the better. I've also got some other pain pills here. Like one? You could get some rest till I get back."

Kaowa opened his eyes. "Where the hell are you going?"

"To try and find another way out." Toby had popped the pill into Ching's mouth and held the canteen up to his lips until the semiconscious man gave a convulsive gulp. Toby eased him down so that he was lying flat and propped one of the coils of rope under his head.

"You're crazy," Kaowa informed him.

"It's worth a try. We could hold out until help comes, but I'm not sure he will," Toby said grimly, getting up and collecting one of the ropes and his big flashlight. "I'll leave the canteen with you, but go easy on it—it's all we have to last us three days."

"Before you go hand me one of those spears," Kaowa said. "The one next to the *kahili*." Toby handed it to him and, balancing himself with it, the big man gradually heaved himself up, his head almost touching the roof of the cave. He winced as he tried his weight on his injured leg, but gave a satisfied nod and expertly hefted the spear, one hand braced against the cave wall. "Well, if those shots don't keep the bastard off, at least if he gets this far I'll get him as he gets me. I may not be any use with a gun but I'm one hell of a spear thrower."

Toby smiled faintly at him. "I'll bet you are. But I'm hoping he'll stay quiet for now and suggest you do the same."

"For God's sake be careful!" Kaowa's voice was husky. "And above all, if you find the cave, touch nothing."

Toby nodded, switched on the flashlight and started to thread his way into the crowded darkness. His light illumined a series of coffins, and the deeper he went the more mouldering the relics. The tube narrowed and then flared out in a rounded cul-de-sac, the back wall of which had been plastered up. He was wondering how he could hack through it to the passage beyond, when his scanning light picked out an incongruity among the grave goods— a large flat slab, its entire face covered with petroglyphs. He put down the flashlight and pushed at the slab with all his strength. It started to slide, and with a final mighty heave he managed to roll it entirely away from the dark hole it covered. Grabbing up the light he shone it into the hole and saw a narrow flight of rough-hewn basalt steps leading downward. Something flew out of the hole straight at him and he recoiled, his heart pounding, then caught the flash of small black bodies and heaved a relieved sigh. "Bats!"

He edged down the stairs and after some thirty feet suddenly came out on a larger staircase that soared away to his right, while from below came the sound of dripping water. He climbed on down, his light picking out a small pool of water in a natural basin at the side of the stairs. He tasted it gingerly; it was brackish but drinkable. One problem solved, he thought, his spirits soaring. At least we'll not die of thirst.

Just beyond the pool the steps stopped abruptly and he found himself in a wide vaulted passageway. His excitement mounted as he hurried along it, for he could now hear the soft surge of the sea. The roof of the passage suddenly soared upwards to a higher cave roof and he came to the beginning of another stairway; he ran down a few steps, then his foot struck a flat plane and he almost fell. Trembling with anticipation he shone his light around, and froze. "Well I'll be double-damned," he murmured. "So that's how it is!"

Chapter   20

"What do you mean they're *all* gone? Even Giles? Where? When?" Penny ran a frantic hand through her hair so that it stood up in spikes around her worried face, as the other hand gripped the phone with vise-like intensity. The phone crackled some more. "How could you *possibly* let this happen?" she cried.

"I am most terribly sorry. I had no idea . . ." Roger Rogers' voice was abject in apology. "You see it was like this . . . when we got in last night, dinner was very late in arriving and they kept pressing drinks on us—very strong drinks I may say. I did say everything Sir Tobias had suggested I say to them, but what with one thing and another, well, once I got up to bed I'm afraid I just passed out. Didn't surface until nine o'clock. Went down and found they had all *been* there—their breakfast things were still on the table, and so I thought they were out showing Giles the ranch or something. So I had some myself and then wandered out after them, but couldn't find a soul. Asked the servants and they didn't seem to know anything, except that Gregory had gone out earlier and had come in again in a raging temper and had gone off in his car again."

"Well then, quickly, hop in your rented car and go down to the ranch hands' settlement, they might know," she said in exasperation.

"I can't, the car's not here. Nothing is here but a station wagon and that's not working."

"No helicopter?"

"No, I checked the pad. That's gone too." Rogers sounded as anxious as she did.

"Oh, dear God, I don't like this!" Penny's fears were in full flood.

"Neither do I. I think I'll get in touch with Lyons right now and try and light a fire under him. Shall I come over? Is there anybody there who could pick me up?"

"No, you stay right where you are and phone me every hour on the hour until something breaks. Check the bunkhouse, check the servants again, check everything—and yes, get Lyons in on this if you possibly can." She slammed the phone down and glared around the Laolani's kitchen in search of inspiration.

The Laolanis, alerted by Kaowa to the importance of the day's operations, had tactfully taken themselves off to Hilo for the day to visit a married daughter, leaving Penny a clear field to their house and telephone, and she had set up her communications HQ in their kitchen. The door opened and Brad Field came in, an expression of eager enquiry on his face that was now a symphony of brown, green and yellow bruises. The momentum of events had led him to abandon—albeit reluctantly—his role of suffering invalid; an eventuality that evidently did not suit Griselda too well, by the disgruntled expression on her face as she followed him in. "What's cooking?" he demanded.

"Plenty! Rogers says they're all gone, and he doesn't know where." Penny was tight-lipped with fury.

"I noticed a strange car by your cottage," he said mildly.

"*What!*" she jumped up. "I'd better check that out. You man the phones, but *no* calls to your paper, remember?"

The evening before a delegation had visited Brad, headed by Ching, and other than allowing him to phone his paper to tell them of his whereabouts and condition, and that he was on top of a headline story that was just about to break, had elicited a vow of silence until they gave the go-ahead. He had agreed in return for the exclusive they had promised him, but Penny was so much on the jump that at the moment she trusted no one.

"I promised didn't I?" Brad said in an injured voice. "Go on—I'll hold the fort."

She hurried out and over to her cabin. There was no one in the car, so she cautiously poked her head around the edge of the cabin door, expecting she knew not what. Giles Shaw was sitting in an armchair smoking a cigarette, and by the butts in the ashtray had been there for some time. She was torn between relief and extreme irritation at the sight of him. "What the hell are you doing here?" she demanded.

He looked up, a tentative grin on his long face. "Why I came to see you, me darling! I got the distinct feeling that you were angry at me about something, and I came to mend fences. What have I done? What can I do to make amends?"

She plonked herself down in the chair opposite him and glared. "That's it, I don't *know* what you've done, but I'm more upset by what you *haven't* done! You've not been straight with us, Giles, not from the very first. You haven't lifted a finger to help yourself or us, in fact, quite the opposite. We've spent what was supposed to be a restful vacation rushing around—at vast expense, I may add—

trying to get you out of the predicament your own stupid folly had got you into in the first place. And what do we get from you? Nothing! Not a word to put us on the right track, not even a thank-you. Toby is out there at this moment putting his obstinate neck into God knows what kind of noose to try and resolve this mess, and, by God, if anything happens to him, I'll hold *you* directly responsible, and I'll see to it that, even if you walk away a free man, what's left of your dubious reputation will be in ashes. I'll hound you out of here and I won't stop hounding you till I die, and that's a promise. I dragged Toby into this and I got into it because of my friendship with Emily, and I felt I owed it to her memory. She adored you— though God knows why! But once this is over, Giles, we are *through*. I don't give a damn what you do with the rest of your miserable life—you can drink yourself to death, make yourself the laughing stock of our little world, whatever. You've become a poor excuse for an anthropologist and, for my money, you're not much of a man either, Giles. You may have enough of the old charm left in you to con good, dedicated men like Kaowa, but you no longer con *me*." She had run out of breath, but felt markedly better after her tirade.

He had wilted under her barrage of words and sat slumped in his chair gazing at the floor, his large hands hanging limply. He suddenly covered his face with them. "Oh, dear God, Penny, I don't blame you for being so upset. The truth of it is that, since Em went, I haven't been a damn bit of good to myself or to anyone else. I'm a straw man and with brains to match." He put his hands down and looked pleadingly at her. "But I swear to you I had no hand in Freyer's death or this other man's, and there is nothing more I can tell you now that would help— you've already discovered it on your own. I'm sorry I've been such a fool, but I realize it's too late for that now.

Here . . ." he fumbled in his pocket and produced a crumpled check. "I know that this is no compensation for what you and Toby Glendower have been through, but at least let me make up to you for all the expense you've been to on my account. And you know you have my deepest thanks. Please, is there anything I can do now, anything at all, to help? Just say the word."

He handed her a check for ten thousand dollars, which caused her to raise her eyebrows at the large amount, but she pocketed it without comment and said, "Yes, there is. First you can start acting responsibly for a change. Get back to the Payson ranch and Rogers who, after all, is sticking *his* neck out on your behalf, and stay close to him until we get word from Toby—that way you should both be safe. Second, tell me what you heard them saying this morning at breakfast. I'm certain now that it has to be one of them, maybe all of them, so this is vital."

He looked blankly at her. "I can scarcely believe the Paysons could . . ." he started.

"Believe it!" she interrupted. "Tell me what went on."

"Well, it's all a bit foggy," he confessed. "You see we had a lot of drinks and dinner was very late. . . ."

"I've heard all that from Rogers," she cut him off. "But you were there for breakfast, so tell me what they *said*."

"I only came in just as they were finishing. There was an argument going on. . . ." He ran a hand over his forehead, trying to concentrate. "Philip was saying something to Mildred about her helicopter license being up for renewal and that she'd have to get in some air time—he was offering to come with her if she felt nervous. Gregory was going on at him about getting back to Waikulu. Said he would need the helicopter and Philip would have to drive back. Philip flared at him and Gregory flared right back. Said he's just about had enough of him and that he'd show him who was in charge. Philip and Mildred stamped out. Gregory said something apologetic to me like he'd have to leave us to our own devices today, but since we had a car at least we could go sightseeing or whatever. Then he left in one hell of a hurry. Said he had an important appointment. There was still no sign of Rogers, so I thought I'd come over and see you. That's all."

A cold feeling was growing inside of Penny. "But Gregory came back. Rogers told me that," she whispered. "After you left he came back—so they *did* take the helicopter. That has to be the way of it. Oh, I don't like this, I don't like this at all!"

"But they may just have been giving Mildred a flying lesson, just like they said," Giles exclaimed.

"Let's hope so, but my guess is that they were going to the Hale Iliili to go after Toby." She looked at him with anxious eyes. "Look, Giles, the minute you get back to the Paysons, check Gregory's gun case. See if any of them are missing and call me right back. Now go, I've got to get back to the phone."

He got up and smiled tentatively at her. "So it's all right now? Friends again?"

"Nothing will be all right until Toby, Kaowa and that nice Chinese inspector are right here and all in one piece," she said severely. "Just do your bit from now on, and we'll talk about it later." She hustled back to the Laolani's, where she found Brad and Griselda holding hands and murmuring sweet nothings at each other. "This is no time for canoodling," she snapped. "Any messages?"

"A call for the Laolanis about renting a cottage," Brad grinned at her. "I made the booking. Who was it?"

"Giles Shaw—so he's off the hook, thank God! But it looks as if Philip and Mildred may have gone after Toby." And she explained rapidly what had developed. They both sobered. "Anything we can do?" Brad asked.

"At the moment, nothing. Yes, there is. Bring me a

carton of cigarettes. There's a store down the road. There's no sense all of us sitting here fretting our heads off. Go be an invalid, or have Griselda take you for a drive or something. Just check in from time to time to see I haven't keeled over." They left, looking relieved.

When the phone rang again she pounced on it like an eager terrier after a rat. It was Giles. "I checked the case—there are two rifles gone, I'm afraid. Can't tell what they were though. Rogers says he got on to Lyons who is tied up with something in Honolulu for now, but will be down later this evening. Best he can do. He says the police drag of the islands hasn't come up with any sign of Hapili."

"I see," she sighed. "Well, let me know the minute any of the Paysons show up at the ranch." For want of anything better to do, she put in a call to the helicopter rental company at Ke'ahole, but was told the pilot was out on a Waimea trip, but that the early morning drop on Hale Iliili had been made without incident. "Have him call me the minute he gets back, will you?" she said, and gave the Laolani's number.

He called back within the hour and repeated what the girl had already said. "Well, I just wanted to alert you to the fact that there may be trouble, so be careful this evening when you go back to make the pick-up," she told him.

"What kind of trouble?" he demanded.

The last thing she wanted was to put him off from making the run, so she said, "There just might be another helicopter around, so just watch yourself."

"Oh, okay." He sounded mystified. "I'm due back there at seven." She looked at her watch—it was just on noon. Seven hours to go! She wondered if she would last that long without bursting a blood vessel.

She drank endless cups of coffee, and for about the fiftieth time fell off the "no smoking" wagon and started to chain smoke. The hours dragged by. A subdued Griselda appeared with the peace offering of a dainty lunch at which Penny pecked with no appetite, a sense of calamity growing within her. She had not felt this badly since Toby had been lost in the wilderness in Israel, but this time there was no gifted psychic at her elbow to bring succor, and she raged inwardly at her own helplessness.

At two o'clock the phone rang again. This time it was Rogers in a high state of excitement. "A rider has just come in. The helicopter is down on a remote part of the ranch. Some kind of accident. It buckled a skid on landing. Mildred was piloting it. Knocked herself out. We've called an ambulance and I'm going out there now, leaving Giles to man the phone."

"What about Philip?" she cried.

"They made no mention of him. He may be trying to walk in for help." But in the hours that followed there was no sign of either of the Payson brothers as Mildred was carried off to hospital still unconscious—the diagnosis, a concussion and bad whiplash.

Brad, who had rejoined Penny in her vigil, tried to calm her down, for by this time she was raging to get into a helicopter and get out there. "Look, we've just checked Ke'ahole, and there's no chance of the pilot getting there earlier than he said. And aren't you underrating Sir Tobias? After all, he's a very clever and able man, and I'm sure he can cope with any situation. Besides, there are three of them together, and you can't even be sure Philip is out there."

"But if he *is* there, he's stuck and desperate by now!" she hurled back, and refused to be comforted.

"Well, let's wait and see what happens at the pick-up and take it from there," the young reporter soothed.

But when the call from the pilot came in it did nothing to calm her. "I got there a bit early and put down," he reported. "But there was no sign of anyone. No sign of trouble either. One odd thing though. I left an orange jerrycan of water there as a marker this morning—and there was no sign of it. I looked all around. They must have taken it with them, though I can't imagine why. Anyway I'll be back tomorrow."

"I'd like to alter that," she said with decision. "Can you make a very early trip? I'll be at Ke'ahole say about six thirty in the morning? I think the party may be in trouble. Please, this is urgent!"

"Well, okay, but if it's for all of you I'll have to take the bigger chopper. It'll cost."

"Fine, fine—anything you say! We'll be there at first light," she cried, and for the first time felt a glimmer of relief.

Brad promptly volunteered, but after much toing and froing between them and the Payson ranch, it was decided that Giles should go with her. "I'd like to," he declared firmly. "And besides, I'm pretty good with a rifle. I'll bring one of Gregory's." This was okayed by Lyons who had just arrived at the ranch and was shortly to depart for the hospital and Mildred. He had issued an all-points bulletin on Philip and Gregory.

At crack of dawn the next morning the pilot eyed his two so very disparate passengers, the small, dumpy, frantic-looking woman and the tall, gangling redhead. His eyes riveted on the rifle Giles was carrying. "Look, I don't know what all this is about, but I sure in hell want to know exactly what kind of trouble you're expecting," he said. "I don't usually carry armed passengers."

"It's just a precaution," Penny shrilled. "And all we want you to do is fly over the whole area as low as possible, to see if we can pick up any signs of them. You don't even have to land if we don't see anything. Otherwise we'll just come back here and we'll make the run again tonight as originally scheduled. Okay?"

"Okay," he agreed reluctantly, and they climbed aboard. They circled the promontory and he hovered above the ruins, but there was no sign of movement in the pale morning light. The throb of the engine as he skimmed low over the bush thickets elicited nothing but the soaring of startled birds, until they were following along the ridge that ran like a protective arm guarding the peninsula from the sea. Then the pilot gave a sudden convulsive start. "Jesus!" he exclaimed. "Down there at the foot of the cliff—it's a body!" He jerked the helicopter savagely away to avoid the ridge.

"Who? Where? What color?" Penny cried, peering frantically down.

"White I think, but I only got a glimpse. Hold on! I'm going in for a landing." And it was at that moment that Mauna Loa, after brooding about it all week, burst into fiery, angry eruption.

Chapter 21

"You have found it?" There was both anger and fear in the demand as Kaowa looked up at the dirt-stained figure before him.

"A way out? No," Toby said wearily, and slumped down beside him. "But some of my news is good. I have found a water supply, so there is no longer a need to skimp on the water." He took a long swig from the canteen and handed it to Kaowa who drank thirstily. "And to put an end to your fears, my friend, I did find the cave but I have not gazed on the treasure of Kamehameha, nor will any mortal man—Pele has seen to that. She has guarded the king for all time."

Kaowa gaped at him in amazement, as Toby fished in his pocket and extracted his mini-camera, which he handed to the big Hawaiian. "You must be the guardian of this, for with it I have the proof that will convince the world to leave this place in peace. The burial cave is now half-filled with solid lava. I am not a vulcanologist, but it looks like an old happening to me; possibly when Mauna Kea was still active and sent its molten streams down the ancient lava tubes. Anyway, the great king lies sealed beneath tons of lava rock and our quest is done. Now we just have to get ourselves out of here."

It was as if the great cloud of fear that had encompassed Kaowa dissipated at the sound of his words, and Kaowa seemed to swell as he beamed upon Toby. "Then whatever happens now I can rest easy," he breathed, then sobered. "But you found no way out?"

"No, I followed the old main staircase up to the spring, but that is totally blocked—possibly by an earthquake or even a man-made explosion. There is no way we could ever move it in time, and though I searched all the tubes leading from the cave, there was nothing, so . . ." Toby heaved a sigh. "It will have to be by the way we came in here." He looked at the opening where the light was slowly beginning to weaken. "Maybe I can make a try for it when it gets dark."

Kaowa gave a derisive snort. "Find your way down the cliff face in the dark? You'd break your neck for sure. And if you showed a light, he'd pick you off like a fly."

"If he's still out there. Have you heard a helicopter?"

Kaowa shook his head. Toby looked over at Ching. "How's he doing?"

"Out of it, but he's been stirring and moaning a bit the past half hour."

Toby went over and felt Ching's pulse; it was still rapid but perceptibly weaker and now his flesh was hot to the touch. "He's worse," he muttered. "We can't wait it out, we simply *have* to get out for his sake." He stood looking down and pondering, then turned back to Kaowa. "I have an idea. How big a risk are you prepared to take on me, for if it backfires we may both end up dead?"

The big man shrugged. "If it is my time, then it is my time," he murmured. "I am with you."

Toby came back and sat down again. "Then listen. The man out there *knows* he has shot you and Ching, and for all he knows you may both be dead already. That just leaves me. If I can persuade him that I also am dead or badly injured, he just might be drawn up to the cave. If we can get him here we'd have a fifty-fifty chance of getting him before he gets us."

"But how are you going to do that?"

"It will mean a certain amount of play-acting, and I'm not too good at that I'm afraid," Toby said apologetically. "Can you yell or scream on cue?"

"You bet I can," Kaowa grinned at him. "Why?"

"Well, when it is almost dark I propose to show myself, or at least my hat, with a flashlight, as if I was trying to get along the ledge. If that draws no fire then I will go down the cliff and make for the road to get help. But if he does shoot, then *you'll* scream and I'll chuck the flashlight and the hat over the edge. It might convince him I am dead or injured, so that at dawn he may come up to see his handiwork or to finish it. It will mean spending the night in absolute darkness, of course, but it's all I can think of. What do you think?"

"Sounds reasonable to me." Kaowa's spirits were mounting by the second and he patted the great spear beside him lovingly. "I would surely relish getting one shot at the bastard with this."

"In that case I had better get our water supply replenished." Toby got up with the canteen.

"Why don't you take that as well?" Kaowa said grandly, indicating a huge gourd studded with shark's teeth that leaned against the bigger coffin. "It holds a lot more, and you could decant it into the kava bowl. I'm sure great-grandfather won't mind since it's in such a good cause." He was now firmly a man of the twentieth century, all his atavistic fears banished.

"All right. With Ching's fever mounting it may come

in handy," Toby agreed and wound the tortuous path back to the spring.

By the time he got back Ching was starting to thrash and moan as the morphine wore off. Toby looked at his watch in the dimming light and grimaced. "He is going to be in pretty rough shape by morning. I have only one morphine tablet left; after that it will have to be pain pills, and they aren't going to do much, still. . . ." He repeated the process of popping the pill in and getting some water down the injured man's throat; then sponged him all over with the cool water from the kava bowl to sooth his fever.

"That's a thick tapa cloth on great-grandmother's coffin," Kaowa observed. "Why not cover him with that? It's going to get pretty chilly in here now the sun is down. She won't mind either."

Toby duly covered Ching with the beautifully patterned cloth, then straightened up and braced himself. "You ready?" he asked Kaowa, who nodded.

He took two short stabbing spears from the head of the coffin, propped his hat on top of one of them and lashed a flashlight to the other, then lit another flashlight which he placed on the ground near the cave mouth. Like a puppeteer he angled his two props around the cave entrance, one held head high, the other waist high. He had extended them as far as he could reach along the ledge and was just about to follow them himself, when the response came; a rapid volley of wild shots. Kaowa unleashed a gargantuan banshee shriek of anguish that sent echoes reverberating through the cave as Toby hastily withdrew the spears, tossed the loose flashlight cartwheeling over the edge and chucked his hat in its wake. He switched off the light on the spear and groped his way back to Kaowa. "Well, that's it. We shan't know until dawn if it worked," he murmured. "I don't think we'll have anything to worry about during the hours of darkness, so we may as well get some rest. I'll take first watch, and I'll wake you in four hours or thereabouts. Would you like a pain pill?"

Kaowa snorted gently beside him. "Keep them for Ching. With Pele's fire burning in my leg I'd rather talk. Who do you think is out there? How did you put all this together? If I'm for it tomorrow I'd like to know."

"Oh, alright. Maybe that's a good idea, in case you make it and I don't," Toby mumbled. "Lord, what I would give for a smoke, but I left my damn pipe in the knapsack!"

"Smoking is bad for your health." Kaowa chuckled. "Go on—it will take your mind off your terrible addiction."

"I still don't know if all the Paysons were in on it, but I think Philip murdered both Freyer and Hapili. I have a contact lens in my pocket I found by Hapili's body which should confirm that."

"How about Manua?" Kaowa demanded.

"No, I believe that's where the double-crossers were double-crossed and things started to go wrong," Toby said. "I'm sure Hapili murdered Manua, but to make any sense of this I'd better start from the beginning. I learned from the Donelson papers that Hapili had been one of the old man's Oahu informants and, as such, had got some inklings about this place. Then Donelson died and his papers, to Hapili's dismay, went to Freyer. Hapili approached Freyer, thereby diverting him from his anti-Menehune campaign on Van Norkirk's behalf. Freyer came down to Kona to check things out himself, thereby drawing attention to himself *locally*. Philip may already have been aware of him and his dealings with Van Norkirk, via Paea Young, a cousin of Manua and Lalai, one of them Philip's crony, the other his mistress.

"By the high quality of the Hawaiian artifacts in the

Payson house, I think Manua had already been doing some quiet tomb robbing in this area of his *kahu* and selling the proceeds to his bosses. Enquiries in the area about the present *kahus* of the tomb by Hapili led him to Manua, whose *local* knowledge Hapili needed to supplement his own. Manua confided in his gambling/drinking buddy Philip that the big prize might be theirs, so Philip comes in on the deal. Whether he met Freyer directly, I'm not sure, but I think it probable. Then Freyer started to have second thoughts and they became suspicious of his overtures of peace to Giles Shaw. Philip set up this schoolboyish scheme of murdering Freyer and framing Giles by the ridiculous 'Menehune murder' scenario, not having the sense to see that the African poison he got from his father's collection would be a dead giveaway that it was not a *native* murder at all. And he moved too soon, for Hapili had not got some of the vital bits of the treasure puzzle from Freyer—hence the break-ins by Manua and the *kahuna*. They must have got *something* from the map folder, because Hapili left Honolulu in a hurry, came down here and quickly went into hiding.

"Then we came into the picture and Philip contrived through Mildred to see we stayed with them in order to keep tabs on us, and, unfortunately, at the luau Penny recognized and asked about Manua, thus alerting Philip, and so in turn Manua had to 'disappear'. Probably he came out here with Hapili while they searched for the missing bits of the puzzle, while Philip was keeping an eye on us. And here I think is when things went seriously wrong for them.

"Hapili and Manua must have found the two other markers, and at that juncture Hapili considered Manua expendable and so killed him. But he still needed Philip for the transport and possibly the sale of the treasure, and so set up a rendezvous here with him to make final arrangements. I don't think he dreamed that Manua's body would have been found so soon or that his death would be recognized as a murder. Before this Philip and Manua must have decided that *Hapili* was expendable, having culled all his knowledge, and so Philip, thinking Manua now had all the necessary information, went ahead and blew Hapili away. That's why the news of Manua's death so upset him, for it meant he still lacked the final bits of the puzzle. But then he learned we were after it too, and so, in a last desperate bid, he followed *us*—and here we are." He was so weary that his words were beginning to slur.

"But Philip couldn't have been responsible for that third break-in," Kaowa pointed out. "Thinking back over it, that must have been on the very day he murdered Hapili."

"Oh yes, I realize that—yes, it means Mildred or Gregory or both of them must have been aware of what was going on and followed me to the Freyers. So Philip now may just be waiting for reinforcements. I'm gambling that, with his reckless nature, he'll be tempted to come and find out before they arrive. If not . . ." he trailed off into a weary sigh.

A huge arm encircled his sagging shoulders. "Rest now," Kaowa commanded. "Rest, and I'll keep vigil."

"Well, just for a little then," Toby muttered, his eyes closing. "But wake me in a couple of hours . . ." and went spinning down into a dark vortex filed with the murmurous surge of the sea.

He was recalled from its comforting depths by a hand pressing his shoulder and Kaowa's voice murmuring in his ear. "It is almost light and we have to do something about Ching. . . . " Toby opened his eyes to see the cave entrance greying into light. "You should have wakened me long since," he reproached and, flexing his cramped limbs, crawled over to where Ching was moaning and thrashing under the heavy cover. Now the inspector's pulse was thready and his whole body bathed in sweat. Toby managed to get two more pain pills into him and once more sponged down his burning body. He shook his head. "If we don't get him out of here soon, he's not going to make it."

He looked around and froze, for Kaowa was no longer sitting by the wall. He sprang up and whirled around to find the big man sitting on his great-grandfather's coffin and thoughtfully hefting the great spear. "What in heaven's name are you doing? You'll be in direct line of fire from the opening!"

"And so will he—and I need a clear shot at him," Kaowa returned. "I suggest you take the gun and hide just to the right of the cave mouth. If he comes along the ledge, he'll swing left instinctively as he gets to it, and at point-blank range you'll get at least one shot off before he starts riddling the cave. Now we'd better shut up, because it's light enough for him to see his way up."

Toby nodded and picked up Ching's gun, then produced the small silver brandy flask from his pocket and offered it to Kaowa. "A final toast to our success," he whispered. The Hawaiian grinned, tossed down a slug and handed it back to Toby, who finished it off with a satisfied sigh and took up his position.

The minutes dragged endlessly by as the light strengthened; then Kaowa held up a warning hand and nodded. Toby had heard nothing, but after a few seconds picked up the sound of a stone falling and tensed. Then, before he could draw breath, a figure sprang into the opening, its rifle pointed right at him. His finger tightened on the trigger, but before either of them had time to get off a shot, Kaowa, with a full-throated yell, had hurled the spear and caught Philip Payson full in the chest, its impact hurling him backward off the ledge. He plummeted without a sound, and there was a dull crunch as he hit the ground. Toby peered cautiously out and down to see him lying motionless, the spear skewering him through so that its blade stuck out between his shoulder blades. Sickened, he turned back to Kaowa. "Well, it worked," he said heavily. "I'll get out now and be back with help as soon as I can."

Again Kaowa held up a warning hand, "No, not yet. We may not be out of the woods. Listen!"

"Holy hell!" Toby swore, as there came the unmistakable throb of a helicopter. "And we were so close, so close. . . !" He ducked back inside and crouched down as the throb became a roar, as the helicopter swept over the ridge and circled. He snatched up his glasses and trained them on it as it started to settle into a landing close by. Then he started to chuckle, for there was no mistaking the pixie face that was peering so frantically out of the window. Still laughing, he turned to Kaowa. "It's all right! We've done it. The Old Guard to the rescue. Penny Spring has arrived with the relief column."

To Penny, whose horrified gaze was fixed on the body as she leapt from the helicopter and started to run frantically toward it, the voice from above came as a heart-jolting shock. "Ahoy there! Up here." She looked up to see a nightmare figure framed in the cave opening, a bloodstained bandage drooping over its left eye, the sun shining pallidly on the bare chest beneath the blood-spattered coat, but to her the vision was more beautiful a sight than the whole of the heavenly host. "Oh, Toby!" she choked, as the horror-stricken pilot and Giles caught up with her and Mauna Loa roared its anger in the distance.

"Get on your radio and get the police and medical rescue team here with a doctor as quickly as you can," Toby called down. "I have two wounded men up here—one in a very bad way. We'll need basket-stretchers to get them down. It's going to be damned difficult, the only way up here is by some footholds in the rock face five caves to my left along here."

"Got you!" the pilot yelled, and raced back to the chopper.

"Kaowa?" Giles called up anxiously.

"Kaowa took a bullet in the leg, but he'll be all right. Ching took a bullet in the back and it is still in him, so he's in very bad shape."

The pilot rejoined them. "We're in luck. An Hawaii Five-0 inspector was at Ke'ahole. Help is on its way. Shouldn't be more than fifteen minutes," he panted.

"I'm coming up," Penny cried, having spotted the footholds.

"No, stay right where you are," Toby boomed back. "It's possible Philip may have had his own reinforcements coming in."

"Hapili?"

"Hapili is long dead—his body is about a quarter of a mile to our east. Philip finished him too. The 'hunting trip' he came back from when you were in Hilo. But Mildred and Gregory are unaccounted for."

"Mildred's out of it," she shouted. "She crashed the helicopter and is in hospital."

"And Gregory?"

"No sign of him."

"What about the treasure?" There was an avid eagerness in Giles' voice.

Penny glared at him, as Toby said blandly. "The treasure is safe—safe for all time and from all men, Dr. Shaw. But that reminds me, there is something I must do." And he disappeared from the opening to be replaced by the

249

huge figure of Kaowa, using yet another of his great-grand-father's spears as a crutch; he grinned cheerfully down at them and waved.

"Now what's Toby up to?" Penny demanded crossly. "That man is the living end!" as the distant throb of engines signalled the arrival of the rescue mission.

The next hour was a whirlwind of frenzied activity, meticulously organized by the tight-lipped Inspector Lyons. The quiet promontory became a droning hive of helicopters, as one crew went off in search of the remains of Hapili, another occupied itself with the body of Philip Payson, and Ching was lowered from the cave on a basket-stretcher and whisked off for an immediate operation. "What are his chances?" Toby demanded anxiously of the doctor who had climbed up to examine them in the cave. "About fifty-fifty," the doctor said grimly. "Another hour and there would have been no hope at all."

A slight glitch arose when it was found no stretcher was big enough to accommodate Kaowa, and a faintly comic solution was found, whereby a harness was fixed around his massive torso and he was lowered slowly down the cliff face. Since he refused to be parted from his spear, he looked like the Demon King descending from the skies in an English pantomime.

It was not until the injured had been safely whisked away that Toby consented to come down from his lofty aerie. He had already replaced the petroglyph stone over the hidden entrance, but before he left he carefully spread the tapa cloth over the smaller coffin and replaced the artifacts around the larger one. "Thanks," he whispered. "We wouldn't have made it without you." And with a final look around the cave that he knew would now forever be part of his dreams, he edged back along the ledge.

Penny and Inspector Lyons were waiting impatiently for him at the bottom, and he fished in his pocket and produced the envelope with the contact lens. "I found this by Hapili's body," he explained. "Philip must have lost it after the shooting. Fortunately for us, I might add. He wasn't quite so much of a marksman with his glasses."

Lyons grunted. "I'll need a full statement from you as soon as you are up to it. I am not at all amused by all this, Sir Tobias. I did warn you and you ignored me."

"Neither am I," Toby murmured, making with single-minded determination for his knapsack and extracting his pipe and pouch. "I feel as badly about what has happened—especially about Inspector Ching—as I'm sure you do. On the other hand it *has* cleared up three murder investigations, hasn't it? Though there is still the matter of Gregory's involvement to be settled."

"I just got word over the radio," Lyons said gruffly. "Gregory has been picked up in Hilo. He claims he was over there selling the Waikulu ranch to Van Norkirk and knew nothing whatever about any of this. We've let him go for the moment."

Penny looked at him in astonishment. "Why?"

"Because our information is that Mauna Loa's latest eruption is sending one of its rivers of molten lava right into his K'au ranch. Had to give him the chance to get over there and save what can be saved. We can pull him in again any time we want. By the way, there's a police chopper waiting to take you to Kalaoa when you're ready."

A policeman hurried by with a message from Oahu and the inspector excused himself and hurried off after him, leaving Penny glowering at Toby. His gray-stubbled face now wore an expression of bliss as he puffed hungrily away on his pipe.

"A fine old mess you got yourself into this time," she said at length. "Just look at you!—no shirt, filthy, blood all over you—and I suppose you're now going to tell me how clever you've been!!"

"Yes, well, it's a long story . . ." Toby said amiably. "Shall I tell you en route? I could use a drink—several in fact. By the way, thanks for jumping the gun in such a timely fashion."

"Don't mention it!" she said sarcastically. "You're entirely welcome."

Chapter 22

"I'm exhausted!" Penny declared. "Never in my life have I done such a sight of travelling in such a short space of time—whizzing around in cars, bucketing about in helicopters and planes and now whooshing through the ocean on this thing!"

Three days had passed and they were once more aboard *The Dancing Lady*, who strained restlessly at her precarious mooring in the remote spot—suggested by the invaluable Chris Bullard—close by the Amelia Earhart monument, with the vast bulk of Diamond Head towering over them. The remote location had become a vital necessity, for the publication of Brad Field's "exclusives," complete with Toby's pictures of the lava-filled treasure cave, had almost pushed the wrathful antics of Mauna Loa off the front pages, and had set the rest of a very disgruntled press corps baying at their heels without respite.

Toby looked up from his unending battle of keeping the yacht's decks free of the ash that was now spreading over the rest of the islands in a fine cloud. "Yes, well, I agree it hasn't been very restful, but you must admit it's been—er—different." The bandage over the gash in his forehead gave him a faintly rakish air that had been a bonanza for the press photographers.

"It's all very well for you," she grumbled. "The hero of the hour and all that, but I'm *tired*. And the motion of this boat is driving me bananas."

"Ship," he corrected doggedly. "And you are equally the *heroine* of the hour, as Brad Field has so eloquently stated in his overblown prose." He indicated with his scrubbing brush the pile of papers beside her; the banner headline on one trumpeted "World-famed Anthropologist Leads Rescue to Party Imprisoned by Murderer in Treasure Cave." "After all, if you hadn't arrived when you did Ching would never have made it. As it is, he is safely past the crisis and should be up and about in a month or so. And if it hadn't been for your persistence in the first place, and all the things you found out along the way about Philip *et al*, Giles would still be in prison for a murder he did not commit, and the real murderer would have gotten away with it."

She snorted. "That reminds me, what do you want to do about this check Giles gave us? I've totted up our expenses and I put out about a thousand dollars and you spent about three thousand."

"I don't want any of it," Toby said loftily.

"Oh, very altruistic of you, I'm sure! But may I point out that Giles won't even feel it, and that what he has saved in lawyer's fees alone more than compensates for it."

"Then take your whack and give the rest to Kaowa. He deserves it and I'm sure it will be used to further his worthy cause."

"There's another high-minded idiot for you! Do you know that Rogers took such a fancy to the big lunkhead that he offered him a position in his firm? And Kaowa turned him down flat!"

"Quite right too," Toby rejoined. "Kaowa is a man with a mission, and accepting such an offer would have compromised him. Maybe he can use the money to do something about Van Norkirk and his schemes."

Penny rolled her eyes heavenward. "Much as you admire him and vice versa, the sad fact is that the Kaowas of this world can rarely trounce the Van Norkirks. The world wags against them. However, for the moment, I am hoping you are right and that enough dust has been raised—and I intend to keep it stirred up—to put Van Norkirk off that particular area. But there is equally no doubt that he'll find somewhere else for his tacky designs. If you really want to do something to help fight Van Norkirk, you ought to put a bug in Benedict Lefau's ear. It's the sort of battle his father would adore, and Jules has got the clout to do it."

Toby brightened. "That's a good idea! I'll do that. Maybe we can chase Van Norkirk back to South Africa."

"Speaking of South Africa—here's a final irony for you. I heard from Brad that Gregory, after all this scandal and with Waikulu gone and his K'au ranch in shambles, is planning to sell up and go back there. Poor Philip! It was all he wanted: to get enough money of his own to get out of here and back there."

It was Toby's turn to snort. "Poor Philip indeed! He murdered two people in cold blood—and by all accounts that wasn't the first time he'd done so—and he almost got three more. The man was a highly dangerous idiot."

"Despite all that I still feel some sympathy for him—and for the equally dim Mildred, who was fighting for the same thing—they both were striving for a place in the sun away from the suffocating shadow of Gregory. They were victims too—victims of an outdated cultural system that for my money has little to commend it." Penny said stubbornly.

"Did you find out if they are going to charge her with anything?" he asked.

"No, they aren't. Not worth the effort with Philip dead. Proving she was an accessory to all this would be well-nigh impossible. She has her own life sentence as it is—there'll be no escape from Gregory now. I pity the silly bitch, just as I pity Lalai. They were both of them fond of Philip, with all his faults." She sighed dolefully.

Toby thought it was high time to change the subject. "Well, at least there have been some happy endings. With all the spread his paper has been giving him, young Field should be set for life."

"Oh yes, he's the fair-haired boy of Hawaiian journalism at the moment alright—and for a journalist he's not a bad kid," Penny said. "He certainly has done a good job in buffering Griselda from his fellow journalists."

"Do you think he'll marry that girl? She struck *me* as a very hysterical type," Toby disapproved, as he went on with his diligent scrubbing.

"Oh, there's nothing basically wrong with her," Penny sailed to her defence. "She's been brainwashed all her life into being dependent by an overbearing father, so it's small wonder she's like she is. But underneath it all she's a very bright and determined young woman. The patient Griseldas of this world can be very determined, and I shouldn't think Brad has a hope in hell of *not* marrying her if that's what she has in mind. Should work out very well for both of them: he'll get an adoring, frugal and efficient wife, and she'll get an attractive manly shoulder to lean on. Takes care of the situation very nicely, I'd say. A lot to be said for Griselda's approach to life—men find the 'weak woman to be protected' role irresistible. Even you fell for it, and you're a particularly hard nut to crack."

Toby snorted indignantly but did not deny it. A small silence fell and Penny returned to the attack. "You know this is just plain ridiculous. Just look at you! What would the Athenaeum say, what would your fellow Fellows of All Souls say, seeing you going on like this? At this rate you'll end up with housemaid's knee *and* dishpan hands! What kind of a vacation is that!"

Toby sighed, got up stiffly and came to sit beside her in the cockpit, groping for the comfort of his pipe. "Alright then, what do *you* want to do?"

Having got his full attention at last, Penny took her time. "Well, I don't know about you, but frankly I've had enough of this island paradise for now. In fact I have a sudden yearning for the grey skies of England, the peace and quiet of Oxford in vacation time and the comforts of my own little pad in Littlemore, far, far away from erupting volcanoes, multiple murders and the hawk-like eye of the press that will be fixed on us the whole time we're here. So my vote is to sail this thing quietly back to Honolulu, fix up with the agents to clean it up again and have it all nice and shiny when the Lefaus get here in three days' time, while we quietly slip away to the airport and head for home. In short, it's *aloha* time."

Toby, whose secret thoughts had been turning hungrily in the same direction, was inwardly relieved. "Well, alright, if it's what *you* want," he condescended. "But we can't just slip off without a word—shouldn't we say a lot of goodbyes?"

"I've already said all mine," she said promptly. " 'Thanks a million' to Chris Bullard, 'Bless you my children' to Brad and Griselda, and 'Get your act together or don't bother to call me, I'll call you,' to Giles. You've given all your statements and evidence to Lyons, so he's done with. And if you want to stop off at the hospital to say goodbye to Kaowa—fine! We can give him the money at the same time. And I don't think Ching is viewable yet. Who else is there?"

"The Lefaus—they were expecting to see us." His tone was so doleful that she almost laughed.

"You can write them a nice long letter on the flight back explaining all this—you know how bored you get on airplanes, so it'll fill in the time nicely," she comforted.

He sprang up with relieved alacrity and looked at the westering sun. "In that case, I'd better get a move on. Have to get beyond the reefs here before it's dark, but we should be back in Honolulu by dinnertime. Give me a hand, will you?"

"With pleasure," she jumped up. "What do you want done first, captain, my captain."

And so, bickering happily, they sailed off into the sunset.

About the Author

Margot Arnold is the pseudonym of a writer and educator living on Cape Cod. The author of numerous thrillers and novels of romantic suspense featuring exotically far-flung locales, Ms. Arnold's work bears the unmistakable veracity of first-hand knowledge of her settings. She is comfortable in the classroom, the archaeological dig, or in the realms of mayhem and murder.

The Menehune Murders is the first new adventure of Penny Spring and Sir Toby Glendower in nearly a decade, and it marks the debut of the beloved and peripatetic sleuths in hardcover.